D1474958

the PIG, the PRINCE & the UNICORN

KAREN A. BRUSH

AVON
PUBLISHERS OF BARD, CAMELOT, DISCUS AND FLARE BOOKS

AVON BOOKS
A division of
The Hearst Corporation
105 Madison Avenue
New York, New York 10016

First Avon Printing: June 1987

AVON TRADEMARK REG. U.S. PAT. OFF. AND IN OTHER COUNTRIES, MARCA REGISTRADA, HECHO EN U.S.A.

Printed in the U.S.A.

K–R   10   9   8   7   6   5   4   3   2   1

Praise for

the PIG, the PRINCE & the UNICORN

by

KAREN A. BRUSH

"Charming, entertaining!"
Elizabeth Scarborough, author of
The Christening Quest

"A delightful surprise, by turns charming and totally wacko!"
Craig Shaw Gardner, author of
A Malady of Magicks

"Karen Brush has a fine command of character and story, her style is engaging, and you find yourself thinking about the book long after you've finished reading it."
George Alec Effinger, author of
The Nick of Time

"A Disneyesque quest!"
Gregory Frost, author of *Lyrec*

Worlds of Fantasy from Avon Books

THE CHRONICLES OF THE TWELVE KINGDOMS
by Esther M. Friesner
MUSTAPHA AND HIS WISE DOG
SPELLS OF MORTAL WEAVING
THE WITCHWOOD CRADLE

100 GREAT FANTASY SHORT SHORT STORIES
*edited by Isaac Asimov, Terry Carr,
and Martin H. Greenberg*

UNICORN & DRAGON
(trade paperback)
by Lynn Abbey

UNICORN VARIATIONS
by Roger Zelazny

WINDMASTER'S BANE
by Tom Deitz

WOLF-DREAMS
by Michael D. Weaver

Coming Soon

TALKING MAN
by Terry Bisson

VALE OF THE VOLE
by Piers Anthony

To my father, Charles Francis Brush,
a traveler and explorer.

But in Man's dwellings he became a thing
Restless and worn, stern and wearisome,
Drooped as a wild-born falcon with clipt wing,
To whom the boundless air alone were home:
— George Gordon, Lord Byron
Childe Harold's Pilgrimage,
Canto III, St. XV

ACKNOWLEDGMENTS

-

I gratefully acknowledge all the friends who helped Quadroped on his way. Frances Kennedy, Patricia Renard, Sidney Offit and Francine du Plessix Grey taught me. Charles Brush, Sylvia Karas, Amy and Sarah and William Goodhart, Jane Rodgers, Florence Lambourne, Robin Rue, Amanda Taylor and Carol Croswelle were patient readers. Oscar Collier and John Douglas helped turn the manuscript into the book and Barbara and Christina Wright helped name it.

Special thanks are due to Ruby Waiters who helped create working space in the midst of my room and to my mother, Ellen S. Brush, for fairy tales and, most especially, for Morrag.

Chapter One

There was a young pig who found the Key to Chaos and became the only barrier between his land and the malevolent forces of Ravenor.

Quadroped was brooding under an acorn tree at the edge of Whistlewood Forest when a thieving magpie landed on a bough above his head. The bird had stolen a key from a blue jay's nest and was afraid to return home. She had flown south all day, the heavy key clutched in her yellow claws. When the air cooled with afternoon she decided to rest a while and examine her newfound treasure.

The acorns had just ripened. They hung in huge, golden clusters amongst the thick green leaves and the air was filled with their delicious scent. The magpie soon forgot the key and began to gobble up every acorn within reach. As her thin, greedy claws grabbed at the nuts the key slipped and fell with a loud *thunk* onto Quadroped's tender snout.

"Ouch! Damn chipmunks!" squealed the young pig. He rubbed his nose and looked accusingly upwards, but the dense foliage hid his attacker from view. He began to feel very sorry for himself, and a tear coursed slowly down his cheek. He scuffled in the dirt for the acorn, for such he supposed the misguided missile to have been, and popped it into his mouth. Fortunately, he was a delicate eater; he chewed his food rather than gulping it down in true pig fashion. Even so, he almost cracked a tooth and, howling dismally, he removed the hard object from his mouth and glared at it reproachfully.

The key in Quadroped's hoof was forged of silver and dark with age. It was shaped like an *L* and its stem was engraved with a curious design of twisting lines. Quadroped studied the lines carefully. *I wonder if they're some kind of writing,* he thought. *I don't recognize any of the symbols but perhaps Father will be able to read them.* He put the key into his mouth for safekeeping, rubbed his snout once more to assure that there would be no bruise, and resumed his gloomy reveries.

Quadroped was directly descended from a herd of fairy pigs, lost long ago by the shadowy King of the Underworld. His whole family was magical; they could cast spells, talk to the wind, even change the weather. But Quadroped had inherited no special powers; he was just a pig.

Even my name is ordinary, Quadroped reflected unhappily. Once he had tried to change his name to something unusual and exciting such as Gwarwyn a Throt, or Coluin gun Cean. But these hopeful suggestions were crushed by his mother, who remarked in an offhand manner that Coluin gun Cean meant the Headless Trunk, and was quite unsuitable. Unabashed, Quadroped had squeaked, "Great Uncle's name was Gwarwyn, so what's wrong with *that?*"

"Yes, dearest," Mother Pig had replied, "but Great Uncle was a warrior. You're too small to be a Gwarwyn; Quadroped suits you." She had ruffled his ears and sent him off to play.

It was true, Quadroped decided; he *was* too small for a heroic name. He was only fourteen inches high and resembled a round ball with a pink snout and four tiny hooves attached. His only unusual feature was his coloration. He was snow white and his eyes were a deep shade of purple. "But what," he complained bitterly, "is the point of *looking* different if inside I'm just an ordinary pig?" He looked around the small yard with its twig hut, duck pond and vegetable patch and sighed. The huge moss-covered trees of the forest stretched away on all sides. To the south, only a few miles away, there was a great ocean and wonderful lands lay on its far shores. Quadroped wanted, more than anything, to leave home and travel to the countries beyond the sea and forest, but his parents would not let him go.

"How would you protect yourself?" his father always asked. "You don't know any magic and you're too small to fight."

"But I'll never have any magic," said Quadroped, "and I never *will* grow any larger. I don't *want* to stay here forever. I want to have fun and adventures."

"Being roasted for supper isn't fun," said his father. "You'll stay home where I can protect you." And that had been that. So, as the shadows lengthened and the light began to fade, Quadroped sat despondently under the acorn tree.

"Quadroped? Quadroped!" Mother Pig called across the yard.

"Coming!" said Quadroped. He got up and ambled across the yard towards the small twig hut. As he approached the duck pond the light dimmed and the yard became shadowy and strange. Quadroped hesitated, shivering uneasily in the sudden shade. He glanced quickly upwards. "Oh." He smiled with relief. "It's only a cloud." He shook himself slightly and hurried towards the kitchen.

The forest whispered and the cattails and rushes beside the pond began to rustle. The sounds swelled to a roar as a gust of wind swept off the water and into the clearing. The blast caught Quadroped by surprise, picking him up and spinning him roughly into the bulrushes at the water's edge. Clouds of dust and spray whirled into the air, hiding the house and yard from view.

Help! Quadroped thought, as he rolled backwards into the prickly weeds. "Uggh," he gurgled as the key in his mouth almost choked him. With difficulty he managed to stop rolling. Grabbing hold of the rushes with his mouth and hooves he began to pull himself free of the slippery, slime-crusted mud. He had almost succeeded when he had a horrible premonition that there was Something Else in the rushes with him. Alarmed, Quadroped sat down and looked cautiously about. The duck pond always made him uneasy. Its brackish waters were said to well up from a spring on the floor of the Southern Sea, and strange creatures had been caught in its depths. The dark waters were choppy with waves now. The wind smelled of salt and fish.

There's nothing there; at least not that I can see, Quadroped thought. But the rushes were tall and stood close together; something could be hiding just out of sight. *I'm being silly,* he thought, and began to feel frightened. His efforts to climb out of the weeds became more frantic. The leaves seemed to wrap and tangle around his legs, and the mud became softer and more treacherous. A breath of cold air blew into his ear, and he froze. The Something Else stood beside him.

"So, a pig," hissed an invisible voice. "Good evening, piggy. How nice to meet you."

Quadroped did not think it was possible to *meet* a voice, but he refrained from comment. The voice had an unpleasant, serpentine quality, and he did not want to see its owner. The odor of decaying fish grew stronger.

I wish Father would come out and chase this thing away, Quadroped thought. He pushed hard against the wind and weeds and managed to advance a few paces towards the house. A long shadow fell across him and he squealed. A ghastly form was slowly precipitating from the gloomy air. As it solidified it assumed a vaguely human form and began to flow, with silent menace, towards the small pig.

"No manners, no manners," lamented the visitor, halting barely a foot in front of his terrified audience. As suddenly as it had arisen, the wind died.

The dust settled, and Quadroped saw the creature clearly for the first time. He was tall and thin, shrouded from head to foot in a black cloak. Dripping strands of seaweed clung limply to his shoulders. His face was nearly hidden by a deep cowl, the shadows pierced only by three pale and gleaming eyes. Ivory claws, stained with mud, peeked out beneath the dark hem of his garment. Quadroped studied the claws with dismay. The creature, he concluded, was a carnivore.

"Good day, sir. Can I help you?" Quadroped whispered timidly. His mother had always advised him to mind his manners when faced with difficult situations.

"Help me?" the sinister visitor repeated with a repellent chuckle. The unwavering eyes glared down at the hapless pig. "Certainly you may help me, little piggy; you have the Key."

I hope he doesn't mean my key, thought Quadroped nervously, running his tongue across the carved metal. He was afraid to give it to the visitor. It would be death to venture too close to those slender claws. *If I don't tell him about my key, maybe he'll go away,* Quadroped decided. "Key?" he asked. He tried to look innocent, offended and faintly bored. He managed instead to look slightly deranged. His voice, due to the presence of the key in his mouth, sounded muffled and abnormal.

The visitor hesitated and examined Quadroped carefully. "No Key?" he cooed. Quadroped took a step backwards and contrived to look vacant and dumb, the one facial expression he had perfected. The visitor bent towards the pig and began to slowly describe the Key.

Quadroped's throat felt sore and tight. *He's looking for my key,* he realized. *He'll never go away now. I should give the key back, but what if he attacks me? He'll be angry if he learns I've lied. Oh, I wish I'd never tried to hide it.* The key tasted bitter and cold against his dry tongue.

"I *need* that Key," the visitor breathed urgently.

Oh dear, thought Quadroped.

"And," the visitor continued, "I am sure that such a nice, *honest,* piggy would not want to keep something that was not rightfully his?"

I don't want to keep it, Quadroped pleaded silently. *But how can I give it back now?*

"Give me the Key," said the visitor, "and I shall reward you richly and as you deserve."

He licked his lips when he said that! thought Quadroped. The creature gave an unfriendly smile, and he shivered. *What an awful lot of teeth.* Quadroped took another step backwards. Soft mud squished under his hooves and water ran up around his legs; he was cornered. He gazed up at the horrifying creature and endeavored to look stupider and more bewildered than before. The visitor paused again in confusion. Then he lunged towards Quadroped, his cape flying back to reveal a black fish-scaled body.

"Father!" screamed Quadroped. "Help!" The key fell out of his opened mouth and lay, glinting in the sunlight, directly in front of the visitor.

The visitor halted, transfixed by the sight of the little key. With a gasp Quadroped leapt and grabbed the key with his mouth. He dashed between the creature's widespread legs and ran towards the house, ears flat against his head and eyes wide with fright.

The visitor whirled around and sprang after the fleeing pig. "Give that to me. Now!" he cried.

Quadroped ran faster than he had dreamed possible, but the visitor was quicker. His talons swept towards Quadroped's head, forcing the pig to roll sideways and run in another direction. Again and again Quadroped barely escaped capture. Too late he realized that the visitor had turned him completely around and he was now running towards the duck pond. He tried to turn, but the creature was right behind him. With a snort of desperation, he plunged into the pond and paddled awkwardly from the shore. The visitor howled gleefully and dove after his prey, webbed feet propelling him swiftly through the water.

"I have got you, horrible piggy," the visitor whispered. He whipped his black cloak around Quadroped's head and dragged him beneath the surface of the duck pond.

They sank swiftly into the depths. Quadroped kicked furiously, trying to escape and regain the surface. But his frenzied struggles only tangled him in the heavy folds of the black cloak and the stems of long, thin waterweeds.

The visitor grabbed his tail. He turned to free himself and stiffened in shock. Through the muddy, yellow haze he saw the creature's cloak twist and move as though it were alive. The visitor's arms dissolved. The cloak fused to his shoulders and began to fragment into a writhing mass of dark, suckered tentacles that sprang from the shoulders where a man's arms should grow. The hood melted away, exposing three lidless eyes that gleamed with pale, persistent madness. The visitor opened his wide froglike mouth and laughed.

Quadroped stared at his captor, mesmerized by his glowing eyes. His struggles grew weaker and eventually ceased altogether. He lay motionless in the monster's grasp, powerless to move or even think. He never felt the tentacles wrap tenderly around him. They enmeshed him in a thick, fleshy blanket and tightened imperceptibly, slipping past each other with a soft gelatinous sound. One crawled across Quadroped's face, leaving a trail of slime; three more slithered over his eyes. His empty lungs hurt, but twitching arms covered his mouth and nose.

The visitor's tongue caressed his teeth with a slippery sound; he sloshed gently, pleased with himself. He had found the Key; soon he would appease his hunger. The pig was almost tenderized and seemed plump. His Master would be pleased, would reward him, give him power, *feed* him . . .

A faint musical sound crept through the layers of crawling night. It awakened Quadroped. He listened and felt the soft jellied appendages clutch his skin. His body ached and burned where the monster held him. He tried to struggle again, but the tentacles were wrapped too tightly to permit motion.

The music became a wild song that made the visitor snarl and cringe. The three eyes narrowed, searched for the source and saw nothing. Tentacles groped through the muddy water, weaving through the weeds and crawling over rocks towards the tormentor. The tentacles around Quadroped tightened unmercifully until he was sure he would die from the pain.

The music changed again to a single piercing note that

stabbed the creature's eardrums like a silver needle. The
tentacles writhed, whipping the water into foam. One by
one they went limp, paralyzed by the sound. The visitor
clutched his prize tightly until his last arm died, then the
dazed, bewildered pig fell slowly to the bottom.

Quadroped narrowly avoided a patch of orange fire
corals and settled instead into the soft interior of a large
basket sponge. He lay there gazing up at the paralyzed
monster above his head. He took a deep breath and realized, too late, that he was under water. He waited to choke
and die as his lungs flooded with water. But after a moment his panic subsided; he was still alive. He inhaled once
more; air rushed in. He swished a tentative hoof around
and felt water; he was still in the pond. *Maybe*, Quadroped
thought, *I'm dead; a spirit doomed to float through the
pond forever*.

"You may come out now, Master Pig," said a deep reso-
nant voice, interrupting Quadroped's visions of his spectral
form, a tragic yet noble expression on its face, drifting
transparently through the weeds while his weeping family
dragged the pond for his body. Quadroped peeked carefully
over the rim of the sponge. The voice belonged to a pair of
quizzical grey eyes, and a delicate golden harp perched
high above his head on a coral-encrusted boulder. After a
moment he added the figure of a tall slender man.

"Come here," the man called, "and be quick about it.
We haven't got all day."

All day for what? wondered Quadroped. "How?" he
asked, eyeing the steep sides of the boulder.

"Swim," said the man.

Quadroped recalled that things worked differently underwater. He took a deep breath and started to paddle upwards. When he finally reached the top, he was out of
breath and had to sit still for several moments. The man
quietly studied him, a thoughtful frown marring his pleasant features.

"And now," said the man, when he saw that Quadroped
was no longer winded, "you may tell me why you were
being squeezed by a Water Demon."

"Why should I?" asked the ungrateful Quadroped. He

was frightened and upset. He was not about to tell anyone, no matter *how* kind, about the key in his mouth.

"No reason," came the cool reply. "It would merely be a common courtesy. It is, of course, your own business." The man looked disdainfully down at Quadroped.

Quadroped blushed slightly and mumbled that he had strayed into the pond accidentally and the monster had grabbed him. The man raised an eyebrow and looked extremely displeased.

"If," he said sternly, "you're not going to tell the truth, you shouldn't say anything at all."

"Oh but . . ." began Quadroped, only to be silenced by a haughty look.

"I know you're lying," the man continued. "I have been following this Water Demon for days. He was searching for something. He would not have paused in his search for a mere snack."

"Maybe he mistook me for someone else?" suggested Quadroped ingeniously.

"*Not* likely!" snapped the man. "You must have something his Master wants. That probably means that *I* want it too. I suspect that you are holding it in your mouth. Unless, of course, you have a speech impediment, in which case you have my deepest sympathy." He did not look sympathetic in the least.

"Why were you following that creature and how do you know so much about him?" asked Quadroped timorously. He looked warily around for an escape route just in case the man turned into something hostile.

The man watched Quadroped's expressive face with some amusement. "The Water Demons are old enemies of mine," he said gravely, "and their Master is an even older one."

"Oh," said Quadroped. He paused to consider this statement.

Observing the worried wrinkling of the young pig's snout, the man addressed him in a milder tone. "I know that you're scared," he said, "but you must tell me why you were attacked. You escaped once; you won't be so lucky next time."

"*Next* time?"

"Next time," repeated the man. "You have something they want and they will follow you until they have it. There are worse monsters than Water Demons."

Quadroped received this appalling news with a mounting sense of dread. *Who or what are 'they'?* he wondered. "My father is a warlock," he said. "He'll protect me. Anyway, they can't want it so very badly. It is such a very *small* key, after all."

The man sat up very straight and stared sharply at Quadroped. *"What* did you say?" he demanded.

"I said 'pea,'" Quadroped improvised brilliantly.

"You said 'key,'" the man stated firmly, "and if you have found *the* Key you are in serious trouble. Unless you —and your family—seek an early grave you had better tell me about it."

Quadroped protested weakly that *his* key could not be *the* Key, whatever *it* was. The man merely raised his eyebrows as though he questioned how anyone, even a pig, could be so foolish. "Show it to me," he said, *"now."*

Quadroped stared at the man's face. It was a nice face, strong and kind with laughter lines around the mouth and eyes. *I can trust him,* he decided with relief. *He'll know what to do with it.* He placed the key in the man's outstretched hand. He recalled that dinner awaited him at home and plunged swiftly into his tale.

"Well," said the man when the tale was done, "it *is* the Key." He tied the Key to a spare harp string he pulled from his knapsack, and hung it around Quadroped's neck with no further explanation whatsoever. "And now," he said, rising to his feet and stretching slightly, "it's time for us to go."

"Us?" asked Quadroped dubiously. *"I* am going home. You can have the key; I just want my mother and some dinner."

"I can't carry the Key," said the man. "Now come along."

"Oh, but I can't!" cried Quadroped. "My mother must be frantic by now and—"

"Can't be helped," came the unhelpful reply. "You're

coming with me. Now hop to." The man turned and began to walk away.

Quadroped did not move. *He* wasn't going anywhere, except home. "You," the man declared, "are stubborn. I can't abide stubborn people. If we're to be friendly companions you'll have to break that habit."

Quadroped remained where he was; he had no intention of breaking his habits, and said as much. "Besides," he added petulantly, "why do I have to obey you?"

"Well," said the man, "because I'm Glasgerion."

"Oh," sniffed Quadroped.

"The Glasgerion," the man said.

Quadroped began to worry. *I wonder,* he thought, *if he's the* very *famous bard who wrote all those songs Mother sings at bedtime? That Glasgerion is a real royal Prince.* He looked doubtfully at the man.

"Yes, I'm *that* Glasgerion," said the man, having apparently read Quadroped's mind. "Even if I weren't," he added, "I've just saved your life. I'm only trying to do what's best for you."

Quadroped felt very churlish and scuffled a hoof through the sand. Glasgerion stared pensively at him. "It's unfortunate that you were chosen to be the Key Bearer," he said, "but that can't be altered now. As long as you carry the Key you'll never be safe from the Warlords. The only thing you can do is to come with me. There may still be time to lock the Gate and stop the Black Unicorn."

Quadroped did not know who the Warlords or the Black Unicorn were, but he guessed they were evil. If he went home his family might be killed; suddenly he missed them very much. He started to cry.

"Will you come now?" asked Glasgerion gently.

"Yes," sobbed Quadroped. He tried to look brave but only looked more woebegone than ever.

"Good." Glasgerion laughed. "If you hadn't agreed I might have crunched you up for dinner myself."

Quadroped gave a watery smile. "You can call me Quadro," he offered shyly. They shook hand and hoof and set off into the murky water.

*   *   *

Quadroped tried to study his new companion while they swam. Glasgerion did not look like a Prince, Quadroped decided. His clothes were wrinkled and patched and their color had faded from a dark blue to indeterminate grey. His white hair was too long and it was ragged at the ends, as though he had tried to cut it himself. The only thing princely about him was his harp. The instrument was carved with strange beasts and flowers and covered with gold leaf. Rare gems winked in the animals' wide eyes.

I wonder how old he is, thought Quadroped. *Old humans have white hair, but he doesn't have any wrinkles. He's probably somewhere between thirty-five and fifty,* Quadroped decided. "Are you a magician?" he asked.

"No, just a bard," came the disappointing reply.

"How did you defeat the monster?" asked Quadroped. "Are you a warrior?"

"No, I used my music. It can't kill, but it's mildly effective on lesser horrors." Quadroped secretly wondered how Glasgerion dealt with major horrors. "I don't," said Glasgerion. "I avoid them."

"Where are we?" asked Quadroped after a short silence. Huge corals grew all around him, and brilliantly colored fish swam among their branches. It did not look like a duck pond.

"At the bottom of the Southern Sea," said Glasgerion.

"How *can* we be here?" Quadroped asked. "I fell into the duck pond in my front yard."

"The duck pond is where a subterranean branch of the ocean surfaces," said Glasgerion.

"But it's fresh water."

"Fresh water is lighter than salt water," said Glasgerion. "Rain and spring water float in a lens above the sea water."

"If you're not a magician," said Quadroped pensively, "how can I breathe underwater?"

"You *do* ask a lot of questions." Glasgerion laughed.

"Sorry," said Quadroped, "but—"

"I don't know," said Glasgerion. "I was taught by the sea people. Perhaps you were born with the talent?"

"I don't have any special powers," said Quadroped morosely. "Even Mother says so."

"Then it is the Key which is protecting you," said Glasgerion. "It is a very powerful talisman in the hands of its Key Bearer."

Glasgerion abruptly decided it was getting dark too quickly. He began to lengthen his stride, forcing Quadroped to gallop along behind him until he was quite out of breath.

"Wait! Wait! Oh, *stop!*" cried Quadroped dismally, when he could run no more.

"What *is* the matter with you?" demanded Glasgerion. *He* had found the pace brisk and refreshing.

"I'm sorry," gasped Quadroped, "but I'm smaller than you are, and I'm rather fat. I just *can't* run anymore."

"Too many acorns," pronounced Glasgerion. He stooped and lifted Quadroped onto his right shoulder, admonishing him to hang on tightly.

"Where are we going?" asked Quadroped, as soon as he had accustomed himself to his elevated, if somewhat precarious, position.

"Hopefully to a friend's house," said Glasgerion. "Stop pulling at my ear like that. If you have to hold on, put a hoof around my neck."

Quadroped let go of the ear and wondered what Glasgerion meant by "hopefully." Did Glasgerion hope the house owner was a friend? Or did he hope the friend had a house? When asked, Glasgerion just snorted and told him not to be sillier than necessary. Quadroped fell silent and studied his surroundings.

The bottom of the ocean was a strangely silent place. Gigantic coral columns stretched upwards into the green haze until they were lost from sight. Quadroped supposed that the columns eventually reached the surface. He imagined the great blue waves crashing over their jagged tops, sending rainbows and sea spray high into the air. Tall, pale weeds waved with monotonous regularity in the gentle swells. Schools of small fishes mimicked the motion, floating back and forth with the water until some unseen danger startled them, and they dashed away in an explosion of bright fins.

Sponges of all shapes and colors grew upon the corals. Quadroped looked into the center of a lime-green tube sponge. A pair of milky blue eyes glared suspiciously at him from the ends of two fragile pink stalks. A crab waved its orange claws threateningly, danced away sideways on six hind legs, and hid in a dark crevice.

Black sea urchins inched across the coral walls, their rippling black spines revealing flashes of indigo blue. The spines were long and sharp; Quadroped was glad he had not landed in them when the demon had dropped him. Once, Quadroped saw a black tentacle wrapped around a lavender sea fan, and gave a cry of fear. Glasgerion laughed, and told him it was nothing but an octopus.

"They are shy creatures," Glasgerion informed the startled pig. "That one would be insulted if it knew you'd mistaken it for a demon."

Though the sea floor was lovely, it was also faintly disturbing. As the night approached the water became colder, and the bright colors faded into somber browns, maroons and dark greens. The small fish disappeared, vanished into the reef. Large, silver predators appeared and hung silently overhead; their black mouths gaped to expose rows of thin teeth.

"Those are barracuda," said Glasgerion with a frown. "Put the Key in your mouth, Quadro If they see it, they may swim closer to investigate."

A dark shadow streaked over the sand. Quadroped looked up and saw a huge fish shaped like a *T*. Dark, soulless eyes glittered on either end of the crossbar.

"Hammerhead," said Glasgerion, his jaw tightening.

"What?" asked Quadroped.

"A shark." Glasgerion began to walk faster, Quadroped holding on as tightly as he could.

The journey ended abruptly in front of a long wall of corals. Glasgerion stopped so suddenly that Quadroped was flung from his perch. He landed headfirst in a patch of ruby sea anemones. He emerged squealing, for the soft creatures had stung him rather badly, and was advised by

Glasgerion to rub some sand across the welts. Glasgerion turned callously away and began to study the wall. Quadroped watched in curious silence while Glasgerion peered into dark holes, glanced inside sponges and thumped loudly on coral heads.

"What are you doing?" asked Quadroped.

"Looking for the door." Glasgerion's tone implied that this should be obvious to anyone with a little sense.

"Door?" repeated Quadroped blankly.

"Door," said Glasgerion, his voice muffled by a clump of gorgonians.

"Door to what?" asked Quadroped. He had thought all doors were rectangular, wooden, brightly painted and with yellow brass knobs. Glasgerion was examining a thicket of delicate purple sea fans and did not reply.

After an hour of searching, Glasgerion cried, "Hah! I've found it." He was looking into the interior of a pale-pink sponge the size of a large barrel.

"Is that a door?" asked Quadroped, trotting over to inspect the sponge. "It doesn't look like one."

"It's been disguised," explained Glasgerion patiently. "The witch doesn't like visitors, so she hides her front door."

"Oh," said Quadroped, alarmed by the mention of a witch. "Are you going to jump into that sponge?" His eyes implored Glasgerion to deny this dreadful suspicion.

"Of course," said Glasgerion with depressing cheerfulness. "Now, I want you to stay right here until I come back. I must be sure this is the right address. We must not be caught by the Warlords' minions now."

"Oh . . . but I don't *want* to stay out here alone," wailed Quadroped. "What if the Water Demon comes back to get me?"

"He won't," said Glasgerion. He vanished headfirst into the sponge with a muffled oath and an encouraging, "Be back soon."

When Glasgerion had gone, Quadroped crept to the rim of the sponge and peered inside. The sponge concealed a bottomless hole that stretched down into the ground beneath the reef. He shuddered and settled down on a soft clump of seaweed to await Glasgerion's return. He hoped Glasgerion would not stay away too long; he felt unprotected, and it was growing dark.

"I wonder," Quadroped mused, "what kind of person would live at the bottom of the sea at the end of a black tunnel? Glasgerion said she was a witch." His vivid imagination conjured up an unsettling picture of a slime-covered hag with long yellow teeth; he thought about dinner instead. He was dwelling on thoughts of buttered toast when the idea of hungry witches crept unbidden into his mind. *I do wish Glasgerion would hurry,* he thought, and nibbled on a stalk of seaweed.

Quadroped waited patiently for Glasgerion. He waited, and waited, and waited, until it was pitch-dark and his muscles ached from sitting still too long. He was very worried, and the icy current that swirled past made him shiver. All around he could hear and feel strange creatures swimming past. Some, especially those with the glowing eyes, came uncomfortably close, one going so far as to nip his ear. He recalled the lurking predators glimpsed at twilight and was grateful that he had only been lightly nibbled. *I wonder,* he thought pessimistically, *how long it will be before I am devoured whole?*

Glasgerion must have forgotten me, Quadroped decided. A tear formed and dissolved in the water around him. He thought about all his mother had told him about the famous bard, as well as his own impressions, and rejected that idea. *Maybe he's in trouble,* he thought. *I'll have to go into the tunnel and find him before a hungry something finds me.* A long, scaly body chose that moment to curl around his legs, sending him scrambling towards the sponge.

Quadroped hesitated and gazed uncertainly at the sponge which glowed with an unhealthy phosphorescence and reconsidered his decision. But the memory of eyes seen and nips received swiftly convinced him that if he stayed out in the open he would not live until morning. *Anyway,* he reasoned, *Glasgerion went in and he wasn't scared. Although, he hasn't come out either; maybe he's dead*. Quadroped ignored this thought and stepped closer to the sponge. One sniff, two sniffs; no, there was nothing lurking just inside. He jumped in and tumbled down the tunnel.

Chapter Two

The tunnel stretched far below the ocean floor. Quadroped plummeted through the darkness, spinning and tumbling until the motion made him dizzy. "This is terrible," he moaned as he collided with the stony walls of the shaft. "I'll be crushed when I hit the bottom." He had just abandoned all hope of landing when he suddenly bounced onto a soft sandy floor. He quickly discovered that he was alive and uninjured, so he picked himself up and looked around. He was in the middle of a spacious cavern. Globular sponges grew on the ceiling, bathing the chamber with cold silvery light and casting strange blue shadows on the white sand. Long straight rows of evil-looking fungoid plants covered the floor.

It looks like a garden, thought Quadroped. *I wonder if anything's edible?* But the plants looked poisonous and he was afraid to try them. Glasgerion was nowhere in sight, but he found a set of deep footprints stretching towards a delicate gold gate set in the far wall. *Glasgerion must be in the next cave*, Quadroped decided.

Quadroped stood on his hind legs, forelegs braced

against the gate, and tried to reach the latch with his nose. He had just succeeded in pushing the bar back when a sharp voice said, "Go back. Go back, you are *not* welcome and we don't want any."

"Any what?" asked Quadroped, dropping to the ground.

"Any anything," elucidated the voice in an uncompromising tone. "We're not at home to salesmen."

"But I'm not," said Quadroped timidly, searching for the speaker. "My companion is inside."

"Do you know the password?" asked the voice peevishly.

"No," said Quadroped.

"Or do you have a written invitation?"

"No but—"

"Do you *even*," the voice persisted, ignoring Quadroped's protest, "know the name of the owner?" Quadroped reluctantly admitted that he did not. "*Well* then," said the voice, "you can't come in. Private property. No vagabonds, salesmen or stray livestock permitted." A cloud of sand rose into the water as a gigantic moray eel, possessing two rows of razor sharp teeth, swam into view. "Go away," he hissed. "Go away or I'll *eat* you." He glared malevolently at the unwanted pig.

"But I *can't* go away," wailed Quadroped. "I have nowhere else to go. And anyway, I won't." *If the eel eats me,* he thought, *at least I'll know what killed me. I don't even know what the things outside are.*"

"Well, well," said the eel, "you *are* spunky, aren't you? I never would have thought it of such a *round* creature. Still, you can't come in; but I suppose it would be all right if you slept in the ornamental sponge patch." He indicated a plot of rainbow-hued sponges in a far corner. "Nothing will harm you in here," he added benevolently. "Everyone is scared of me." Quadroped replied that he could quite see why and the eel, looking pleased with the compliment, glided back into the shadows.

Quadroped returned to the garden and stared longingly at the plants. They smelled like food and he was very hungry. *The witch will be angry if I eat them,* he thought. He recalled his mother's hatred of the turtles that ravaged the garden each year. He nibbled tentatively at a fleshy pink leaf; it was juicy and sweet. Hunger vanquished his common sense. *I'll only eat a few,* he thought.

Half an hour later Quadroped finished his meal and curled up in the middle of the ornamental sponge patch. *I wonder what* did *happen to Glasgerion,* he thought, but he did not worry for long. He was warm, safe, and well fed. The sponges were very comfortable, and it had been a *long* day.

Quadroped was rudely awakened next morning by a woman's furious cry. The witch had entered her garden to find a series of ugly, gaping holes where her favorite plants had grown. It was not long before she discovered the perpetrator of this foul crime curled up comfortably on the squashed remains of her ornamental sponge patch. Her skin and hair began to glow, and the water was suffused with a flickering crimson light.

"Wretch! Abysmal pig!" she cried, her luminous red eyes narrow with rage. "Remove yourself from my sponge patch at once!" She prodded him forcibly in the ribs with one elegant foot.

"Ouch! Help!" yelped Quadroped, exploding to his feet.

The witch towered over him, her hair and scarlet robes swirling around her slender form like flames. "What are you doing here?" she said.

Quadroped cowered under a sponge and babbled a confused apology.

"Glasgerion!" called the witch, ignoring Quadroped's muddled speech. "Come and get rid of this repulsive pig for me. Glasgerion!"

"There's no need to shout, Morragwen, I'm right behind you," said Glasgerion quietly. Quadroped looked cautiously up as Glasgerion approached the witch. The bard looked unpardonably healthy.

"Well, get rid of it." Morragwen kicked Quadroped again.

"Please stop kicking my companion," said Glasgerion. "He's not, despite appearances, a ball." He smiled reassuringly at Quadroped and slipped a conciliatory arm around Morragwen's trim waist.

"Oh, so he's yours, is he?" demanded Morragwen, brushing Glasgerion's arm aside. "Look what your monster's done to my garden." She gestured towards the multitude of half-eaten plants that littered the ground.

Glasgerion surveyed the horrible destruction with dismay; his lips thinned with irritation. "Really, Quadro," he said, "*must* you be so messy?"

"Messy!" raged Morragwen. "Is that what you call it? He isn't messy; he's a destructive menace. *Why* was he left in my garden all night instead of safely locked up in a cupboard?"

"Yes. Why *was* I left alone?" asked Quadroped.

Glasgerion scowled at him to be quiet. "I left Quadroped by the front door," he said. "You witched me asleep before I could collect him. If he hadn't found his way into your garden, he would have been killed." Glasgerion looked very stern, and Morragwen lowered her eyes.

"You looked tired. You needed to rest," she defended herself. "I couldn't guess that you'd left a pig outside." She shrugged angrily and stalked away.

"You should *not* have eaten Morragwen's garden, Quadro," said Glasgerion when the witch was gone.

Quadroped glared indignantly at the bard. "You *forgot* me," he said. "An eel almost ate me. I was *cold,* and *hungry,* and *frightened* and you *promised* to come back. Why shouldn't I have eaten her nasty mushrooms?"

"They're not really mushrooms," said Glasgerion, momentarily sidetracked, "but a unique suborder of the phylum Porifera. However," he continued severely, "it was wrong to eat them. I'm *very* sorry I didn't return. Morragwen put a spell on me, but that doesn't give you the right to destroy her whole garden."

"I didn't mean to. I only ate a few," said Quadroped earnestly.

"*Quite* a few," said Glasgerion drily, contemplating the wasteland around them. "You really *must* apologize, Quadro."

"All right," agreed Quadroped. He was secretly appalled by the enormity of his crime; the garden hadn't looked so bad in the dark. "You won't forget me again, will you?" he asked.

"Never again," Glasgerion promised fervently. He scooped Quadroped up and gave him a quick hug.

They found Morragwen setting out breakfast dishes in a small parlor tastefully decorated with yellow corals. Her demeanor was less formidable, for her complexion had changed to a serene azure hue. She smiled bewitchingly when she saw Glasgerion. The look she gave Quadroped was, if not welcoming, at least resigned.

"I'm very sorry I ate your garden," Quadroped apologized politely, eyeing the dishes with interest. "I'll never eat your garden again."

"I'll never let you near enough to do so," retorted Morragwen, but she smiled faintly.

Quadroped was encouraged enough to ask, "Is there any breakfast?"

"Breakfast?!" exclaimed Morragwen indignantly, a frown darkening her delicate features. "You've devoured my lovely garden, you awful creature, and still you hunger for more? Do you intend to eat me out of house and home? Glasgerion, take your unruly pig and speak sternly to him." Quadroped's ears drooped and Morragwen relented. "Oh, very well, abominable piglet," she said, "you shall have some breakfast. I'll have to find you a cushion; you won't reach the table otherwise." A silk pillow was swiftly produced. Quadroped squirmed happily out of Glasgerion's arms and clambered onto his chair.

"So now, Glasgerion," said Morragwen when all save Quadroped had eaten his fill, "tell me why you are here. And *what* are you doing with a baby pig?"

"He *is* an unusual companion, isn't he?" asked Glasgerion, deftly removing the jam cakes from the vicinity of his small but voracious charge. "Creatures from Ravenor have been sighted in this vicinity. I was on my way to visit you. I thought you might know what Goriel was up to. When I saw there was a Water Demon skulking about I followed him. He was after Quadroped."

"He was attacked by a *Water* Demon?" asked Morragwen. "Glasgerion, that was not Goriel's doing."

"Whose then?"

"Only the Manslayer can control the creatures of the sea," she said. "Someone has released him, but who? Only the Sea Lords knew his whereabouts."

"There must be a traitor in Seamourn," said Glasgerion. He looked upset and Morragwen changed the subject.

"Why were the Warlords after Quadroped?" she asked.

"He's found the Key."

"What?" Morragwen gasped. "He *can't* have found the Key, Glasgerion, he's a piglet." She reached across the table and captured Glasgerion's hands in her own. Their eyes met. "Are you sure it's the Key?" she asked gently. "You've searched so long . . ."

Glasgerion chuckled. "Quadro," he said, "show Morragwen the Key." Quadroped obediently placed the Key in Morragwen's outstretched hands.

"It *looks* right," agreed Morragwen. She studied the symbols etched on its surface, brows knit with concentration. Her low voice shook slightly as she read the inscription aloud.

" 'There is Intelligence and Mind
Out in the darkness of the void
That thinks, that listens, and that waits,
The opening of unwatched Gates.'

"The inscription is so melodramatic it *must* be real," said Morragwen.

"I told you so," said Glasgerion ignobly.

"Quadro has gotten jelly on it," said Morragwen absently. "How did he find it?"

"It dropped on him," said Glasgerion ruefully. "The world's greatest heroes have searched for a century and a baby pig finds it by *accident*. I'll have to get him to the Gate before the Warlords catch him."

Morragwen studied the young pig pensively. "Quadro," she said, "the way to the Gate is very dangerous. Are you certain you want to go?"

"Yup," mumbled Quadroped over a mouthful of pancakes. He had absolutely no idea what she was talking about. He had not understood the conversation from the first and had wisely devoted himself to the food.

Morragwen placed a hand beneath Quadroped's chin and raised his head until their eyes met. "Quadro, do you know what the Key *is?*" Quadroped looked blank. "Do you know *anything* about the Key?"

"Nope," said Quadroped. The Key was connected with Water Demons, Warlords and unpleasant Unicorns; he really didn't *want* to know anything more about it.

Morragwen released him and turned on Glasgerion. "How can you let Quadro go to the Gate when he doesn't even know the dangers involved? Explain them to him."

"I *was* trying to avoid doing that," complained Glasgerion. "A terrified pig is a useless pig."

Oh dear, thought Quadroped. *Now I am getting scared.* He began to fidget nervously.

"Stop squiggling, Quadro," said Morragwen as she removed the apple tarts from his reach. "Glasgerion is going to tell you a story." Quadroped reluctantly lifted his ears.

Glasgerion showed little sign of beginning. He tipped his chair against the wall and stared at the ceiling as though he had never seen one before. "Glasgerion," said Morragwen sweetly, "we're waiting."

"It's very complex," said Glasgerion, eyes still fixed on the stuccoed trim. "I suppose I should start at the beginning?"

"Most likely," agreed Morragwen, "but you're the bard."

"Well, I don't want to scare Quadro unnecessarily." Glasgerion brought his chair down with a heavy *clump*. In a deep, serious voice he told Quadroped the story of the Key.

"Long ago the Black Unicorn of Ravenor declared war upon the Kings of the World. Why he did so no one knows. In the hundreds of bloody years that followed, the origins of the war were forgotten. Perhaps he desired the fertile green lands beyond his own kingdom. For Ravenor is a desolate land, lying west of the Crystalline Mountains, and nothing grows there but monsters and minerals. Whatever the reason, he swore that he would not rest until the world lay crushed beneath his hooves.

"The Kings of the World combined their armies to meet this threat. They chose a Prince of Essylt, the largest of the Kingdoms, as their warlord. The ensuing wars lasted for over a century. Generations of Kings grew up and died defending their lands against the immortal Black Unicorn and his four terrible Warlords.

"A thousand years ago the sorcerer Rhiogan, another Prince of Essylt, brought the Great War to an end. In the caverns below the forgotten city of Illoreth, he forged a key and unlocked a gateway into the half-formed world of Chaos. He tricked the Black Unicorn through this Gate, imprisoning him. But before Rhiogan could complete his work and lock the Gate forever he was slain by the evil Warlord Goriel.

"Chaos still touches our world and once every hundred years the passage between the worlds is opened. Then Rhiogan's Key must lock the Gate once more or the Black Unicorn will be freed and the Great War begin anew.

"There have been many Key Bearers since the Gate was first locked. Their stories are too lengthy to tell you now. A hundred years ago the Key vanished from the vaults of Essylt—stolen, it seems, by nothing more sinister than a bird. For ninety-nine years men have searched for the Key without success. Now the Gate is about to open and the Kingdoms are preparing for war. The Prince of Essylt is already gathering the armies together to face the Black Unicorn when he breaks free. Now that you have found the Key, the Gate can be locked. If we travel fast we may reach Illoreth in time to prevent another war."

"Is my key really the Key to Chaos?" asked Quadroped softly.

"Yes," said Glasgerion.

"Tell Quadro about the Warlords," said Morragwen. "It is they who will try to stop him from locking the Gate. The Black Unicorn is still trapped in Chaos and can do him no harm." Her voice was melancholy and her eyes were sad. Quadroped supposed that Glasgerion's story had upset her as much as it had him.

Glasgerion sipped his orange juice. "The Black Unicorn has four demonic Warlords," he said, "chosen for their power and their loyalty to Ravenor. They are Goriel, Toridon, the Manslayer and one who remains anonymous. The Manslayer sent the Water Demon to kill you." Quadroped turned pale and Morragwen put him on her lap for comfort.

"Toridon and the Manslayer," Glasgerion continued, "were defeated in the last days of the war and imprisoned deep inside the Mid-Oceanic Mountains. The nameless Warlord vanished, possibly slain or banished to Chaos with the Black Unicorn. In the past, only Goriel remained to oppose the Key Bearers from his palace of ice, high on a summit in the Crystalline Mountains."

"You must never underestimate Goriel's powers, Quadro," added Morragwen grimly. "He was ever the strongest Warlord, second only to the Black Unicorn in power. He is a brilliant and pitiless opponent. The success of the former Key Bearers was largely due to fortune, and none lived long after locking the Gate. You have a harder trip ahead of you than any Key Bearer before you. You must face two Warlords, for it seems that the Manslayer is free. Quadro, do you really want to go to the Gate?"

"Not really," said Quadroped, "but I have to, don't I? Glasgerion can't carry the Key. If I don't go, the Black Unicorn will destroy the world."

"No," said Glasgerion, "he won't do that just yet. We'll fight him again; perhaps we'll win this time. I won't force you to risk your life for a world you've barely seen or lived in yet."

Quadroped stared at the crumbs on his plate. "I'll go," he said at last. He was not descended from a herd of fairy pigs for nothing.

"Good," said Glasgerion; he clapped Quadroped warmly on the back. Quadroped felt very small indeed and looked about hopefully for another piece of toast.

"Will you start for Illoreth at dawn?" asked Morragwen.

"I'd like to," said Glasgerion, "but I don't know where Illoreth is. It was abandoned in the early days of the Great War and there are no maps left that show it."

"You must go to Seamourn," said Morragwen. "Illoreth's location is a sea secret and Angmar, the Sea King, knows the way."

"What's Seamourn?" asked Quadroped.

"Seamourn," said Glasgerion, "is the submarine city of the sea people, largest of the Southern Cities. We're going to ask the Sea King how to get to Illoreth. Illoreth," he added patiently, "is where the Gate to Chaos stands."

"You should travel in disguise," said Morragwen. "The Warlords may not know who the Key Bearer is but they know where he is and where he must go."

"How did they find me?" asked Quadroped. "I only had the Key for a few minutes before the monster attacked."

"Key Bearers are not selected at random," said Morragwen. "I don't understand how they are chosen, but Goriel does. He has always been able to predict where and when a new Key Bearer will be chosen. That power makes him particularly deadly." Quadroped gulped; hostile eyes were watching his every move.

"Goriel can't see you, Quadro," said Morragwen. "The Key is hidden, and hides its bearer, from spells. That is why no one was able to find the Key when it was lost. Goriel knew where it would be found and when but with any luck he does not yet know who found it. But while magic cannot see you, eyes can and the Warlords' spies will be waiting for you. Goriel knows the Key Bearer must go to Seamourn. If he recognizes you, Glasgerion, he will look for the Key Bearer nearby. He may even suspect that you are the Key Bearer."

"I'll become a poor traveling minstrel," said Glasgerion. "I'll dye my hair and wear old clothes. You can turn Quadro into my faithful hound."

"But I don't want to *be* a faithful hound," said Quadroped loudly. "Can't you dye me pink? Then I'll look like an ordinary pig. In fact I'll *be* an ordinary pig because I don't have any magical powers."

"No," agreed Morragwen sympathetically. "But a minstrel accompanied by his pet pig is bound to attract attention. Even," she added over Quadroped's protests, "if it is a *very* ordinary pig."

"Don't be difficult," said Glasgerion. "You'll be a dog,

and that's that. And you mustn't talk, the sea people's dogs don't."

Quadroped glowered at Glasgerion. *Really*, he thought, *not only are they going to change me into a horrible dog, they won't even let me talk*.

"Glasgerion," Morragwen objected, "you always wear old clothes. You'll be recognized as soon as you sing."

"You are *not* going to alter my voice."

"Then I'll have to transform your body," said Morragwen. "Don't frown, Glasgerion, changing shape is fun." She became a mermaid with long blue hair.

"I like that one," said Glasgerion.

"How will you arrange to see Angmar?" asked Morragwen.

"His jester, Caelbad, is a good friend of mine," said Glasgerion. "He will recognize me through any disguise. It will not be hard to arrange a meeting with him and he has the power to arrange an audience with the King."

"Then I think," said Morragwen, thoughtfully twitching her tail, "that the enchantment should only be broken by Angmar's gaze. Otherwise Goriel could undo the charm before you can reach him. Of course," she added doubtfully, "if you don't reach Angmar, you'll be changed forever."

"If we don't reach Angmar Goriel will have found us," said Glasgerion grimly.

"You won't escape Goriel for long," Morragwen warned him. "It is a long way to Illoreth and you are an abysmal warrior."

"I'm an abysmal magician too," said Glasgerion frankly. "Reander will have to help us if we're to reach Illoreth alive. Can you contact him?"

"The spell is not too arduous," said Morragwen.

"Who's Reander?" asked Quadroped.

"My nephew," said Glasgerion.

"Reander," said Morragwen, "is the current Prince of Essylt and a thoroughly loathsome man."

"He's not that bad," said Glasgerion. "He's in Essylt gathering an army together to fight the Black Unicorn.

Let's send Quadro out to play before we call. I don't want Reander to know our Key Bearer is a piglet."

"Why not?" asked Quadroped.

"Because he wouldn't like it," said Glasgerion.

"You'll have to tell him eventually," said Morragwen.

"I'll deal with that problem when it arises," said Glasgerion. "He'll be angry enough when he learns where I am. He's told me to stay away from you, Morragwen. He's convinced that you're from Ravenor."

Morragwen sniffed and rang a small silver bell. The eel of the night before swam silently into the room in answer to the summons. "Morrag," she said, as the eel glided up to Quadroped, "that is Quadroped. Show him the reef and keep him entertained until dinner. Glasgerion and I have unpleasant work to do."

"So," said Morrag as they went into the garden, "you were invited after all. I'm sorry you had to sleep outside. Were you comfortable?"

"Very," mumbled Quadroped. Morrag was still formidable, though he did not seem about to pounce. "The sponge patch was very nice."

"I'm glad you think so. You must be very important if Morragwen forgave you for destroying it."

"I didn't mean to," said Quadroped. "I'm not important at all, or I wasn't until yesterday."

"What happened yesterday?" asked Morrag.

"Oh, *lots* of things," said Quadroped. "I met Glasgerion, I was attacked by a Water Demon and I found a little key."

"You found *the* Key?" Morrag asked. "How did you do it? Are you a magician? Glasgerion has been looking for it for *ages*."

"It fell on me," said Quadroped simply, and told Morrag his story.

"Well, Key Bearer," said Morrag, "good luck. It's a great honor to be a Key Bearer, but I don't envy you."

"I *am* a bit frightened," said Quadroped, "but Glasgerion will protect me."

"Maybe," said Morrag doubtfully, "but be careful, Key Bearer."

"Please call me Quadro," said Quadroped earnestly, "'Key Bearer' is so formal. I'm not large enough for a title like that."

"Quadro it is then," said Morrag affably. "Come along, Quadro, I'll show you the reef."

The reef was lovely in the daytime; all of the frightening creatures had crawled off to sleep. Everyone respected Morrag; they bowed and called him "Lord Morrag" when he addressed them. Quadroped met many strange beings, including a spiny fish with seaweed growing all over its back.

"I'm a toad fish," the creature said. "It's not a nice name, but it's the only one I have. I nipped you last night."

"Oh," said Quadroped.

"I am not always sweet tempered," said the toad fish. "You were sitting on my favorite patch of weed. I like to sit there and trick minnows into swimming too close. If I'm very quiet it's almost impossible to tell me apart from the weeds."

"Oh," repeated Quadroped politely. "I didn't mean to sit on your weeds; if you hadn't nipped me I might never have found Glasgerion."

"A nicely behaved youngster, that," said the toad fish to Morrag. "A pity he is so round."

"True," Morrag replied, gazing at his own slender, cylindrical body with renewed appreciation.

At four o'clock, Morrag took Quadroped back to his own, elegantly furnished hole for tea and cake before dinner.

"Morrag," asked Quadroped, as he polished off the spice cake, "who is Reander?"

"How did you hear about *him?*" Morrag asked, looking slightly disgusted.

"Glasgerion says we need his help to reach the Gate," said Quadroped. "He asked Morragwen to contact him and then he sent me away so Reander wouldn't see me.

Doesn't Reander *like* pigs?" Quadroped's eyes were dark with worry.

Morrag searched desperately for something that would reassure Quadroped without being a downright lie. "I'm sure Reander doesn't hold anything against pigs, Quadro, but he's, well . . . he's *heroic,* if you know what I mean."

"I don't really," said Quadroped. "I thought all heroes were good and noble, like Glasgerion."

"Reander *is* good and noble," said Morrag helplessly. "But he's also stern, proud and . . . formal. He's only thirty and already he's the ruler of Essylt, a great warrior and one of the greatest sorcerers alive. He won't be impressed by you, Quadro, you're too round and too young. But don't worry too much, he'll probably ignore you. You'll have Glasgerion for company."

"Maybe he won't help us," said Quadroped.

"Not a chance," said Morrag with awful certainty. "He would do anything to stop the Black Unicorn's escape. Besides, Glasgerion is his uncle and one of his only close friends; he can't let Goriel slaughter him."

"Oh," said Quadroped.

"Cheer up, Quadro," said Morrag. "Glasgerion is no protection against beings as powerful as the Warlords. With Reander along you'll have a fair chance of reaching Illoreth alive."

"Can't you and Morragwen come with us instead?" asked Quadroped.

"Morragwen wouldn't stand a chance against Goriel, and Reander would never allow it. Morragwen is seven hundred years old and a witch. He thinks she's from Ravenor."

"But Morragwen is so *nice,*" said Quadroped.

"Lots of people are nice, Quadro," sighed Morrag. "That doesn't mean they're on your side. Reander *is* on your side and he's downright unpleasant."

"But Glasgerion trusts her," said Quadroped.

"Glasgerion is in love with her," said Morrag. "And Reander thinks he's bewitched. If Morragwen ever agreed to marry Glasgerion I don't know what Reander would do." Morrag paused reflectively then said, "I guess he'd kill her."

Quadroped fell silent, then he said, "If Morragwen could contact Reander, could she tell my parents that I'm all right?" asked Quadroped. He had been worrying about his parents all day.

"Spells like that only work when both parties are exceptionally powerful magicians," said Morrag. "Besides, Quadro, if your parents knew what you were doing they'd be just as worried as they are now." Morrag paused, interrupted by the deep tones of a bell.

"What's that?" asked Quadroped, perking up his ears.

"The dinner bell," replied Morrag. He uncoiled and glided towards a large mirror that covered an entire wall.

"Dinner? Oh goody," said Quadroped, his ears wagging and his eyes acquiring a happy shine. "Let's go."

Morrag was not about to stir from his mirror. Slowly he polished his gleaming olive skin; languidly he filed each of his one hundred teeth to a razor point and applied pearl drops and toothpaste. With deliberate ease he attached glimmering gold and emerald patches along his body-tail. Quadroped watched these proceedings in silent amazement but eventually his hunger got the best of him. "Oh, Morrag, let's *go*," he pleaded.

"Not yet, not yet," murmured the eel, applying eye drops and scent. "How do I look?" he asked after a prolonged moment.

"Wonderful, marvelous," said Quadroped quickly, hoping to speed the eel up.

Morrag appeared to think so too for he muttered, "Too true, too true," flicked an imaginary speck of dust off his immaculate fin and began to glide majestically towards the door, the gems on his tail flashing with every graceful undulation.

Luck was not with Quadroped that night. "*You*," said Morrag, coming to a dead halt and regarding him icily, "certainly look a mess! What do you mean, may I ask, by coming to dinner with *me* in *that* state of dress!"

So Quadroped, who did look rather muddy and disheveled, was pushed into a large soapy tub and scrubbed briskly by the offended eel. As the dirt disappeared, the eel became more cheerful.

"I suppose"—he smiled—"you are marveling at the nicety of my tastes and my air of genteel refinement?" Quadroped admitted that he was, all the other eels on the reef had been encrusted with barnacles and slime. "A natural surprise," agreed the eel. "You see, Morragwen once turned me into a cat for a week."

"Glub?" asked Quadroped, getting a large dollop of soapy water in his mouth.

"Yes," said Morrag calmly, "and it was so wonderful to feel clean that I was incapable of becoming a normal eel again. Once I was as messy as you," he said with a shudder and scrubbed at Quadroped's ears till they hurt.

"Why did you change back?" asked the sodden pig. "Couldn't you have become a catfish instead of an eel?"

"A catfish. Certainly not!" cried Morrag indignantly. "It is my duty to protect Morragwen and who, may I ask, would be scared by a belligerent catfish?"

"I would," admitted Quadroped.

"Oh *you!*" scoffed the eel, grabbing a towel off the hook and beginning to dry Quadroped off. When he had finished, Quadroped, who had been a dull grey color, shone pure white and almost looked dignified. Pleased, Morrag gave him a silver chain on which to hang the Key, rather than the old harp string.

Morragwen's tastes were expensive and exotic. The dining room walls were fashioned of black coral, the floors paved with mother-of-pearl. A long marble table, heaped with delicacies, ran down the center. Morragwen had even supplied a bowl of acorns. Garlands of glowing sponges swung from carved rafters, bathing the room in a lavender glow.

Glasgerion and Morragwen were seated, arms entwined, at the head of the table, their heads bent together in conversation. They stood up when Quadroped and Morrag entered, and Quadroped was glad Morrag had given him a bath. Morragwen was violet and she wore white satin hemmed in gold and covered with tiny amethyst and pearl

flowers. Glasgerion had cut and combed his hair; he wore
the deep blue and silver of the bardic tradition. They
looked just as Quadroped had thought heroes and great
ladies would. Dinner was delicious and Quadroped ate
much too much for a pig his size. Eventually, when he
could eat no more, he settled back and began to quietly
suck his hoof.

"When is Reander coming?" asked Morrag.

"In a week or so," said Glasgerion. "We'll have to reach
Seamourn on our own. When I told him we needed help
sooner he told me the Key Bearer couldn't possibly be a
worse swordsman than I am." He chuckled.

"Enough talk of Reander," said Morragwen. "Play
something for us, Glasgerion. Sing the song about Eorlahelm."

"It's depressing," objected Glasgerion.

"But beautiful." Morragwen snapped her fingers and the
harp appeared in Glasgerion's hands.

Glasgerion's strong fingers strayed almost idly across
the taut strings, extracting a melancholy air. His voice was
rich and deep, his ability to evoke emotions in his audience
almost magical. Quadroped found himself sniffling sleepily
though he had no idea what the song was about. In a
sombre voice Glasgerion sang:

Eorlahelm took to the sea one night
To follow the paths
That the ghost fish make,
Into the North where the ice is a light
Reshed from a foreign star;
Follow the phosphorescence forth
As it streams from the backs
Of the winter whales,
Find Eorlahelm in his small boat
And bring him home to his sad kinfolk.

Glasgerion laid his harp aside and rose from the table.
"Quadro, you should go to sleep now," he said. "We must
be on our way at dawn." Quadroped yawned. Glasgerion
scooped him up and carried him off. With some difficulty,

Morrag and Glasgerion succeeded in squeezing the sleepy pig down Morrag's hole and popping him into bed.

"Good night, Quadro," said Glasgerion softly. "Wake him up no later than four-thirty, Morrag."

"I'll do my best," said Morrag, eyeing the somnolent Quadroped doubtfully.

"Up!" cried Morrag at an unfashionably early hour. "You leave soon and Glasgerion has already breakfasted."

"Ugh, food!" grunted the snout under the coverlet. "I'm sleepy, go 'way!" He tucked his head under the pillow and curled into a tight ball.

"Oh *no* you don't!" said Morrag, advancing to the bed. "Up you get. Now!" He pounced on poor Quadroped and tickled him savagely until he was forced to rise.

"Nasty," said Quadroped, and proceeded to wash his ears. Twenty minutes later found Quadroped at the breakfast table consuming the remains of a bran muffin.

"Ready to go?" Glasgerion strode into the room, his harp and knapsack slung over his shoulders.

"Yup," chirped the bane of the breakfast table and hopped down from his stool.

"Not so fast, you two," said Morragwen, hurrying into the room. "I have to disguise you. Now, who wants to be first?"

Glasgerion grinned. "I will."

Morragwen drew a slender ivory wand from her sleeve and waved it over Glasgerion. Her eyes twinkled mischievously. "Grey and greasy," she said. Glasgerion's silver hair darkened and hung limply over his eyes. "Blue eyes, one squints. Smaller nose, wart on side. Rough skin, not so tall, crooked teeth." In an instant a short, troll-like being crouched where the handsome bard had been.

"Morragwen! Take away the warts and the squint at once!"

"Don't be vain, Glasgerion. Nobody will recognize you now," said Morragwen.

"And how am I supposed to find lodging in Seamourn?" asked Glasgerion. "People will run away sooner than sit and look at me, no matter how good my voice is."

"Oh, very well; no wart, no squint, straight teeth. And now for Quadro."

"No!" Quadroped took refuge behind Glasgerion's left foot. "I don't want to be a dog! I hate dogs!"

"Don't be silly," said Morragwen. "This won't hurt a bit." She waved her hand and said, "dog."

"Oh good *god!*" said Glasgerion, surveying the transformed pig.

"Sorry," said Morragwen. "I tried for a dog, but he's so young."

Quadroped looked up anxiously. "If I'm not a dog, what *am* I?" he asked.

"A puppy," said Glasgerion. "Puppies," he added "are more trouble than piglets! We'll have every child in the kingdom chasing after us." He glared at Morragwen and her eyes began to flash.

"What are you going to do about the Key?" asked Morrag quickly.

"I can't work a spell on it," said Morragwen.

"Just as well," said Glasgerion. "You might turn it into a frog by mistake."

"Can't we make a dog collar with a hidden pocket on the inside for the Key?" asked Quadroped.

This suggestion met with approval from all concerned. Morragwen promptly conjured up a neat little red collar, which Glasgerion, much to her displeasure, described as "showy."

"Now," said Glasgerion, when the collar had been fastened on and the Key and chain hidden, "let's be off. We have a long journey ahead of us."

"Wait a moment," said Morragwen. "I have a present for you." She handed him two gold buckles in the shape of dolphins. "Put them on your belt, one on either side."

"What are they?" asked Glasgerion suspiciously.

"Put them on."

Glasgerion attached the buckles. "Now what?"

"Think 'forward.'"

Glasgerion obeyed and found himself shooting towards the ceiling. His head hit the roof with a sickening crack. "Get me down!" he cried.

"Think 'down,'" instructed Morragwen. "They'll carry you wherever you want to go."

"I want to travel sideways, not straight up and down," said Glasgerion crossly.

"Then point sideways, as if you were swimming," said Morragwen.

Glasgerion fell forwards, tried again. The experiment was more successful and, after the destruction of several lamps, he learned how to steer. "They're wonderful," he said. "Thank you."

Glasgerion wrapped his arms tightly around Morragwen and kissed her, much to Quadroped's embarrassment. "We must go," he said, pulling reluctantly away.

"Be careful," whispered Morragwen. "Remember, there's a traitor in Seamourn." She placed Quadroped gently between Glasgerion's shoulders. "Hang onto the knapsack," she instructed, "so you don't fall off."

"Good-bye," said Quadroped. Glasgerion tipped forwards and they swam away into the soft green light of dawn.

Chapter Three

The journey to Seamourn passed uneventfully. The scenery was beautiful and undramatic. Fat, complacent fish grazed on meadows of sea grass. Fields of varied seaweeds divided by white fences and winding lanes stretched to the horizon. Farmhouses, perched on tall, twisted coral heads, gazed out across the land.

"How do the sea people get to their houses?" asked Quadroped. There were no stairs and the rocks were too steep to climb.

"They swim," replied Glasgerion, "just as we are doing. Sea people never walk; they can swim as fast as I do, even without magical buckles."

"If they always swim, why do they have roads?" asked Quadroped.

"They're farmers," said Glasgerion. "Each week they carry their goods to market. It's hard to load a wagon so that it floats horizontally. Usually, the wagon tips and the load spills to the ground or floats away. It's easier to pull the wagons along the roads."

They spent the nights by the roadside where the sand

and weeds were thick and soft. Glasgerion would sing or talk of his travels and life in the courts of Essylt. Quadroped began to forget the Warlords; they did not belong in such a gentle land.

They swam for three days and on the evening of the fourth they reached the outskirts of Seamourn. The road became crowded with wagons and the water was thick with sea people swimming to and from the metropolis. Quadroped held tightly to Glasgerion and his fears returned in force. The sea people scared him. Their strange yellow eyes gleamed from faces blue and green. Their ears and eyebrows rose to points and their teeth were long and bright.

Glasgerion swam through the busy streets, past white buildings guarded by leering gargoyles. As he approached the center of the city the streets became shady avenues bordered by graceful galleries and arcades. He stopped before an elegant house with doors of pearl. A gaily painted sign swung in the current indicating that this was the Jovial Lobster Inn. Glasgerion rapped sharply on the door.

The innkeeper, a thin nervous man, appeared to ask their business. "A minstrel?" he asked when Glasgerion told him his profession. He frowned at Glasgerion's torn clothes. No minstrel of any talent wore rags in the Sea Kingdom.

"People are not as fond of music on the surface," said Glasgerion.

The innkeeper accepted the explanation with a nod. "I'll listen to a song," he said, "but I don't think you'll do. We have a very elite clientele."

The innkeeper's expression changed from gloomy resignation to interest when he saw the quality of the instrument. Glasgerion sang a love song in a deliberately mediocre voice. Master Harpers were rare, even in Seamourn, and he had no wish to attract undue attention. Nevertheless, the song impressed the innkeeper. He agreed to give Glasgerion a room and three meals if he would sing at night.

The room was small and cosy; Quadroped immediately jumped into a large, velvet armchair near the window. The innkeeper looked disapprovingly at the small puppy curled up in a good armchair.

"Surely, sir," he said, "your pet would be more at home in the kitchen with my own dogs?"

Quadroped almost told the innkeeper that he was *not* a dog but a pig in disguise. Then he realized the man might have stronger views on the subject of pigs in his armchairs. He satisfied himself with a short *yip*.

"My puppy," Glasgerion said, "always sleeps with me. If you are unwilling to let him share my rooms I shall find lodgings elsewhere."

The innkeeper paled and assured Glasgerion that he had no objections to dogs in the rooms. His archrival, the owner of the Slippery Egg, would be only too happy to grab this gifted performer.

Glasgerion closed and locked the door. Then he sat down on the bed to compose a note to his friend. Glasgerion did not wish to reveal his identity in a letter. With a traitor in the Royal Family itself he had to be very careful. He wrote in an ancient language, known only to a handful of scholars, and merely requested to see the jester on a matter of research. It would convince Caelbad that the author of the note should be granted an interview but would not endanger Quadroped should it be read by anyone else. The water was dark when Glasgerion finished writing and the innkeeper returned to inform him that the inn was almost full. Glasgerion gave the note to the innkeeper for delivery and went downstairs, Quadroped running behind him.

The taproom of the Jovial Lobster was noisy and crowded. Tables and chairs covered every conceivable inch of floor so that there was no room even for the serving maid to walk and drinks had to be passed along from hand to hand. The only space left was in the center of the room where the innkeeper had placed a large chair for Glasgerion. Quadroped sat beneath the chair and stared nervously at the loud, boisterous crowd.

The inn did indeed cater to an elite clientele. The audience's gem-encrusted garments astonished Quadroped. By comparison, Morragwen's clothing seemed tasteful but inexpensive. He stared, fascinated, at a particularly resplendent couple nearby. The man's powerful chest was bare save for a massive collar of topaz and gold that gleamed against his azure skin. Black opals winked on the man's long pointed ears and from the golden circlet on his brow, brilliant against the snowy whiteness of his hair. He was gazing at Glasgerion with an expression of boredom and his long fingers drummed impatiently on the tabletop. His companion was a pretty young woman dressed extravagantly in gold silk. A diadem of sapphires held her seagreen hair, and sapphires shone on her neck, arms and hands.

The woman, as though aware of Quadroped's gaze, suddenly turned and looked s raight at him. Her yellow eyes grew large and a delighted smile transformed her haughty face. "Oh, look Aodh," Quadroped heard her say to her companion, "that puppy has purple eyes. I've never seen a puppy with purple eyes."

Quadroped shrank under Aodh's contemptuous regard. There was something wild and frightening about his thin face. Aodh looked at the woman and a smile softened his harsh expression. "Shall I purchase the beast then, love?" he asked.

"Oh *would* you?"

"Certainly, dear heart," said Aodh smoothly. He rose gracefully to his feet and approached Glasgerion. The landsman, he noted with displeasure, was slow to rise and bow. "You play well, for a landsman," said Aodh. His voice was deep and velvet soft. Glasgerion accepted the compliment with a wary nod.

"The lady at my table," Aodh continued, indicating the woman with a languid hand, "desires the puppy beneath your chair. I will pay any reasonable amount for the beast."

"I'm afraid that I can't sell him, sir," said Glasgerion.

Aodh sighed. "Perhaps," he suggested, "you will change your mind when you learn our identities. I am the Prince Aodh and the lady my cousin, the Royal Princess Adjurel. The Princess is a kind lady, she will treat the dog well."

Glasgerion forced a smile. "I'm sure, Your Highness,"

he said, "that the Princess is both kind and good, but I can't sell the puppy."

"That is most unwise," said Aodh slowly. "Your refusal could have . . . unpleasant repercussions."

Quadroped buried his head in Glasgerion's boot. "I regret to disappoint the Princess, but I will not sell my dog," said Glasgerion firmly.

"You are a fool, landsman," said Aodh, his eyes hard and flat. "Keep the dog. But you will leave Seamourn before dawn if you are wise."

"You are useless!" said Adjurel petulantly when Aodh returned to her table empty-handed. "I *want* that puppy." She tossed her bright hair. "I shall just have to get him for myself."

"The man won't give it to you," said Aodh.

"He will not dare to refuse me," said Adjurel confidently. She arose with a sinuous grace and glided towards Glasgerion. "Minstrel," she said with a sweet smile, "won't you give me your puppy?" She bent and tried to scratch Quadroped between the ears. Quadroped scuttled away from her. "Oh," she cried, "the poor thing's frightened. He's *cowering* behind your boot. Don't be afraid, little puppy, I won't hurt you." She stretched out her hand once more. Quadroped cringed and refused to look at the terrible Princess.

"An inn is no place for a puppy," said Adjurel imperiously. "The noise frightens him. Sell him to me; I shall give him a silken cushion and a collar of gold." Quadroped flattened himself against the floorboards and whimpered.

Glasgerion picked Quadroped up and held him tight. "This puppy is not for sale," he said again.

Adjurel looked at him, surprised that anyone would refuse such a reasonable request. "Please?" she asked prettily. "I'll give you a kiss." Glasgerion slowly and firmly shook his head. Adjurel's surprise turned to anger. "No one refuses me!" she cried. Glasgerion gazed steadily at her and a slow flush of embarrassment suffused her cheeks. A quick glance around revealed that she had become the center of attention. Adjurel turned and, head held high, returned to her table. A few minutes later she and Aodh left the inn.

"Those children have grown into very high-handed adults," remarked Glasgerion when the royal pair had gone. "Angmar must have spoiled them dreadfully. I hope this does not lead to trouble, Quadro."

"You wouldn't have *sold* me?" squeaked Quadroped, staring unhappily up at Glasgerion.

"No, never that," Glasgerion assured him. "I'll deliver my note to Angmar in the morning. We'll be in the palace by noon and I can apologize to Adjurel. She will understand when she learns what you are. Just think, Quadro," he added as he mounted the stairs to their room, "you'll be able to talk again."

"Yip!" said Quadroped. He was tired of being a puppy.

Heavy footsteps rang in the hall, waking Quadroped and Glasgerion. The room was dimly illuminated by the first rays of dawn. "What is it?" asked Quadroped. The footsteps were coming closer.

"Trouble," said Glasgerion. He got out of bed and stood listening.

The footsteps stopped and a heavy fist crashed against their door, causing the strong wood to vibrate. "Open," cried a deep, hoarse voice. "Open in the name of the King!" Glasgerion hastened to comply and was knocked backwards as the door swung violently open and four imposing warriors rushed into the room. Their glimmering armor and drawn swords were richly figured in gold and jewels. On their crested helms they bore the insignia of the Royal Family of Seamourn.

"Arrest the man," commanded the foremost man. His gigantic stature proclaimed him their captain. "Grab his belongings and that mutt, too." Quadroped tried to dash under the bed but a huge hand swept him up into the air and held him there, helpless. Two soldiers fell upon Glasgerion and subdued him without much difficulty.

"Why are you arresting me?" demanded Glasgerion, as the men bound his arms tightly behind his back.

"You stand accused of treason," said the captain shortly.

"Who has accused me?" insisted Glasgerion as the guards hauled him roughly towards the stairs. "Prince Aodh?"

"Does it matter?" asked the captain with a savage smile. He gave Glasgerion a vicious kick. "Keep quiet or I'll kill you."

The guards dragged their captives down the stairs onto the shadowy streets of Seamourn. Quadroped gazed over his shoulder and saw the frightened face of the innkeeper peeking from the parlor window. The city was quiet and the soldiers' boots rang loudly against the cobblestones. Sleepy citizens peered out then closed their shutters quickly when they saw who marched below.

Glasgerion and Quadroped were forced through a small unmarked door that led to a labyrinth of tunnels beneath the Royal Palace. The water was murky with dirt and algae and bitterly cold. Slivers of pearly light fell on the slimy floor from the narrow skylights. Widely spaced torches cast shadows on the walls and provided a feeble, bloody light. The fire, if fire it was, shed no warmth. Quadroped wondered what kind of magic could make fires burn under the ocean.

The captain gave a great shout, his harsh voice echoing through the halls. A tiny man appeared at the captain's shout. Translucent yellow flesh stretched tightly over his cadaverous frame. His black eyes glittered speculatively when he saw Glasgerion. "Traitors," said the captain tersely.

The jailer's bloodless lips twisted in semblance of a smile. He produced a set of heavy manacles from a black chest and fastened them over Glasgerion's wrists. "I don't have anything for the dog," he said.

"It's only a puppy," said the captain. "It can't cause any trouble. It will stay close to its master." He turned and led the warriors away.

The jailer grabbed Quadroped by the collar and pushed Glasgerion down a dark passage. The ceiling was so low that Glasgerion had to stoop to avoid hitting the jagged prongs of corals. Rows of narrow, cramped cells opened onto the tunnel. Their bars were covered with mucous weeds, barnacles and shells. One cell was sealed shut by the encrustations. Quadroped hoped that there was no one imprisoned inside. The jailer stopped before a cell smaller and darker than all the rest. The lock was stiff with age and took all his strength to open.

The jailer thrust Glasgerion inside and flung Quadroped roughly after him. The floor was thick with weed and silt. Glasgerion slipped and fell, cutting his head on the sharp shells of the dark blue mussels hidden in the wrack. The blow rendered him insensible. Quadroped crouched miserably over the silent bard and watched his jailer lock the heavy wooden door.

"You'll be safe in there," chuckled the gnome malevolently. He walked away, the keys on his belt jangling dismally.

Quadroped began to lick Glasgerion's face, trying to revive him. This eventually had the desired effect; with a groan of pain, Glasgerion sat up and gazed around him. A pink cloud rose from the cut on his head and a school of small unpleasant fish circled him, attracted by the blood.

"This *is* a mess," groaned Glasgerion, waving the fish away. "The Gate will open long before we escape from this place."

"Can't you send a message to the King?" asked Quadroped.

"How?" asked Glasgerion. "Who would help me, an accused traitor? No one will believe that I'm Glasgerion; Morragwen's disguise ensured that."

"What about the letter you sent to your friend? Won't he try to help us?"

"I didn't tell him who I was," said Glasgerion. "I thought it would be too dangerous."

"Won't your nephew try to rescue us?" asked Quadroped, reluctant to give up hope.

"Eventually," said Glasgerion, "when he finds us. But dungeons are guarded by powerful spells to prevent outsiders from locating prisoners. It will take Reander time to trace us and break those spells. He won't even miss us for a week or more. It is a long way to Illoreth; I fear he will free us too late." Glasgerion began to brood and for a long while the cell was filled with melancholy silence. Then Quadroped gave a hesitant *yip*.

"*Must* you make that insipid noise?" snapped Glasgerion.

"Sorry," said Quadroped.

"I hope it doesn't become a habit."

Quadroped thought it already had but he said only, "There's a little window in the ceiling. I think you can reach it."

Glasgerion looked at the window and sighed. "It's too small for me," he said. He looked at it again and grew thoughtful. "You could fit through it, Quadro," he said. "If you could sneak into the palace, find a way to see Angmar..." he stopped and studied Quadroped. "No," he said. "It's too dangerous. You've never been inside a palace and the Warlords are looking for you. You'd get lost or be killed."

"I can try," said Quadroped. "Lift me up. It's better than staying here."

"You may be right," said Glasgerion. "Goriel might find and 'rescue' us before Reander can." He stood and examined the window; it was well within his reach. "All right," he said at length, "we'll try it. I don't remember much about the palace—I visited it only once when I was a child —but I recall that there are many doors. You should be able to sneak through one. Once inside, try to find the throne room. It is a busy room, you should be able to follow someone there. Wait until the King arrives—he probably holds an audience twice a day—then show him the Key. He will recognize it and help you."

The plan sounded very simple when Glasgerion explained it and Quadroped's spirits rose. "Be very careful," said Glasgerion. "And tell no one, no one at all, who you are. Someone in Seamourn freed the Manslayer and the palace will be full of Goriel's spies. The Warlord knows we must speak to Angmar and he will be waiting." Glasgerion picked Quadroped up and pushed him gently through the window. He emerged underneath a large and prickly bush.

Quadroped struggled through the bush, wincing as the sharp branches scratched his hide. He crawled out onto a wide lawn of cut seaweed, surrounding the palace. The palace was a fantastic arrangement of airy spires and thin bridges arching through space. Bright gardens occupied myriad terraces, and their colorful vegetation crept down the building's pearly walls. There were guards on the ramparts; he could see the sun flash on their steel armor. He narrowed his eyes against the brilliance and looked for a door.

Quadroped wandered through the formal gardens all day trying to find a way into the palace. Armed guards patrolled the lawns and heavy iron bolts secured all the doors. As evening approached he gave up and sat down under a coral shelf to rest.

"How odd, a dog," said a small voice near his ear. "I wonder if it talks."

"Of *course* I talk," said Quadroped. He looked half-heartedly for the speaker and could not, as usual, find him.

"How unusual," said the voice moving closer. "Dogs don't usually talk. As a general rule, I have found you creatures rather stupid. Much too dumb to grasp even the barest rudiments of speech." This was delivered in a *very* superior tone of voice.

"I," said Quadroped loftily, "am *not* a dog."

"No?" asked the voice.

"No," snapped Quadroped. "I'm an enchanted pig."

"No offense intended," said the invisible creature. "But you can't expect people to guess that. After all, you don't *look* like a pig."

"Well I am!" said Quadroped. He wished the voice would go away and leave him alone.

There was a moment of silence, then, "A pig! Dear me!" A small, sea anemone–like polyp walked forwards to observe Quadroped more closely.

"What are you?" asked Quadroped, for he knew that real sea anemones cannot walk.

"I am Pseudo-Polyp," said the tiny creature importantly, "a unique species of intelligent coelenterate. Who are *you?*"

"Me? Oh, I'm Quadroped," said Quadroped dismally.

"Why so unhappy?" asked Pseudo-Polyp. He hopped off his ledge onto Quadroped's snout.

"My companion's been arrested and thrown into prison," said Quadroped.

"If he's a criminal then you're better off without him," declared Pseudo-Polyp sagely.

"You don't understand," said Quadroped. "He's not a criminal. He's a very great man. He's on a mission to the King, only he's disguised so the King doesn't know about it. He wouldn't sell me to a Princess, so now he's been accused of treason."

Pseudo-Polyp pondered this information. "Why doesn't he take off the disguise?" he asked eventually.

"Can't," came the dreary reply, "it's magical. He can only regain his true form in the presence of the King. I'm also doomed to remain in this dismal shape until I can see the King. If we don't see the King soon, our mission will fail and the world be plunged into war." This last was uttered with a sort of gloomy satisfaction. Quadroped felt the world was an unfair, unfeeling place and deserved to be trampled a bit.

Pseudo-Polyp decided to trust Quadroped. The pig-puppy looked so honestly upset, it was impossible to believe him a liar. "Why then," he said, "you'll just have to see the King as soon as possible."

"As soon as possible may be never," said Quadroped. "There are guards all around the palace and the King never sees traitors."

"Ah," said Pseudo-Polyp, "but what if the charges were dropped? Then your companion would have every chance of seeing the King, *if* he's who you say he is."

"How *can* the charges be dropped?" asked Quadroped. "Nobody will listen to me; I look too silly. If only I were a pig . . ."

"Don't be so gloomy," said Pseudo-Polyp. "I have many friends in the palace; one of them is Prince Aedh."

"Prince Aedh?" said Quadroped. "He's the one we met in the tavern—he put us in prison. He'll never help me; he was scary."

"You must have encountered Prince Aodh," said

Pseudo-Polyp. "Prince Aedh would never be seen in a common tavern. We had better rescue your companion fast. Prince Aodh is unpredictable when angry."

Quadroped shuddered. "Who is Prince Aedh?" he asked.

"Aedh is Aodh's identical twin," said Pseudo-Polyp. "But he's as quiet and wise as Aodh is wild and cruel. If your friend is innocent I'm sure Aedh will help him."

"That," said Quadroped, "depends on whether I can convince him. Anyway, I can't get into the palace."

"Leave that to me," said Pseudo-Polyp. He jumped onto Quadroped's ear and attached himself firmly.

"You tickle!" complained Quadroped. He twitched his ear violently, hoping to dislodge Pseudo-Polyp.

"Stop that at once!" snapped Pseudo-Polyp, "or I shall become quite dizzy and refuse to help you. You won't be able to hear my instructions unless I sit here and I'm too small to walk all the way to the palace. Surely an itchy ear is a small price to pay for my valuable assistance."

"Sorry," said Quadroped. He tried valiantly, but without notable success, to still his shaking ear.

"Follow that path," commanded Pseudo-Polyp, waving an imperious tentacle. Without another word, the two set off towards the palace.

The palace was a labyrinth and it was easy for Pseudo-Polyp to find a way to enter secretly. Once inside, Quadroped quickly became confused by the twistings and turnings of the long marble hallways. Around every corner the halls branched in a thousand directions. Behind every door lay a maze of rooms, gardens and interconnected courtyards. There were stairways that ascended flight after flight, only to start descending again without having gotten anywhere.

"Are you *sure* we're not going around in circles?" asked Quadroped as they passed a lovely door of green malachite for the fourth time.

"I know what I'm doing," said Pseudo-Polyp huffily. But when they passed the door for the fifth time he relented and explained that they were currently in the wing of the palace assigned to Caelbad, the Royal Jester. "Caelbad loves to play tricks on people," said Pseudo-Polyp. "All the halls are identical. People who are new to the palace can wander for hours thinking they are going in circles, whereas they are actually walking straight ahead."

"But how does anyone find his way around?" asked Quadroped.

"If you look very carefully," said Pseudo-Polyp, "you will notice a subtle change in the predominant color of each area. If you know the color code, navigation becomes quite simple. Of course, Caelbad does change the code from time to time; otherwise it would be no fun."

"Oh," said Quadroped. Caelbad sounded like a strange individual. He pitied the color-blind members of the court.

They turned down a small passage and entered a series of cloistered gardens and cool, spacious hallways. Rich tapestries depicting scenes of courtly love covered the walls. Sweet perfume scented the water and brilliantly colored fish swam among the colonnades. *The fish are behaving like birds*, thought Quadroped.

"These apartments belong to the Princess Adjurel," said Pseudo-Polyp, "so try to be quiet. There'll be trouble if she catches us here." Quadroped gulped nervously and tried to obey. This was difficult because, as a puppy, he had little claws which clicked noisily upon the hard gold tiles. He gave a great sigh of relief when they left Adjurel's rooms behind and entered the section of the palace that belonged to Prince Aedh.

Here the halls were white marble inlaid with black onyx in severe geometrical designs. The walls were filled with dark wooden doors with square, unornamented brass nameplates. Between these were niches filled with statues of important men, whose severe expressions did nothing to lighten the general atmosphere of sobriety. The floor was covered with a deep maroon carpet that silenced all footsteps, creating the unnatural silence of a library. There was no confusion of twisting passages here, only a single long hall with smaller passages leading to the right and left at orderly intervals.

"He must be a very stern man," Quadroped whispered.

"He is," Pseudo-Polyp whispered back, "but he's very just."

They came at last to a door that was bigger and plainer than all the rest, bearing only the words MAIN OFFICE on the small plaque. "This is it," said Pseudo-Polyp. "Open the door, Quadro, and try to slip in quietly. If the secretary sees us all is lost."

Quadroped did not have much faith in his ability to outwit secretaries. Standing up on his hind legs he turned the knob until he felt the latch click open. Then he dropped down and nudged the door open with his nose. The secretary was standing by the window with his back to the door. Quadroped bounded into the room and hid beneath a large chair. "What now!" he gasped.

"We wait awhile," said Pseudo-Polyp softly. "The secretary will go into the inner office"—he waved a tentacle at another large oak door beside the central desk. "When he does we'll slip in after him. Aedh spends his days in there handling most of Angmar's administrative duties." He fell silent; the secretary had turned from the window and noticed the open door. The man peered suspiciously around the room, then shrugged and closed the door.

"Why can't we just sneak over and open that door ourselves?" asked Quadroped. It was very cramped under the chair.

"It's kept locked at all times," said Pseudo-Polyp.

"Why?" asked Quadroped, trying to stretch his legs.

"Assassins!" said Pseudo-Polyp enigmatically.

"Assassins?" Quadroped looked violently around, half expecting to find one sharing their hiding place.

"Shhh," said Pseudo-Polyp, "we'll be heard. And stop shaking your head around, it's unsettling."

"Sorry," said Quadroped. "Who wants to kill him?"

"Oh, lots of people," said Pseudo-Polyp.

"He can't be a very good Prince then," said Quadroped.

"Don't be silly," snapped Pseudo-Polyp. "Aedh is the most capable man in the kingdom."

"Then who wants to kill him?" asked Quadroped again.

"Well," began Pseudo-Polyp, "there are criminals who

have suffered from his rigorous justice. But his worst
enemy is his brother, Aodh."

"His brother?" said Quadroped, aghast.

"Aedh and Aodh are the only male heirs to the throne.
Aedh is the elder and so he will inherit the throne. He will
also get Adjurel's hand in marriage. Aodh covets both, and
they will be his if Aedh dies."

"How horrible," said Quadroped.

"Yes, it is rather," said Pseudo-Polyp, "but it's not unusual in royal families. To do him justice, Aodh truly
seems to love Adjurel. She is the only person he cares for."

"Would Adjurel marry him if he murdered his brother?"
asked Quadroped. He tried to remember the Princess. She
had not looked evil, only young and spoiled.

"Aodh is too smart to be implicated in the murder," said
Pseudo-Polyp. "And Adjurel loves him in return. Aedh has
never tried to woo her; he is more concerned with business.
Hush now and get ready to move."

The secretary had withdrawn a large key and was approaching the door to the inner office. The door swung
silently open and the secretary disappeared inside. "Now!"
cried Pseudo-Polyp.

Quadroped dashed across the room into the inner office
and hid under a leather sofa.

The inner office was, if possible, more somber than the
outer office. Redwood shelves covered with dusty books
lined mahogany walls. A deep brown carpet covered the
floor and heavy curtains covered the windows. The room
was dimly lit by glowing yellow sponges set in tall vases.
A massive desk, covered with neat, orderly stacks of
paper, dominated the far wall, but the chair behind it was
empty.

Aedh stood by a window, lost in thought and apparently
oblivious of his secretary's entrance. The secretary quietly
placed a document on the desk and left, closing the door
behind him. When he had gone, Aedh turned and stepped
out of the shadows.

Quadroped recoiled as Aedh's arctic eyes fastened on
his hiding place. The Prince looked exactly like Aodh and
Quadroped could find no kindness in his thin face. In a

quiet, emotionless voice Aedh spoke. "Come out," he said. A slender dagger glittered in his hand.

"You'd better do as he says," advised Pseudo-Polyp. "I think he thinks you're one of Aodh's assassins. He has good aim; if you don't move fast, he'll kill you."

Quadroped exploded into the center of the room, knocking over the sofa and a sponge vase in the process.

"A puppy!" gasped Aedh, falling back a pace. His voice was sharp with anger. "How did you get in here?"

"Say something, Quadro," said Pseudo-Polyp, "or he'll have us thrown out." But Quadroped was too frightened to do more than squeak. "Prince Aedh," cried Pseudo-Polyp as loudly as he could, "it's me, Pseudo-Polyp. We need your help!"

Aedh's long ears twitched forwards. "Pseudo-Polyp?" he asked, bending down to stare at Quadroped's head. "What are you doing here? If this is a joke—"

"It's not a joke!" shouted Pseudo-Polyp. "We need your help. Aodh's thrown Quadroped's companion into prison for treason, only he's really a friend of the King's. If he isn't rescued soon he'll be executed."

Aedh looked confused, but he had regained his composure. "That sounds most unlikely," he said. "Even Aodh is not fool enough to throw Angmar's friends into prison. Who is the man?"

"I don't know," said Pseudo-Polyp. "Oh, Quadro, say something!" The intrepid creature reached out a tentacle and gave Quadroped a good sting on the nose.

"Ouch!" cried Quadroped. "My companion is in disguise," he said. "Aodh doesn't know who he is."

"Well, who is he?" asked Aedh again.

Quadroped shifted from foot to foot in an irritating manner. "I can't tell you," he said. "It's a secret."

"You can tell me," said Aedh. "All of Angmar's friends are my friends, too."

Quadroped studied Aedh. The Prince looked reserved and somewhat scholarly, not like a monster at all. But Glasgerion had ordered him to remain silent and he dared not disobey.

Aedh began to frown again; he shuffled the papers on

his desk impatiently. "I can't help the man unless I know who he is or who you are," he said, glancing sharply at Quadroped. "Dogs don't talk in Seamourn."

"I'm not allowed to tell you," said Quadroped miserably.

"He and his companion can only regain their true forms in sight of the King," said Pseudo-Polyp suddenly.

"Magic," said Aedh darkly. "That is most disturbing. There is too much magic afoot, now that the forces of Ravenor draw near. Are you truly friends, I wonder, or two of Goriel's creatures?" Quadroped looked at Aedh in dismay. The Prince advanced steadily towards him and he began to back around the room.

Aedh grabbed for Quadroped who leapt out of his way and jumped up on the fallen sofa. "Come here," said Aedh, running after him. Quadroped was suddenly glad he was a puppy. Puppies run much faster than baby pigs, and they can jump.

"Get out of here, Quadro," said Pseudo-Polyp. "If he catches you he'll throw you back into prison and you'll never escape."

Quadroped ran to the door and was thrown backwards as it burst open. A wild figure ran into the room and sprang onto Aedh's desk, pushing all the papers onto the floor. "Caelbad!" said Aedh with disgust. "Get out of here, jester." Caelbad settled himself more comfortably on the desk.

Quadroped stared curiously at Glasgerion's friend. Caelbad was certainly very peculiar. He was dressed in a tattered rainbow of silk adorned with ribbons and small silver bells that chimed merrily when he moved. Caelbad noticed Quadroped's intent gaze and grinned. "What's this, Aedh?" he asked. "Running a zoo?"

"Get off my desk," said Aedh. "You look absurd."

"Jesters are supposed to look absurd," said Caelbad peaceably. "I thought I'd disturb you for a while; you work too hard. What are you doing? I thought you objected to small dogs. Is this one of Adjurel's lot?"

"I do," said Aedh. "This isn't a dog, but some creature in disguise. I suspect that Goriel has sent him."

"Impossible," said Caelbad. "Goriel doesn't have a sense of humor. What are you going to do with it?"

"If I could catch him, I'd throw him in the dungeon," said Aedh.

Caelbad looked at Quadroped closely. "Why, hello, Pseudo-Polyp," he said, catching sight of the small creature on Quadroped's ear. "Let me have the puppy," he said. "I'll keep him out of trouble."

"No," said Aedh. "If he is from Ravenor it's too dangerous to let him go free."

"He isn't from Ravenor," said Caelbad. "Trust me. In my youth I traveled through that forsaken land in company with Prince Glasgerion."

"You know more of Goriel than I," said Aedh thoughtfully. "Very well, take him. But keep him close. I will question his companion tonight. If they are spies they must be killed."

"Come here, puppy," said Caelbad with a cheerful smile.

"Go with him," whispered Pseudo-Polyp. "He might even help you."

Quadroped walked to Caelbad and allowed himself to be picked up. "Take him and leave," said Aedh abruptly. "I have work to do."

"When do you not?" asked Caelbad impertinently.

"Out!" said Aedh, pointing imperiously towards the door, "before I throw you out!"

"Yes, Your Majesty." Caelbad tucked Quadroped under his arm, bowed and left.

"That boy," said Caelbad presently, as they walked down the hall, "is becoming too autocratic. He isn't King yet." He shook his head and turned his attention to Quadroped. "How did you get into the inner office," he asked, "and why did you bother? I'd suspect it was an elaborate joke, but Pseudo-Polyp is almost as stuffy as Aedh."

"No, I'm not," said Pseudo-Polyp.

"I'm Quadroped," said Quadroped.

"He needs to see the King," said Pseudo-Polyp, "otherwise he'll be a puppy for life."

"A terrible fate," agreed Caelbad sympathetically. "Who is this companion Aedh spoke of?"

Quadroped decided to tell Caelbad the truth. The jester was Glasgerion's friend and the person he had hoped to contact in the first place. "If I tell you, you have to promise not to tell anyone else," he said. Pseudo-Polyp looked a little hurt to be left out of the secret but Quadroped did not dare tell anyone but the jester who his companion was.

"I promise," said the jester with mock solemnity. He bent his head so that Quadroped could whisper in his ear.

Quadroped felt slightly annoyed. It was apparent that the jester was not taking his predicament very seriously. He placed his front paws on Caelbad's shoulders and whispered, "My companion is Glasgerion." He was pleased to see the jester's face suddenly become very serious indeed.

"How did he get himself in prison?" asked Caelbad.

"Prince Aodh accused him of treason," said Quadroped. "He was singing in an inn—Glasgerion, not the Prince— and the Princess Adjurel saw me. She wanted to buy me but Glasgerion refused. If only he can see the King his disguise will disappear, but now everyone thinks we're evil."

"Oh, I don't think Aedh really thinks you're evil," said Caelbad. "He's just being careful. Why didn't you tell him the truth? I can't release a prisoner accused of treason. Only Aedh or the King can do that."

"Someone freed a monster called the Manslayer," whispered Quadroped. "Glasgerion says that means that someone in the Royal Family is a traitor. He made me promise not to tell anyone who he was except the King. He'll probably be angry at me for telling you."

"Oh, I don't think so," said Caelbad, "but I think I should get you to Angmar as soon as possible. Aedh said he would question Glasgerion tonight, and his methods might be uncomfortable." Caelbad entered a small green room and put Quadroped on the bed. "Brush your fur and then get some rest," he ordered. "I'll return Pseudo-Polyp to the garden and go speak to the King."

"Good-bye, Quadro," said Pseudo-Polyp, "and good luck. Come tell me who you are after you see the King."

"I will," promised Quadroped. Pseudo-Polyp jumped into Caelbad's hand. Quadroped waved good-bye and settled down to worry in a comfortable chair.

Caelbad returned three hours later with a large straw basket in his hands. "Wake up," he said. "It's time to meet Angmar. Are you ready?"

"Yes," said Quadroped, wagging his tail eagerly.

"Climb into the basket," said Caelbad. "I wasn't able to get a private audience and the family will be there. Aedh will stop me if he suspects what I'm doing. I'll release you only when Angmar is watching." Quadroped clambered in and curled up on the scratchy bottom. Caelbad closed the lid and put the basket under his arm.

"I'm going to be a pig again," chanted Quadroped softly all the way to the audience chamber. "I'm going to be a *pig* again!"

They entered a luxurious round chamber of blue marble and Caelbad set the basket down. Quadroped peeked through the slits. A large man sat on a golden throne. A white beard covered his broad chest and his face was old and lined. *That must be Angmar,* Quadroped decided. Adjurel was seated beside her father, looking demure in a gown of carnation pink. Aodh stood behind her, his hand possessively on her shoulder. Prince Aedh was seated some distance away reading a book, apparently indifferent to the loving picture his brother and fiancée presented.

"Well, Caelbad," said Angmar, "what have you got for me now?"

"I don't know," said Caelbad. "Let's see." He removed the basket's lid and tumbled Quadroped onto the cold floor. There was instant turmoil.

"Arrest that puppy!" cried Aedh, dropping his book on the floor and jumping to his feet.

"Give me the puppy," said Adjurel.

"Kill the puppy," suggested Aodh pleasantly.

"Be quiet, all of you," said Angmar, "and look at the dog!"

The family fell silent as Quadroped began to change shape. His ears shortened and developed points while his muzzle squashed up into a snout. For an instant his outline wavered and blurred. It suddenly sharpened again, and there in the middle of the room sat a white, amethyst-eyed piglet.

"Am I a pig yet?" asked Quadroped hopefully.

"You are indeed a pig," said Angmar. "Who are you?"

"I'm Quadroped," said Quadroped. "And my companion, who is in your dungeon, is Glasgerion."

"Glasgerion? Here?" said Angmar. "What is he doing in jail?"

"Uncle," said Aedh, "it's impossible; the pig lies. If Glasgerion had entered Seamourn, I would know. No landsman of rank has entered the kingdom in a twelve-month. And why would Glasgerion travel with a pig?"

"His master is old, ugly and dressed in rags," said Adjurel.

"Glasgerion is disguised, like I was," said Quadroped. "He will regain his true appearance in Your Majesty's presence."

"His story is easily tested," said Angmar. "Bring the man here at once."

"At least let me send my guard for him," said Aedh. "This may be a clever assassination plot."

"I don't care what you do, just bring the man here," snapped Angmar. Aedh bowed and left to fetch Glasgerion.

Fifteen minutes later Aedh and seven guards entered the room, pushing Glasgerion roughly before them.

"Let go of that man at once," said Angmar. "You may be mistreating a Royal Prince. Although"—he looked hard at Glasgerion's dirty face—"he doesn't look like one."

"He is one nevertheless," said Glasgerion, stepping close to the throne. His shape blurred and stretched; a minute later Glasgerion's true form returned.

"Glasgerion!" Caelbad smiled and embraced his friend warmly. "I am glad to see you. It's been too long."

Angmar studied Glasgerion closely. "You've grown up since I last saw you," he commented. "Welcome to Seamourn, boy. But why all the secrecy? The Princes of Essylt have always been welcome here. And who is this pig of yours?"

Glasgerion swept a hand out towards Quadroped. "Meet Quadroped, the new Key Bearer," he said. There was a surprised silence, broken by Caelbad's laughter.

Aedh had paled when Glasgerion spoke but now he had regained his composure. "A pig cannot be Key Bearer," he said. "It is preposterous. Surely it is you, Glasgerion, who has found the Key."

"I wish it were," said Glasgerion, "and so, I suspect, does Quadroped. But he is indeed the Key Bearer. Quadro, show the King the Key."

Quadroped hesitated, aware that someone in the room might want to kill him. He wondered why Glasgerion had told them all the truth.

"Go on, Quadro," said Glasgerion softly. "We can't leave a traitor at large in Seamourn. Whoever he is, I think we've taken him by surprise. He'll give himself away and we can catch him."

Quadroped slowly took the Key out of his collar and held it tightly in his mouth. He trotted up to the throne and showed it to Angmar.

"It *is* the Key," said Angmar when he saw the symbols etched on the silver stem. "I have waited all my life for someone to find the Key and now my prayers have been answered. My army is off the coast of Essylt, waiting to aid Reander if the Black Unicorn escapes. I am glad they will not be needed."

"Do not call them home too soon," said Glasgerion. "We may not live to lock the Gate."

"A Key Bearer has never failed," said Angmar.

"A Key Bearer has never been a baby pig before either," Glasgerion replied, "or had to face two Warlords."

"Two?"

"The Manslayer has been freed."

Angmar was looking at Aedh, his expression grim. "Whoever freed him will die," he promised. "But that can wait. You must start for Illoreth as soon as possible."

Prince Aedh stepped forward. "You must not tell them the way, Uncle," he said.

Angmar looked at Aedh in surprise. "Of course I must, you silly boy; they have to lock the Gate."

"That," said Aedh, "is precisely what they must *not* do. This time the Black Unicorn will be free."

"You are mad," said Angmar.

"No," said Aedh, "but I am pledged to Goriel." He ignored the exclamations that met this pronouncement. "Glasgerion, your journey ends here. The Key Bearer must be stopped."

"It was you who freed the Manslayer," said Glasgerion.

"Yes," said Aedh.

Angmar slumped on his throne, as if exhausted. "Why?" he asked.

"I thought you loved Seamourn, Aedh," Adjurel said, "though you've certainly never loved me." She moved closer to Aodh, and he put an arm around her.

"I do love Seamourn," said Aedh with passion. "I love her too much to allow another war to destroy her. Let the rest of the world struggle endlessly against Ravenor. While I live the Sea Kingdom shall be prosperous and at peace."

"Let the Key Bearer lock the Gate," said Caelbad. "If the Gate is locked the wars will never start."

"I cannot," said Aedh and for a moment his face seemed sad and tired. "Had I known the Key would be found I would not have chosen this path. But war seemed inevitable and so I swore allegiance to Goriel. I cannot break that vow."

"Why do we stand here talking?" demanded Aodh suddenly. "We cannot let him harm the Key Bearer. Guards, seize Prince Aedh!" The Guards remained motionless at their posts.

Aedh stepped away from his irate twin. "Surely you do not think, Brother, that I would attempt to capture a Key Bearer without help? Goriel has given me servants."

Aedh gestured and the guards shuffled forwards until they formed a ring around the company. Slowly their faces began to melt into featureless blobs. Their flesh turned black and oozed to the floor like soggy dough. Clothing wrinkled and collapsed as their bodies melted away. Dark slime pooled over the floor. Slowly, seven cones of tarry liquid rose and twisted into faceless humanoid shapes with burning blue fires for eyes.

"Pitch Fiends!" said Caelbad. Aodh drew his dagger and leapt at the nearest guard but the jester caught his arm and held him back. "Weapons are useless against them," he said.

"It is not an honorable vow that leads you to kill kin," said Angmar.

"You may all leave," said Aedh quietly. "Only the Key Bearer must remain. The Pitch Fiends won't harm him. Goriel wants to meet this new Key Bearer."

"If we leave," said Angmar, "we give tacit support to Ravenor. You will have to kill us to get the pig, Aedh. Let the Key Bearer go. Goriel will slay you as soon as he has the Key."

"You wrong him, Uncle," said Aedh. "Goriel is, perhaps, evil but he is honorable. He will not break his word and I shall not break mine. Leave or be killed by the Pitch Fiends. I give you that choice."

"You'll be hanged for murder if you kill us," said Adjurel hopefully.

"No," said Aedh, "for Aodh will be blamed. I shall say that he tried to seize the throne and I alone escaped his assassins. No one will doubt my word."

"He's right," said Aodh bitterly, "though I never wanted the throne, only Adjurel."

"I leave you now," said Aedh. "There is a proposal for a new grain tax I must study." He smiled and looked at the waiting Pitch Fiends. "Kill them," he said, "and bring me the pig when it's done. I'll be in my study."

The Pitch Fiends slithered towards their prisoners and Quadroped ran to Glasgerion for shelter. Glasgerion would not pick him up or comfort him. "Go hide under the throne, Quadro," said Glasgerion sternly. "And try to escape while the Pitch Fiends are busy with us. Hide somewhere until Reander can help you."

But where can I hide? thought Quadroped as he crawled under the throne. *I don't know the Sea Kingdom well and Aedh rules it. Reander doesn't know I'm a pig. If Glasgerion dies, he'll never find me.*

The company stood back-to-back, daggers in their hands. The monsters merely flowed over them like a black wave, impervious to weapons and blows. They attacked Caelbad first and the others could not free him, for the Pitch Fiends slipped through their fingers like mud.

Quadroped grabbed the Key by its chain and stared at it, trying to block out the horror around him. His eyes began to ache and blur; the intricate designs seemed to creep and curl across the surface of the Key. They grew out of the silver like strange vines, weaving themselves into a long silver tunnel. Quadroped began to drift down the tunnel towards a faint green light. Suddenly he found himself in broad daylight, sitting on the silver rim of the tunnel. The ground was ten feet below him. *I've traveled down a straw into a big bubble,* he thought. *But the bubble seems to be a whole world.* He was frightened, but he was a practical pig so he ignored his fear and began to look around. A stately woman was seated on a low bench several feet away and he shouted for help. The woman rose and turned around. "Morragwen!" he cried. "Morragwen, it's *me!* Quadroped!"

"Quadro, what are you doing up there?" asked Morragwen. "You're a pig again, so you've seen Angmar. What's happened?"

"Oh, Morragwen," said Quadroped, "it's so terrible. Prince Aedh set the Manslayer free. And the Pitch Fiends "

"Pitch Fiends?" Morragwen paled and clenched her hands. In a controlled voice she asked, "Glasgerion?"

"He's still alive, I think," said Quadroped. "At least, he was still struggling when I left."

Morragwen regained her composure. "How many Pitch Fiends are there?" she asked briskly.

"Seven," said Quadroped.

"So many?" exclaimed Morragwen. "We had better hurry or it will be too late. I can't go back with you, Quadro, because only your spirit has traveled here. Go back and call out my name. Go."

Quadroped drifted backwards into his body. He opened his eyes and looked around. The tunnel was gone. Caelbad's broken body lay before the throne; the Fiends were crouched beside Angmar. Glasgerion, Adjurel and Aodh lay facedown on the floor. He slipped the key around his neck, took a deep breath and shouted, "Morragwen!"

The Pitch Fiends glared at Quadroped. They began to glide forwards, their dripping claws extended to tear him. Quadroped squealed and buried his head in his hooves.

"Go no farther. Touch the pig and die!" There was a blinding white flash and Morragwen appeared before the Pitch Fiends, dressed in robes as blue as their arctic eyes.

"Be gone, witch," hissed the boldest of the Fiends. "Our Master wishes you no harm. These people are not your concern; leave them to us."

"These people are my friends," said Morragwen coldly. She raised her right hand, fingers spread wide and flat. The air around her arm began to glow and spark with iridescent fire. A sphere of rainbows formed and floated towards the Pitch Fiends. It grew, flowed around them and trapped them in a shimmering bubble. The delicate walls stretched under their claws but did not break. Then the bubble began to shrink. With a long, low howl the Pitch Fiends and the bubble vanished.

Morragwen raced to Glasgerion's side and turned him over. His shirt had been ripped open and long red wounds covered his arms and chest. Quadroped hurried over. "Is he going to die?" he asked. Morragwen did not hear him. She was bending over Glasgerion and Quadroped suspected that she was crying.

Glasgerion moaned and opened his eyes. Morragwen quickly wiped her eyes and her expression changed to deceptive tranquility. "What are you doing here?" asked Glasgerion, struggling to sit up.

"Don't get up," said Morragwen. "You will hurt yourself. I can heal your wounds but I need time." She pulled him back against her and put her arms around him, hands upon his wounded chest. Glasgerion leaned against her with an exhausted sigh and closed his eyes. Morragwen's hands began to radiate a warm red light. Glasgerion's wounds began to heal and disappear.

"How did you know we needed you?" asked Glasgerion again.

"Quadro fetched me," said Morragwen.

Glasgerion raised an eyebrow. "Indeed?"

"He showed up in a bubble of silver mist, hovering ten feet off the ground. It was an . . . unusual sight."

Glasgerion opened his eyes and stared at Quadroped. "Amazing what resources are hidden behind that unlikely exterior," he said.

"Oh, it wasn't *me*," said Quadroped. "It was the Key."

"That explains it," said Glasgerion. Quadroped's ears drooped. He wanted to explain something to Glasgerion for a change.

"You can't win, Quadro," said Morragwen sympathetically. "He knows more about the Key than you do."

"The Key has unreliable powers," said Glasgerion. "I don't think we can rely on it to help us again."

"No," agreed Morragwen. "There, you can get up, Glasgerion." She removed her hands and gave him a slight push. "I have other patients to attend to."

Glasgerion looked around the quiet room, noticing the bloodstained walls for the first time. Morragwen rose and went to where Adjurel and Aodh lay beside each other. Her hands ran lightly over them. "These two will be all right," she said. She went next to the fallen King.

Glasgerion's eyes fell on Caelbad's twisted body. He rose to his feet and staggered to his friend. "Caelbad," he said. He collapsed on his knees and grabbed Caelbad's shoulders, but he did not have the strength to turn him. "Morragwen," he cried, "come and help me."

Morragwen came, but she did not touch the jester. "I cannot help him, Glasgerion," she said softly. Glasgerion tried again to turn his friend but Morragwen restrained him. "Leave him be, Glasgerion," she said. "He is dead."

Glasgerion pushed Morragwen roughly away. Quadroped jumped as the bard's fist slammed onto the marble floor with crushing force. "No!" he cried. The anger and pain in his voice shocked Quadroped. Glasgerion had always seemed so calm, so assured.

Morragwen wrapped her arms around Glasgerion and

held him, resisting his efforts to be free. "Leave him, Glasgerion," she said again. "You are frightening Quadro," she whispered. "He needs you to be strong."

Glasgerion's shoulders slumped. He smiled at Quadroped, his emotions once again under tight control. "Don't be frightened, Quadro," he said. "I'm not about to crack up on you. After all," he added, suddenly bitter, "it is not as though I have never seen friends die before."

"There will be more deaths before you reach the Gate," said Morragwen. Her red eyes misted with sudden tears. "Glasgerion, I wish you—"

"Angmar," said Glasgerion quickly, forestalling whatever Morragwen had been about to say. "How is he?"

Morragwen's eyes cleared. "The King is still alive," she said, "but he will not live long. The Pitch Fiends did their work too well. I cannot save him."

"Can he talk?" demanded Glasgerion.

"I don't know," said Morragwen. "We should get him to his room." She looked around. "They should all be in bed." She opened the door and leaned out into the hall. "Help," she cried. "The King needs help." There was a sudden commotion and the sound of running feet. A horde of servants, guards and noblemen rushed into the room. They stopped dead, faces falling with dismay, when they saw the bloodstained room. Several brawny young guards grabbed Glasgerion.

"Release me," Glasgerion ordered. His voice was firm and confident, his face calm. He scanned the crowd of frightened faces until he found one he recognized. "Hewas," he said, "tell these men to unhand me."

An elegant old man in the robes of a councilor stepped forwards. "Prince Glasgerion?" he quavered. Glasgerion nodded. "Release the Prince," Hewas ordered. "What has happened, my lord?"

"Never mind that," snapped Glasgerion. "Prince Aedh has allied himself with Ravenor. Find and arrest him, then bring me word. He must be questioned." The guards rushed out and Glasgerion turned to the rest of the crowd. "Carry the wounded to their rooms and send for doctors," he said. "The King is dying; his councilors should be notified and be ready for his summons."

"You should rest," said Morragwen when the room was empty. She pushed Glasgerion towards a low couch. "Lie down; you can do nothing more. I'll call you if Angmar recovers consciousness." She kissed him lightly on the forehead and hurried out.

Quadroped and Glasgerion slept peacefully on the soft couch. They were awakened by a loud shout at the door—the guards had returned. Glasgerion hurried to the doors and threw them wide. "Where is the Prince?" he demanded, when he saw that they had returned empty-handed.

"He escaped us," said the captain. "He took his sea horse from the stables and went east. We followed, but he is the best rider in the kingdom and his steed is faster than ours."

"I see," said Glasgerion calmly. "Dismissed." The captain saluted and hurried off. A servant came quickly down the hall. Angmar was awake and calling for Glasgerion and the Key Bearer.

Angmar's room was bathed in shadows. A silent crowd of people huddled around his bed. He lay propped up on a mountain of pillows, eyes closed. Morragwen was bending over him, her hands still glowing with the strange red light. Aodh stood beside the witch, he looked tired but strong. He looked up as Glasgerion and Quadroped entered.

"He is too weak to speak," said Aodh angrily. "You will kill him."

Glasgerion looked at Morragwen. "He will die," said Morragwen. "It is only a matter of time."

"We must learn the location of Illoreth, Aodh," said Glasgerion. "The Gate must be locked."

Aodh glared at him, then looked away. "Very well," he said.

"I must go, Glasgerion," said Morragwen. "Be careful." Her eyes suddenly began to fill with tears. Glasgerion caught her hand and held it tightly. "You are so terribly vulnerable without Reander," Morragwen said, "and I cannot rescue you again. Be careful, Glasgerion." She raised one arm high above her head and vanished, as she had come, in a blinding flash of light.

"She does like spectacular exits," said Glasgerion with a wry smile.

Aodh turned and ordered the spectators out of the room. He bent over Angmar's still form and shook him, slightly. "Uncle?" he whispered. "Glasgerion is here."

Angmar slowly opened his green eyes. "Are we alone?" asked Angmar weakly.

"The little pig is still here."

"Yes, yes," snapped Angmar, summoning enough energy to look irritable. "But the others, my councilors and that witch, they have gone?"

"Yes, they have," said Glasgerion.

"Good, then I may speak. But first there is one thing . . ."

"What?" whispered Aodh.

"Pull back those curtains and turn up those wall sponges. This place is as dark as a tomb; and stop speaking in whispers! I'm dying but I'm not dead yet." Aodh hastened to comply and the chamber filled with light that lent a deceptively healthy green tint to Angmar's withered face.

"What has been done with Aedh?" asked Angmar wearily.

"He escaped," said Glasgerion.

"Poor boy," said Angmar. "I am glad that he will not die as a traitor. He will lead an unhappy life as an exile."

"It's what he deserves," said Aodh bitterly. "I doubt the guards tried very hard to catch him; he was a popular commander. I only hope he will not cause you more trouble, Glasgerion."

"He will not try to stop us again," said Glasgerion. "He loves Seamourn too much to endanger it further. He will not go to Ravenor. He did his best to fulfill his vow and is no longer honor bound to Goriel."

Angmar sighed and changed the subject. "I had hoped," he mused, "to see the Gate locked; this is a suspenseful time to die. Listen closely, Aodh, for you must pass this secret on to your sons now that you are to be King. To reach Illoreth, leave Seamourn by the western gate and travel northwest across the Abyssal Plains . . .''

Quadroped listened to the faint, clear voice, and new fears rose in his heart. Angmar spoke of the Robber Barrens in the heart of the Abyssal Plains and the dead city of Illoreth where the ancient Gate to Chaos stood. The trip was more dangerous than he had suspected.

"That is all," concluded Angmar, "and I am weary. Play me something, Glasgerion."

Glasgerion nodded and unslung his harp. "This is an old song," he said, "as old as the Gate itself."

I would go home to the faraway lands,
Said Amon to the autumn folk,
To see the cities on the sand
In a world without a sea;
I would return to the rain-free hills
The bright and barren timeless plains;
I would fare me faraway,
To the parched white skies of the burning day.

Angmar closed his eyes. His head slumped on the pillows. "Is he . . . ?" Aodh could not continue.

"No, he's just resting," said Glasgerion. "Watch until he wakens, and call the Princess and his advisors to wait with you. He will wish to address them before he dies. I must go prepare for the journey." He bent and kissed Angmar's wrinkled brow. "Good-bye," he said.

Chapter Four

Quadroped and Glasgerion left Seamourn at dawn, when the streets were grey and quiet. An hour later the city was lost from sight, but they could hear the great bells knelling, announcing Angmar's death. They swam slowly downwards, along the gentle dip of the continental slope. The seascape remained monotonously the same throughout the morning. The increasing pressure in their ears was the only sign of their descent. By lunchtime there was a visible sign. The bright yellows and reds faded away and the land was blue, grey and green.

"The water absorbs sunlight," Glasgerion told Quadroped. "As we descend the light will fade. The longest frequencies, the reds and yellows, disappear first. If I light a torch the reds and yellows will return."

"I wish you would light one then," said Quadroped. "It's so gloomy."

"We have to save them for the Abyssal Plains," said Glasgerion. "All the light will be gone by then."

The tremendous water pressure made swimming difficult, but the magic that enabled Quadroped and Glasgerion to breathe prevented the pressure from crushing them to death. The seaweeds vanished. Corals and sponges were rare and widely spaced. They were not the delicate branching forms of the shallow water but massive, flat growths that could sustain the pressures. When they could no longer see ahead, Glasgerion stopped and pulled out a torch. Quadroped noticed that it was identical to the torches that had burned so eerily in the dungeons of Seamourn. He waited eagerly for Glasgerion to mutter some magical spell that would make it burn but Glasgerion only pulled out a very ordinary-looking match. The ghastly yellow light of the torch revealed flat, unending grey plains. There was no sign of life.

"Does *anything* live down here?" asked Quadroped, holding Glasgerion's knapsack tightly. He was frightened; they were so far beneath the surface.

"Yes," said Glasgerion, "sperm whales dive here from the surface, searching for giant squid, and there are several species of deep-sea sharks. There are also crabs, molluscs and smaller fish."

The temperature dropped steadily. Glasgerion soon stopped to search for his cloak, which was buried in the mysterious depths of his knapsack. Quadroped climbed off Glasgerion's back and sank into a slimy bed of mud. "Ugh," he grunted.

"That's silicious ooze," said Glasgerion. "It only forms here, where there is nothing to disturb it as it settles. You've just stirred up thousands of years worth of sediment."

Quadroped said that he was glad it formed nowhere else. Glasgerion put on his cape; it hung awkwardly over his knapsack and made him look like a grotesque hunchback. Capes, it seemed, were only glamorous if one had nothing on one's back.

Glasgerion floated horizontally beside Quadroped. "Crawl under the cape," he said, "and hold onto the knapsack. There's nothing to see down here anyway."

"I'm bored," said Quadroped after an hour of dark, silent travel.

"Shall I tell you a story?" asked Glasgerion.

"Yes, please," said Quadroped. He laid his head upon the knapsack and listened contentedly to a long, exciting story about a dragon. Somewhere before the story's end he drifted off to sleep.

Midnight came and went. Quadroped awoke and stuck his head out from under the cloak. The landscape had undergone a subtle alteration. The water was warmer. Curious round stones paved the ocean floor. One had cracked open to reveal thousands of thin, concentric rings of silver and black metal.

"What are those?" asked Quadroped.

"Manganese nodules," said Glasgerion. "They only form in one place in the world. We have entered the Robber Barrens."

"What are they?" asked Quadroped.

"The Robber Barrens," said Glasgerion, "are desolate wastelands surrounding the Mid-Oceanic Mountains. We must cross these lands quickly and quietly. Savage bands of outlaws roam the plains and they owe allegiance to the Manslayer. If they catch us . . ." He did not bother to finish; they both knew what the consequences would be.

Quadroped peered around in nervous expectation. The torchlight revealed no sinister figures, but he was not reassured. *They're probably hiding just out of sight,* he thought. His heart began to thump heavily.

They swam silently now; Glasgerion wanted no noise to betray their presence to the outlaws. Eventually Glasgerion stopped and slipped off his knapsack. Quadroped looked around; the seascape looked just the same as it had for the past hours. "How do you know where we're going?" he asked.

"Why do you think I've stopped?" retorted Glasgerion. "I'm looking for my compass."

"Oh," said Quadroped dismally, "I thought we were going to rest and eat dinner."

"We don't have enough provisions for dinner," said Glasgerion. He unfolded a map and held it flat with one hand while he balanced the compass and torch in the other. "From now on," he said, "we'll only eat one meal a day."

"What!" cried Quadroped, aghast. "I'll starve to death."

"Nonsense," said Glasgerion. "You're already too heavy to carry."

"What sort of a meal will it be when we get it?" asked Quadroped. "Will we have sandwiches and cookies?"

"No," said Glasgerion. Quadroped's spirits sank still further. "We'll have bread, water and a high-energy tablet of dried protein-enriched yeast extract."

"Ugh!" said Quadroped firmly. Glasgerion ignored him and studied the map. A few minutes later he folded it up, put Quadroped back on his back and swam on.

"Time to rest," said Glasgerion. "It's dawn."

"How do you know it's dawn?" asked Quadroped; the water was pitch-black.

"Circadian rhythms," said Glasgerion.

"What?" asked Quadroped.

"I just know," said Glasgerion. He began to unpack the provisions.

Quadroped peered over his shoulder. "We have hardly any food at all!" he cried, glancing into the pack.

"It's enough," said Glasgerion shortly. "We have to travel swiftly, and food is heavy." He gave Quadroped a piece of bread and a protein tablet. Quadroped ate his meal in silence. The food was tasteless; extreme hunger did not improve the flavor in the slightest. Thoroughly discouraged, he choked down the dry tablet and curled up in the silicious ooze to sleep.

Glasgerion soon woke Quadroped up and they traveled on. The sea floor began to slope gently upwards. The water grew lighter and Glasgerion extinguished his torch. Soon huge hills appeared, stretching dark and low across the horizon. Behind them soared lines of thin, jagged peaks. "We are approaching the Mid-Oceanic Mountains," said Glasgerion softly. "The Manslayer was imprisoned there. He is probably somewhere nearby, searching for us." Glasgerion began to cast long looks over his shoulder as they swam. At length he stopped and hung quietly in the water, listening to some faraway sound.

Quadroped strained his ears until he could just hear a

noise like a fast heartbeat somewhere far behind them. "What is it?" he whispered.

"Robbers," said Glasgerion and Quadroped felt him shudder. "They may not have noticed us yet," Glasgerion continued. "If we can reach the mountains we may escape. Trolls live in the mountains."

"Trolls?" asked Quadroped uncertainly.

"Trolls," said Glasgerion, "and the robbers fear them too much to venture into the hills."

"Are *we* going to venture into the hills?" asked Quadroped. He thought that he feared trolls also.

"Yes," said Glasgerion, "but we won't go into the caves. Anyway, trolls are trouble but they're not evil. They owe no allegiance to the Warlords."

The robbers continued to follow them. The sounds of the pursuit grew louder as they began to gain on Glasgerion. *I may never eat another acorn,* thought Quadroped. He closed his eyes and buried his head in Glasgerion's back.

They reached the foothills and entered a long narrow valley. The steep sides were covered with huge fallen boulders. The robbers were so close that Quadroped could hear their muffled shouts as they urged their steeds onwards. He looked backwards just as the robbers rode around a bend and into sight. He could not see the men clearly, but their mounts were horrifying. They rode gigantic crabs whose white carapaces shone in the ghostly light. Their six legs moved with jerky speed, picking their way effortlessly over the rough ground.

"How many are there, Quadro?" gasped Glasgerion. His breast was heaving with effort as he tried to outswim the robbers.

"Ten," said Quadroped. The lead crab came steadily closer. Quadroped could see its round black eyes gleaming from the ends of their long, rotating stalks. Its rider was a meaty, hairy man dressed garishly in scarlet silk. Gold hung at his neck and ears, and the wicked sword in his dirty hand was set with rubies. Quadroped guessed he was the robber chief.

The crab's powerful claw slashed through the water.

"Glasgerion, help!" cried Quadroped. He drew his head back under Glasgerion's cloak as the claw fastened about the bard's waist with crushing force.

The crab drew Glasgerion back and dangled him before its master. The man's bloodshot eyes narrowed to thin slits as he studied his captive. "Well, who have we here?" he asked. "Prince Glasgerion, perhaps?"

Glasgerion winced in pain as the crab's serated claw squeezed into his stomach. "I'm only a poor traveler," he said, "not a Prince." He gestured weakly at his ragged clothes.

The robbers had caught up with their leader by now and were studying Glasgerion with interest. "He don't look much like a Prince," said one, scratching his fleshy nose.

"But he's got a harp," said another. "Glasgerion's a bard, ain't he?"

"He's Glasgerion all right," said the robber chief, scowling blackly at his band. "Look at those gold buckles on his belt."

"Well if he's Glasgerion, where's his pig?" demanded the large-nosed ruffian. "We've got the wrong man. Glasgerion's probably miles away already."

The robber chief chewed his thick lips thoughtfully. "We'll keep him just in case," he said at last. "Half'll stay here and watch him." He indicated four men to remain. "We'll wait for the Master to decide his fate. The rest of you go look for anyone else trying to cross the plains."

When their companions had ridden from sight the crab dropped Glasgerion on the ground and the robbers dismounted. "Let's search him," said one. "He might have more stuff like those buckles." He grabbed Glasgerion and started to pull off his cloak. Quadroped huddled closer to the pack and tried to become invisible.

"Get off," snarled the robber chief, pushing the man to the ground. "He's a Prince, he is, and the Master said as how we should treat him decent. At least until he gets here." He chuckled evilly, exposing rows of rotting, yellow teeth. "I reckon we'll have some fun with him then. We'll get his gold when he's dead."

The robbers moved away from Glasgerion. He sat down

and unslung his harp, being careful to keep the cloak around Quadroped. "I could play a song while we wait," he offered. "It would calm my nerves a bit and it might make the time go faster."

"Why not," said the robber chief with a smile that twisted his ugly face. "It might be a while 'fore the Master gets here. Go ahead." The robbers quickly sat down cross-legged in a circle around their prisoner. "Sing something bawdy," instructed the robber chief, "or with a little gore. We don't want no love songs or anything."

Glasgerion complied gracefully. He had a surprisingly large repertory of revolting songs. Quadroped did not understand most of them, but the ones about murders made him slightly queasy. He supposed Glasgerion had learned them for just such occasions as this. The robbers seemed to be enjoying the performance. They were gazing raptly at Glasgerion as though hypnotized. The songs became slower and more melodic but the robbers did not object. When Glasgerion began to sing a lullaby and there was no protest, Quadroped realized that Glasgerion was enchanting them. The music was soft and gentle. Quadroped lifted a fold of the cloak and peeked out. The white crabs sank upon the sand, eyestalks drooping with weariness. The robbers leaned against their shells, smiled and closed their eyes. They were almost asleep.

A black shadow fell upon Glasgerion. Quadroped felt the muscles of Glasgerion's back ripple and tense. "Put down your harp, Glasgerion," said the newcomer. "It's over."

"Manslayer," said Glasgerion. His voice was firm and calm but Quadroped could feel him tremble. Glasgerion was afraid, but he would never let the Manslayer know. Quadroped looked apprehensively up and barely repressed a squeak. The Warlord was nine feet tall. Powerful bands of muscle stretched like hills across his shoulders, arms and chest. Deep-set cat's eyes glittered in a bestial face. Pronged antlers sprang from his broad forehead. War paint, red and black, divided his body with sinister designs. A kilt of human skins circled his hips. The flayed hands of the victims flapped sickeningly against his legs in the current. Around his thick neck hung a string of yellow bones.

The robbers were awake; Quadroped watched them scrambling to their feet. They cringed beneath Manslayer's savage glare. "Fools," he snarled, "how could you let Glasgerion sing you to sleep like babies? I warned you of his power."

"But, Master," whined the robber chief, cringing as the Manslayer's amber eyes fell upon him, "we did not know him. He has no pig."

The Manslayer slammed the robber chief to the ground with a vicious blow. He grabbed Glasgerion, hauling him roughly to his feet, and tore the bard's cloak aside. "There is the pig," he said. He dropped Glasgerion and stepped back. Glasgerion took Quadroped protectively in his arms, and the Manslayer gave an ugly smile. "Stand away from the pig, Glasgerion," he ordered. "I am going to kill you and I don't want the pig harmed. Goriel wants him alive."

Glasgerion squeezed Quadroped tightly and then set him gently on the ground and stepped quietly away towards the Manslayer. He looked small and almost fragile against the Manslayer's towering bulk.

The Manslayer drew a long broadsword and offered it to Glasgerion. "A chance to save yourself," he said with a mocking smile. Quadroped's heart fell as Glasgerion examined the blade with a mystified expression. The Manslayer took the robber chief's sword and tested its balance with expert hands. "An inferior weapon," he said, "but it will serve its purpose. Take off your pack and boots, Glasgerion. You can't fight properly with them on."

Glasgerion removed his pack and boots and placed them beside Quadroped. His expression was bleak as he grabbed the heavy sword with both hands and held it up before him. The Manslayer stepped swiftly forwards, and the robbers fell silent. The two men began to circle each other, ostensibly testing each other's guard. The Manslayer was merely amusing himself; Glasgerion was trying to escape. The Manslayer swung his sword up and brought it slashing down at Glasgerion. The bard barely managed to parry the blow in time and the two weapons rang against each other like bells. Glasgerion staggered and the Manslayer whirled back. Despite his bulk the Manslayer was frightfully agile. The swords came together again. The impact drove Glasgerion to one knee and his arm slipped sideways. The Manslayer's blade darted forwards, leaving a bright ribbon of blood on Glasgerion's shoulder. He drew back again with a low laugh. Glasgerion struggled to his feet and managed to parry the next blow. His face twisted in agony as the muscles of his wounded shoulder contracted.

Glasgerion really is *a terrible fighter,* Quadroped thought as the fight went on. *The Manslayer will kill him whenever he wants to. I have to do something.* Quadroped picked up the Key and stared at it, but the tunnel did not appear. *Morragwen was right,* he thought. *It only works once.* He looked around; the robbers were too intent upon the fight to pay him any attention. He took a deep breath, held it, and rushed into the circle, right under the Manslayer's feet. He took the Warlord by surprise. The Manslayer stumbled and fell heavily to the ground.

Glasgerion sprang forward with alacrity and clubbed the Manslayer on the head with the hilt of his sword. "Good work, Quadro," he cried, snatching the pig into his arms. "Hold on, we're getting out of here." The magical buckles on his belt turned on full force. Glasgerion shot upwards and away before the astonished robbers could catch him. He left behind his harp, cloak, knapsack and boots.

Quadroped looked backwards. "They're not chasing us," he cried. "We're safe."

"They're afraid of the mountains," said Glasgerion. "They only followed us this far because they were scared of the Manslayer." He swam up the side of the valley, staying close to the ground in the shelter of the huge boulders. When they approached the top of the hill he stopped and collapsed, panting, behind a jumble of rocks. "We need a place to hide," he said. "They'll be after us as soon as the Manslayer recovers."

Quadroped dutifully began to explore the pile of boulders for a good hiding place. "Glasgerion," he called a few moments later, "look. I've found a hole and I think it leads into a tunnel. At least, it looks the way Morragwen's tunnel did." Glasgerion crawled over and looked into the pit. It was not very wide but it looked deep enough to hide a man and its mouth was half hidden by a rock. He slithered, feet first, into the hole and pulled Quadroped down after him. There was room enough at the bottom to kneel. He put Quadroped on his shoulder and together they peered over the edge, down the mountainside.

"Glasgerion," said Quadroped suddenly, "it's dry in here!" The hole was filled with damp air, not water. Quadroped looked out and saw a purple fish swim past the opening.

"A troll hole," muttered Glasgerion darkly, "of all the luck! Let's hope it's abandoned. We don't have time to find another hiding place."

"But how can it be dry?" asked Quadroped. "We're underwater."

"Magic," said Glasgerion. "Trolls hate water."

Quadroped tried to jump down but Glasgerion restrained him. "We'll explore later," he said. "Quiet now, I hear the robbers coming."

The robbers swarmed over the hillside searching for Glasgerion and Quadroped. But Quadroped's hole was well hidden under the boulder, its opening obscured in shadows. The Manslayer arrived while the robbers were still searching. "Where are they?" he asked smoothly.

"They're gone," wailed the robber chief. "The trolls must have got them."

"You have failed me twice," said the Manslayer. He lifted the chief off the ground with one mighty hand. "You have allowed the Key Bearer to escape."

"The Key Bearer?" The robber chief's face was ghastly with fear. "We did not know. . . ."

The Manslayer's hand tightened around the man's neck, slowly crushing his windpipe. When the chief was dead he tossed the body aside and turned to address the stricken robbers. "Glasgerion and the pig must not leave these hills alive," he said. "Do not fail me. If they escape your deaths will be excruciating and slow."

"Where shall we look, Master?" asked the boldest robber.

The Manslayer closed his eyes a moment and his body went rigid. He opened his eyes and stared directly at Glasgerion and Quadroped's hiding place. "They are nearby," he said, "but some spell hides them from me. They must have found an entrance to the caves. Search for an opening into the hills."

"We have to move, Quadro," Glasgerion said. "The Manslayer will find us soon. He will break the troll spell that hides this tunnel. We'll have to go into the caves and take our chances with the trolls."

"You said trolls weren't evil," said Quadroped hopefully.

"They're not," said Glasgerion, "but they aren't friendly either. They don't like strangers."

"What will they do if they find us?" asked Quadroped tentatively.

"I don't know; maybe they won't kill us."

Quadroped did not like the sound of that at all. "Isn't there another Warlord in the mountains?" he asked.

"Yes," said Glasgerion. "Toridon was imprisoned somewhere in the caverns." He sighed and patted Quadroped absently. "Don't worry about her, Quadro," he said. "She is powerless. Let's look at this hole you've found." He dug around in his pockets, found a torch and lit it. "I wonder what else we've got," he mused, emptying the contents of his trouser pockets on the floor. They had three torches, some matches, and a packet of harp strings. He picked the strings up and stared at them mournfully. "It was a fine instrument," he said. "Oh well, I'll find another. At least we have a weapon." He touched the Manslayer's sword gingerly.

"Don't we have any food?" asked Quadroped, nervously examining the small pile.

"Doesn't look like it," said Glasgerion. "All the food was in the knapsack. Unless . . . yes." He extracted three protein pills and a squashed piece of bread from his shirt pocket. "It's not much," he admitted, "but it will do. I wish I had the compass. It will be hard to find our way through the mountains without it."

Glasgerion raised the torch a little higher and they

looked around their hole. At first glance, Quadroped
thought there was no way out, but then he noticed a small
hole in the wall, barely large enough for Glasgerion to
squeeze through. Glasgerion lay down on his stomach, his
legs bent at the knees because the hole was too small to
allow him to stretch out. He pushed the robber's sword
through, then he squiggled after it. His feet disappeared;
there was silence and then he called, "Come on through,
Quadro, but be careful—it's steep."

For the first time, Quadroped was glad he was small.
He lowered his head and walked through the hole onto the
top of a gigantic boulder slimy with grey algae and drab
moss. He began to slip towards the edge and Glasgerion
grabbed him. They had descended through the roof into a
vast cavern partially destroyed by some ancient cataclysm.
Massive boulders had fallen from the walls and ceiling.
The huge pile hid the original floor from view.

"Do we have to go down there?" asked Quadroped. The
boulders looked unstable.

"I'm afraid so," said Glasgerion, "but we won't have to
worry about trolls. This room's been abandoned for some
time."

"How do we get down?" asked Quadroped. The sides of
the boulder were curved and very steep.

Glasgerion studied the boulder for a minute. He removed his shirt and laid it flat on the rock. "Step into the
middle, Quadro," he said. "I'm going to make a sling." He
removed his belt, pulled the corners of his shirt up over
Quadroped and tied them to the belt buckle. Then he made
a rope out of the harp strings and tied it to the other end of
his belt. "I'm going to lower you to the bottom," he told
Quadroped. "Sit still, or else you'll spin."

Help! thought Quadroped, as he was slowly lowered
over the edge. He was afraid to look down, but when he
looked up the fragile harp strings seemed about to break.
The bundle began to spin until his head ached. When he
finally bumped onto the floor he was so happy he did not
even say ouch.

Glasgerion descended very slowly, for the boulder was
smooth and treacherous. His wounded shoulder was weak

and twice he almost fell. "I wish I had my boots," said Glasgerion when he reached the ground. Thin red lines crisscrossed the soles of his feet where the sharp volcanic rock had cut. He put his shirt on and tucked the sword through his belt.

Quadroped was too small to climb across the cavern and his hooves slipped on the hard stones. He climbed onto Glasgerion's back. Glasgerion's long legs were well suited for scrambling across the boulders. He rapidly wove his way between the megoliths. In the far wall, a dark undamaged tunnel wound down through the heart of the hills. Quadroped jumped down, eager to stretch his legs again.

"Be very quiet now, Quadro," whispered Glasgerion, "this may lead to inhabited caves and trolls have sharp ears."

The tunnel floor was covered with a thick layer of slime that squished loudly as they walked. The passage was steep and Quadroped's hooves began to slip. He began to fear that he would have to roll, rather than walk, to the bottom. But at last the floor leveled and they emerged into another huge room.

This cavern was undamaged and stretched far beyond the glow of Glasgerion's torch. Tall, contorted pillars of basalt twisted up to the ceiling like black serpents or wound together to form archways. Brown, beige, mauve, rust-red and grey-green algae coated the black rock like a creeping disease. Pools of still, black water reflected the red flames of the torch and threw the flickering light upon the walls until they seemed to move. Quadroped shuddered; the room was like a dark cathedral built for some demon lord.

The sheer magnitude of the formations intimidated Quadroped. He looked at the smaller pillars instead and found that many resembled other objects. He soon found a horse, a dragon, a house with a smoking chimney, a witch and a troll.

It's amazing, thought Quadroped, gazing at this last discovery. *That stone really* does *look like a troll. I wonder if it will look just as real if I get closer to it?* He trotted over to the formation and stared hard at it. Yes, it still looked like a crouching troll. It was made of pale grey stone splotched with patches of beige. It had two sharp black horns and a long cow's tail curled across its knees. The resemblance to the real thing was so uncanny that he shivered and exclaimed, "I'm glad you're not real!" This remark was followed by a sharp *"eek!!!"* The rock had just opened up two large, yellow eyes and given him a toothy grin, exposing twin rows of sharp, pointed teeth.

Quadroped stared at the troll for a long minute, mesmerized by its huge, glowing eyes. They were the color of butter; the pupils were slit like a cat's. He shook himself free of the troll's stare and gasped, "Glasgerion!"

"Yes, what is it?" asked Glasgerion crossly. He was trying to find an exit from the cave and did not want to be distracted.

"There's a *troll* in here with us," said Quadroped. "And it's got *lots* of teeth!"

Glasgerion turned quickly. "Where?" he asked, glancing sharply around the room.

"He's over there, on top of that rock," said Quadroped, waving a hoof in that direction. "See? It looks like a stone column, but the top half is really a troll."

Glasgerion drew the sword and gave the formation a sharp rap with his fist. There was a dull thud, and he stepped back, nursing a bruised hand. "That's a rock, Quadro," he scolded. "Stop playing around and help me look for a passage out of here. If we don't find an exit soon there really *will* be trolls after us."

"But Glasgerion," Quadroped protested, "it smiled at me."

"Nonsense," said Glasgerion, "you're seeing things. Now come along and help me."

Quadroped glanced nervously at the troll; its eyes were closed and it looked just like a rock. "I *wasn't* seeing things," he assured himself. "I know I wasn't." He reluctantly went to look for tunnels.

Half an hour later Glasgerion gave a shout. "I've found our tunnel, Quadro," he said. He was standing on a narrow ledge far above Quadroped's head.

"How do I get up there?" asked Quadroped plaintively.

"I'm coming to get you," said Glasgerion. "I'll carry you up." He climbed down, took the harp strings out of his pocket, and tied them firmly around Quadroped's middle.

Quadroped struggled mightily, but Glasgerion prevailed. He found himself hoisted onto Glasgerion's back with his feet dangling down in the air and nothing but two straps under his belly to hold him there. "This is horrible," he cried, kicking at Glasgerion with his sharp little hooves. "I'm uncomfortable."

"Stop that," snapped Glasgerion, enduring a painful jab from the angry pig. "I can't climb unless I have both hands free, so you have to ride that way. One more kick or complaint and I'll leave you behind in the dark *forever!*" The ominous tone in which this last threat was delivered had immediate effect. Quadroped ceased to fight and hung quietly, looking down at the floor below him.

The journey up the cavern wall was far worse than the trip down the boulder. In his makeshift sling Quadroped could only look down. As he watched the torch Glasgerion had left on the bottom growing dimmer in the distance, he began to feel faint. The climb was difficult. Glasgerion's shoulder had begun to ache unbearably and the weight on his back unbalanced him. Quadroped tried to close his eyes, but that made the trip worse for he never knew what was happening. He began to develop an acute stomachache and wondered dimly whether it was due to the tight straps which encircled him or to the sheer terror of their ascent. At last they reached the safety of the ledge. Glasgerion untied him and sat him on the ground.

"My tummy hurts," said Quadroped.

"Probably just hunger," said Glasgerion. He handed Quadroped a revolting slab of bread. Quadroped looked doubtfully at the dry bread, now battered by their adventures. He dutifully gobbled it up and soon felt quite restored.

When Quadroped was done, Glasgerion got down on his hands and knees and crawled into the hole. Quadroped walked after him. They traveled very slowly, for Glasgerion had to lie on his stomach and wriggle like a lizard. In the middle of the tunnel, Quadroped got the unpleasant feeling that something was crawling along after them. He glanced anxiously over his shoulder and stared into the darkness. He was rewarded by a brief glimpse of two large yellow eyes blinking at him.

It's the troll, thought Quadroped. *Oh help! The tunnel's too narrow for Glasgerion to turn around. If it grabs me he won't be able to save me. It can't be behind me,* he told himself sternly. *It's too big to fit.* But trolls were magical and maybe they could shrink. He began to whimper in fear.

"Why are you making that awful noise?" demanded Glasgerion. He was struggling to get through a narrow spot and wondering if he wasn't hopelessly jammed.

"The troll is behind us," said Quadroped timidly.

"Hmmph," snapped Glasgerion, squeezing free. "There is no troll. I wish you'd stop imagining things, Quadro."

Quadroped thought this was unfair, but he did not want to argue with Glasgerion. *Perhaps if I ignore it, it will go away,* he thought. This seemed to work for he did not see the eyes again. But he was still scared, for he could not shake the feeling that they were being followed.

The tunnel exited onto a series of interconnecting caverns with high vaulted ceilings. Glasgerion became more cheerful now that he could walk upright. Quadroped was increasingly upset for he could see the troll. Once he looked up to find the creature hanging upside-down from the ceiling and grinning like a maniac. Several times it popped like a jack-in-the-box out of holes near his feet. Whenever he tried to tell Glasgerion he was pointedly ignored, so he gave up trying.

The troll did not act hostile and soon Quadroped's fear changed to anger. The troll wouldn't stay put long enough for Glasgerion to see it. When he could stand it no more he took a deep breath and shouted, "Come out, you stupid troll, and let Glasgerion see you!"

"Quadroped!" said Glasgerion, as the echoes of this mighty cry died slowly away in the dark. "How many times must I remind you that these caves are dangerous? There may be trolls here or, worse still, monsters ready to carry news of us to the Warlords. Be quiet or I'll put a muzzle on you."

"Sorry," mumbled Quadroped penitently. He was secretly appalled by the amount of noise he had generated and felt rather ashamed.

"Don't scold the piggy," bellowed a gravely voice.

Quadroped looked up and saw his troll perched atop a large stalagmite. "Can *you* see him?" he asked Glasgerion. He did not want to speak to the troll until he was sure it wasn't a hallucination.

"Yes, I see him," said Glasgerion; his mouth flattened into a grim line.

"Good," said Quadroped. "Couldn't you have shown yourself just a *little* sooner?" he asked the troll.

"I wasn't going to show myself at all," said the grinning troll. "It was fun to tease you. But I hated to see you scolded like that; I'm always being yelled at by the elders."

"Who are you?" demanded Glasgerion.

"Murgatrrasheptolominy!" announced the troll proudly. "Most people call me Murg."

"Well, Murgatrrasheptolominy," said Glasgerion sternly, evoking a whistle of surprise from the troll as he got the name right, "I hope you get a good scolding from the elders for this trick. Quadro and I are on a dangerous mission. Who knows what damage you have done, causing Quadro to yell like that."

"Oh now!" said Murg. "You can't blame *me* if the pig likes to yell. Lots of people talk loudly. I have an uncle who never speaks but he can be heard six caves away. Why he—"

"I do *not* talk loudly," yelled Quadroped.

"You see? He's shouting again." Murg gurgled gleefully.

"Enough," said Glasgerion with an exasperated frown. "We don't have time for these games. We could use some help, troll."

"Yeeps!" said Murg. "He talks like an elder. What can I do?" He climbed down and walked over to Glasgerion.

Glasgerion stared up at Murg. "We must get to the surface as quickly as possible," he said. "Can you show us the way?"

"Well," said Murg thoughtfully, "you'll have to take the tunnel that leads out the other side of the mountains."

"No," said Glasgerion. "There must be another way. We'll be killed if we return to the Abyssal Plains. Is there no tunnel that leads straight to the surface?"

"Yes," said Murg, "but the path is dangerous, horrible; you can't go that way."

"We must," said Glasgerion.

"Nice people," said Murg slowly, "don't travel through tunnels like that; I'm not allowed to talk to the others."

"Do we look evil?" demanded Glasgerion impatiently.

"No," said Murg, "but you could be disguised. I can't help you anyway. That tunnel is secret. I don't know where it is."

"And a good thing too, seeing how freely you talk to strangers," cried a voice like boulders crashing off the cliffs. "Who seeks the path to the surface?!" A tremendous troll strode into sight. He was dark brown; the horns on his forehead were longer than Glasgerion's arms and sharp as swords. He had small red eyes. In his hand he held a spiked club as tall as Glasgerion.

"Golly, an elder," Murg gasped, turning pale. Beside the elder, Murg looked like the youngster he truly was; Glasgerion looked like a dwarf.

"I seek the path," said Glasgerion warily.

"And who are you?" asked the elder. He glared at Glasgerion, who barely reached his waist.

"I'm Glasgerion, a bard by trade," said Glasgerion with a practiced smile.

"Glasgerion . . ." said the elder. "I've heard that name before. A harper? Is this song about you?" The elder sang in a deep monotone:

In the land that sang the songs
Where the rivers trickle on
Silver tongued, when you are gone
Who shall sing the tales?
With your our legends pass away
Be buried bones, be empty thrones,
Broken shutters, broken glass,

Magic melting in the streams
Glasgerion, the guard of dreams.

"That's me," said Glasgerion. He looked embarrassed.

"Hmmph," said the elder. "I knew your father, Peredur. Is he still alive?"

"He died, twenty years ago," said Glasgerion.

The elder sighed. "I forget how fast your people age," he said. "Why are you so desperate to reach the surface?"

"I'm trying to get to Illoreth," said Glasgerion. He dared not lie; trolls had an uncanny ability to recognize lies, and their tempers were uncertain.

"To lock the Gate?" asked the elder.

"Yes."

"Why is everyone always moaning about Keys and Gates," he complained. "Seems to me the Black Unicorn's been locked up long enough."

Glasgerion looked severe. "If the Black Unicorn escapes Chaos the war will begin again," he said. "The resultant bloodshed—"

"Yes, yes, I know," said the elder quickly, forestalling Glasgerion's lecture. "I'll show you the path. The Black Unicorn's fate doesn't concern me. Trolls have no business with Ravenor one way or the other. I'm glad you found the Key; your father hoped you'd be the one."

"He's not," said Murg suddenly. "The piggy is wearing it around his neck."

The elder looked down and eventually found Quadroped, who did not quite reach his ankle. "He's so small." He grinned. Then his expression changed and he turned towards the young troll. "Murg—"

"I didn't do anything *very* bad," said Murg, hiding behind a big rock.

"It is forbidden to speak to strangers," said the elder. "Go home at once. I'll speak to your parents tonight."

"'Bye, piggy," whispered Murg.

"Go," growled the elder. And Murg went, very rapidly. "He's a promising youngster," said the elder, relaxing his stern expression once the young troll was out of sight. "He's my youngest grandson. A youngster should break rules occasionally, though they must be punished when they're caught, of course. Let's go." He turned and strode off; Glasgerion picked Quadroped up and ran to keep up.

"Here we are," said the elder. He stopped before the entrance of a thin, high tunnel. "Just follow the tunnel," he said. "You can't get lost."

"It will be nice to see the surface again," said Quadroped wistfully. He was thinking of acorn trees and summer.

The passage to the surface was not a true tunnel but a huge crack in the mountains. It was very narrow; Glasgerion was often forced to walk sideways like a crab. The walls stretched up into the darkness, sometimes leaning away from each other and sometimes bending so close that they touched.

"I don't like this tunnel," said Quadroped. His voice echoed off the walls.

"*Shhh,*" said Glasgerion. "I don't like it either. If you have to talk, whisper. I don't want anything to hear us."

Quadroped looked up at the shadowy ledges above his head and shuddered. Anything could live up there, waiting to jump down on them. The torchlight flickered and moved so rapidly it was impossible to decide if the shapes crawling over the walls were monsters or just reflections of the flames.

They walked until Quadroped's hooves were so sore that every pebble he stepped on hurt. Glasgerion's feet were bleeding from numerous wounds inflicted by the sharp, volcanic stone. They used up one of their torches and lit another. There was only one torch left, and the passage hadn't begun to slope upwards towards the surface.

Glasgerion suddenly stopped and lifted his hand for silence. Quadroped stood quietly, trying to hear whatever alarming sound Glasgerion was listening to. He twitched his ears around and heard a dull, wailing cry floating out of the darkness to their left.

"Can you hear it?" asked Glasgerion quietly.

"Yes," said Quadroped. "What is it?"

"Maybe only air blowing across the top of the passage,"

Glasgerion said, "but I think it's Death Wings. We'll have to go quickly now, Quadro. I can't fight in such a narrow place. There's not enough room to swing my sword."

They walked on as fast as they could. The sound of the Death Wings' pursuit grew louder and louder, until Quadroped's ears ached from the noise. *They must be right behind us,* he thought. He looked back, but the tunnel was still empty.

"The walls magnify the sound," said Glasgerion. "They're not as close as you think." Then, without warning, the wailing dropped in pitch to low, moaning noises. Then it stopped altogether. In the unexpected silence Quadroped's breath sounded like a whole forest shaking in the wind. Glasgerion's footsteps seemed as loud as the elder's.

"Have they gone away?" asked Quadroped.

"No," said Glasgerion; he looked worried. "They wouldn't abandon the chase now. I think they will try to sneak up on us. Look behind me, Quadro, I don't like surprises."

Quadroped tried to walk and look back at the same time but he bumped painfully into the wall. Glasgerion picked him up and held him against his shoulder. Quadroped stared intently into the shadows, but the passageway remained clear. He was just about to say so when a stealthy movement in the corner of his eye caught his attention. He looked up and turned as pale as a white pig can. "The Death Wings," he gasped. "They're *above* us."

Hanging on the underside of the ledge were five of the most repulsive creatures Quadroped had ever seen—Water Demons, Pitch Fiends and the Manslayer all considered. They were manlike and covered with short, velvety, grey fur. Their fingers and toes were unnaturally long, and they used these elongated digits to cling to the crevasse walls. From their lower jaws protruded a pair of yellowed tusks. Black, leathery wings grew from their shoulders and furled over their backs like capes. Worst of all, they had no eyes, only shallow fur-covered indentations in their skulls where eyes were supposed to be. They hung upside down and sidled rapidly across the walls after the bard and his pig.

"Pretend you haven't seen them," Glasgerion whispered. His breath tickled Quadroped's ear. "The passage is getting wider; soon I'll have room to swing the sword."

The passage abruptly turned and they entered a small room. Glasgerion dropped Quadroped on the floor. Quadroped landed with a thump and began to roll. "Run and hide," Glasgerion commanded. Quadroped raced towards a hole in the wall and squeezed inside. Cackling, whistling cries filled the air behind him as the Death Wings appeared, crawling over the roof. Glasgerion spun around and drew the Manslayer's mighty sword with one hand. The torch burned fiercely in the other.

The Death Wings howled and launched themselves off the walls, black wings spread wide, fingers and toes curled into lethal claws. Glasgerion ducked, jumped back and climbed on top of a flat rock. The Death Wings landed on the rocky floor and crouched there, gibbering angrily among themselves. One by one they turned their sightless heads towards Glasgerion. They began to creep towards him, their wings rasping and scraping on the floor. Glasgerion stuck his torch into a crack in the wall and raised the sword high above his head.

The silver blade shimmered in the red light. The largest Death Wing snarled and sprang into the air, its strange fingers stretched to tear Glasgerion's eyes and throat. Glasgerion swung the sword down hard across the monster's neck and a geyser of grey blood shot into the air. The leader staggered and crashed to the ground. It crawled weakly to the wall as the remaining Death Wings attacked. They landed and clung to Glasgerion with their grotesque toes, hiding him from view.

The red tip of the sword slashed randomly through air, slashing the wide, delicate wings to ribbons. The Death Wings began to drop away from Glasgerion. They retreated to the walls where they sat, weeping and howling over their mangled wings. The wounds were not fatal, but the Death Wings lived by gliding through the passages; without their wings they were helpess. Glasgerion quickly dispatched the last monsters and ran towards the survivors on the walls. Before he could catch them they climbed to the shadowy roof and disappeared.

Quadroped crawled out of his hole and ran to Glasgerion. The bard's clothing hung in ragged shreds. Deep cuts ran across his chest, and his arms and legs were bleeding from numerous puncture wounds inflicted by the monsters' teeth. Black blood oozed sluggishly from the ugly wound in his shoulder.

"I'll be all right, Quadro," said Glasgerion with a weak smile. "I'm still alive." He sat down and quickly tore the tattered remains of his shirt into bandages. "Come along, Quadro," he said when the worst wounds were covered. "The Death Wings may come back."

"Shouldn't you rest?" Quadroped asked. Glasgerion looked terrible.

"I'll rest when this is over," said Glasgerion lightly, "under a tombstone in all likelihood."

"He's probably right," grumbled Quadroped, "but I do wish he wouldn't *say* things like that."

They walked on, but Glasgerion rapidly lost his strength. He began to stumble and his breath was hard and loud. Four hours later, Glasgerion stopped and sank to the floor, eyes closed.

"Glasgerion?" Quadroped poked the silent bard with his nose.

"I'm just a little dizzy, Quadro," said Glasgerion. "I'll be all right in a moment." He fell silent and soon his breathing slowed into the gentle rhythms of sleep. Quadroped sat quietly beside Glasgerion, unwilling to wake him up. After a while he extinguished the torch and curled up against Glasgerion's stomach. Thus secured against all dangers, he drifted off to sleep.

Quadroped woke several hours later. He could hear a loud rumbling noise in the darkness and it was uncomfortably hot. He rubbed his eyes and washed his ears until he was wide awake. Then he realized where the sound was coming from. Glasgerion was talking in his sleep. He pressed his nose against Glasgerion's head; it was hot with fever. He groped for the torch and tried to light it, but his hooves couldn't hold the matches. *I wish I had some water*, he thought. The ocean was far above his head and their flask of fresh water had been lost with the knapsack. He sat in worried silence, hoping Glasgerion would wake up and tell him what to do.

The fever grew worse; Glasgerion began to shout and roll violently around until Quadroped was forced to move away to avoid injury. *The Death Wings will hear him and come back,* he thought. He started to cry but his sobs made Glasgerion more restless. *I have to get help,* Quadroped thought. "I can't go back; there are Death Wings there. I'll have to go on down the tunnel. Good-bye, Glasgerion," he whispered. He pressed one flank against the tunnel wall to steer by and began to walk slowly ahead in the dark.

Quadroped walked for hours. His side hurt where it rubbed against the wall to guide him. He began to see colors, hazy dots of blue, pink and yellow floating in the air before him. He tried to touch them, but they faded from his hoof and he realized they were imaginary. He almost believed that he could see halos of grey light around the walls and stones on the floor. He explored the shapes of the rocks with his nose; they were completely different from the halos. Then he began to see flashes of deep orange and brilliant yellow in the air to his left.

That's odd, he thought. *Those colors don't move when I roll my eyes.* He walked on; the lights grew brighter. *It's a real light,* he thought. He began to run; soon he could see the tunnel walls around him, black and sinister in the golden light. The tunnel grew wider and the left wall dropped away. He was walking along a thin ledge over a deep crevasse.

The air was hot, so hot Quadroped could smell the dryness. He looked down and saw a river of dark lava. It moved slowly, like lumpy oatmeal, down the canyon. Long cracks appeared in its black skin. Brilliant yellow liquid spurted out, cooled to sullen red and turned black. He could hear the liquid crackle and roar as it burned. Lava bombs arced high above his head and splashed back to the river. They left yellow holes and spreading ripples of red on the dark, cinder-coated surface.

The air rising from the abyss shimmered and rolled. Quadroped had to blink his eyes to keep from growing dizzy. It burned his skin and did not satisfy his lungs. He looked back the way he had come and saw a long gallery of thick basalt columns. *That's why I could see flashes of light*, he thought. *I was passing behind those pillars*.

Quadroped ran along the cliff edge; the ground was hot and he was glad he had tough hooves instead of feet like Glasgerion had. He could hear a roar in the distance, but the river twisted like a snake and he could not see very far ahead. He ran on, around a huge bend, and stopped. Before him was the largest fall he had ever seen.

A cliff of sheer, black obsidian rose hundreds of feet above Quadroped's head, its glassy surface reflecting the shooting flames. Frothing lava cascaded over its edge and plunged down to the river far below. A cloud of orange haze, formed of lava droplets, veiled the foot of the falls and rained down upon the path which ran dangerously near the descending torrent. As Quadroped approached, he saw something even more frightening than the fall itself. Chained in the middle of the pounding fires was the giant, ghostly figure of a woman.

Chapter Five

Quadroped looked up at the giantess. She was perhaps thirty feet tall. Her form was nebulous, composed of swirling clouds of fire. A dress of smoke wreathed her sinuous body. Her face was round, surprisingly childlike, and her eyes were closed. Thick golden manacles circled her wrists and long chains held her in the midst of the firefall. *She looks a little like Morragwen,* thought Quadroped, recalling his first sight of the witch. *She must be Toridon.* He looked at the path ahead; it wound right past her. *If she wakes up she could grab me,* Quadroped thought nervously. But he knew that he had to go on, for Glasgerion lay dying behind him. *Maybe she will let me pass,* he thought. *The Manslayer said that Goriel wanted me alive. If I'm very quiet,* he decided, *she will never notice me.*

Quadroped walked quickly and quietly down the path. He tried to breathe very softly, although the burning air made him gasp for breath. The noise of the lava fall was deafening, and Quadroped began to feel safer. He was directly below the Warlord now and a cautious glance showed him that her eyes were still closed. *I'm going to make it*, he thought.

The path ended in a long flight of stairs that stretched up the cliffside beside the falls. The stairs were high and it took Quadroped a long time to climb onto the first step. He was just starting to climb the second, when a fireball whizzed past his head. A flickering wall of flames sprouted from the stone before his nose. With a terrified squeak, he rolled back down onto the path.

"Stop, pig!" said Toridon. Her voice was light and sweet. Quadroped stared up into Toridon's moody brown eyes. "Foolish creature," said the Warlord, "were you trying to sneak past me?"

"I thought you were asleep," said Quadroped in a small voice.

Toridon heard him even over the crash of the lava and laughed. "Who are you?" she asked. "Many Death Wings and trolls have walked this way, even a few men and women, but I've seen no pigs. You're hardly even a pig, just a piglet from the size of you."

"I'm Quadroped," said Quadroped.

"I'm Toridon," replied the woman, "as you have probably guessed. What brings a piglet so far from home? Are you lost?"

"Not really," said Quadroped. Toridon did not seem overtly hostile and he began to relax.

Toridon observed the tiny pig closely. "I know why you're here," she said at last. "You're the little Key Bearer. Goriel told me about you."

Quadroped flattened his ears and once more felt as though a thousand pairs of hostile eyes watched his every move. "Yes," he said. He didn't know what else to say. If he lied, Toridon might throw more firebombs.

"Why are you all alone, Key Bearer?" asked Toridon.

"My companion is sick," said Quadroped. "The Manslayer hurt him and then Death Wings attacked us. I think he's dying. I came looking for help, only there doesn't seem to be any. Are you going to throw more fireballs at me?" He looked anxiously at the Warlord.

"I might," said Toridon cheerfully, "but they can't hurt

you. Your Key will shield you from my fires. So Glasgerion is really dying? That will please Goriel. But where is
the other one, Prince Reander? He was supposed to be with
you."

"I don't know," said Quadroped. "He doesn't know I'm
a pig. He thinks I'm a warrior or something. He's supposed
to join us later. I have to go now; Glasgerion needs help."
He bravely got to his feet and began to climb the first stair
again.

Toridon watched him and began to laugh. "You will
never climb that staircase in time to save Glasgerion," she
said merrily. "There are eight hundred steps." Quadroped
looked at her in dismay. "I could help you save Glasgerion," said Toridon.

"You could?" asked Quadroped. "But you're a Warlord.
I thought you wanted to kill me."

"I want to stop you," said Toridon affably, "and if that
means killing you then I'll do it. But right now I can't do
anything at all and so I'm willing to make a bargain with
you."

"What sort of bargain?" asked Quadroped. He knew he
could not give her the Key even to save Glasgerion's life.

"Release me," said Toridon. "Set me free and I will
carry you and Glasgerion to the surface."

Quadroped gulped nervously and chewed his hoof. *I
can't free a Warlord,* he thought. *But how can I let Glasgerion die?* He gazed bleakly into the falls. *Unless I lock
the Gate the Black Unicorn will escape and thousands of
people will die. But there are already two Warlords loose.
Will one more make that much difference?* He didn't know.
"If I let you go," he asked Toridon, "will you promise not
to steal the Key?"

Toridon's eyes narrowed thoughtfully. "Goriel will be
furious," she mused, "but yes, I'll promise. Once I'm free
nothing will prevent the Black Unicorn's escape. Reander
cannot defeat so many Warlords."

I wonder if I can trust her? thought Quadroped. *Aedh
said that Warlords were honorable but the Manslayer
didn't seem very trustworthy.* He wished that he knew more

about the Key and Reander. He just didn't know whether Reander could fight three Warlords or not.

I can't let Glasgerion die! Quadroped thought. *We'll still have time to lock the Gate and maybe Reander can fight three Warlords.*

Quadroped got quickly to his feet. "How do I free you?" he asked before he could change his mind.

Toridon stretched her hand towards Quadroped. He saw a tiny keyhole in the manacle. "The Key will free me," she said. Her eyes burned with triumph.

"Could you lower your hand a bit?" asked Quadroped. He cringed away as her massive hand moved towards him. For a moment he was sure she would crush him or grab at him. She rested her arm on the ground beside him. Quadroped noticed that the manacle was too tight and bit deeply into her fiery flesh. *It must hurt her,* he thought. He grabbed the Key in his mouth and fit it clumsily into the lock. He had a hard time turning it, for the mechanism was old, but at last he heard a click and the manacle sprang open, throwing him backwards with its force. "Help!" he screamed as he plunged over the edge of the path.

Toridon opened her vast hand and caught Quadroped before he could be killed in the fiery lava. As the flaming fingers curled up to meet him, Quadroped was sure he would be burned alive. But Toridon's hand was cool, almost cold, and he landed safely.

"You aren't going to break your promise, are you?" he whispered, gazing up into Toridon's blazing eyes. She was so large, nothing could stop her if she decided to carry him to Goriel.

For a frightening moment, Toridon hesitated. "The Key will free the King," she whispered. She shook herself. "No," she said, "I will deal fairly with you, piglet." She leapt nimbly onto the path and ran with joyous steps towards the tunnel. Quadroped expected her steps to sound like huge drums—the elder's had—but Toridon made no sound at all as she walked.

"You won't fit into the tunnel," said Quadroped.

"I'll fit," said Toridon. She stretched her arms wide. "It is so good to be free."

When they reached the tunnel, Toridon's body passed like a ghost through the walls. She held the hand with Quadroped in it down at her waist, because he could not fade through stone. Quadroped looked up and saw only a thin section of her body filling the passageway. He could see her lips and nose, but her eyes were moving through the stone. When the walls closed in she became a bodiless orange hand. She reached Glasgerion in minutes.

Quadroped peered down between her glowing fingers and was alarmed to see that Glasgerion had ceased to roll and was lying deathly still. "Is he dead?" he asked in a whisper. It would be terrible if he had freed Toridon too late.

"No," said Toridon, bending close to Glasgerion, "but death is near. We will hurry to the surface." She picked Glasgerion up gently between a thumb and forefinger and laid him beside Quadroped. Then she turned and rushed down the tunnel, her burning hair flying behind her.

Quadroped held tightly onto Glasgerion as Toridon raced up the steep path. He could not feel Glasgerion's heart beating or hear him breathe. The fever was gone and Glasgerion's skin felt cold against his worried nose. *He feels like he's dead,* Quadroped thought, *but Toridon said he wasn't. Oh, I wish she'd hurry.*

At last the darkness turned grey, then blue, then blinding white as Toridon burst into daylight. Quadroped looked down; they had emerged in a forest of ancient oaks and elms. Below them flashed the silver water of a lake. "I leave you here," said Toridon. Her feet steamed as she walked across the cold waters of the lake. She tipped her hand and Quadroped and Glasgerion rolled onto the sandy lakeshore. She reached down and took the Manslayer's sword from Glasgerion's belt. "He won't need this anymore," she said. "The Manslayer will need it soon."

Quadroped looked anxiously around at the silent forest. "But there's nobody here," he cried. "Glasgerion will die without help."

"I never promised to save him," said Toridon, "only to carry you to the surface." She laughed and rose like a burning whirlwind into the air. "Farewell, Key Bearer," she cried and vanished.

Quadroped sat and stared into the sky where Toridon had been. *I've made a terrible mistake,* he thought. He shook himself and ran to Glasgerion. The bard lay half in and half out of the lake. His face was ghastly pale. Dark blood seeped from his wounds, staining the bright waters pink. Quadroped nudged Glasgerion and licked his face, but Glasgerion did not move.

There has *to be someone nearby,* Quadroped thought. *Glasgerion can't die now.* He looked around. The lakeshore looked deserted, and the dark forest stretched away on all sides. Quadroped was about to walk into the woods behind him when he suddenly noticed a tall woman standing behind a thick raspberry bush on the far side of the lake. Waggling his ears about wildly, he galloped towards her as fast as his short legs could propel him, squeaking, "Help! Help! Oh, help!"

The woman dropped her basket in surprise, spilling ripe raspberries over the ground. When she saw that the author of the commotion was only a small pig, she relaxed. She frowned at her fallen berries, pushing a strand of auburn hair out of her chilly blue eyes. "Don't step on them," she snapped as Quadroped ran up to her. "It took all morning to pick them. I don't want them squashed as well as spilled." She gave Quadroped a hard look. "And don't you *dare* eat them."

"I'm sorry," said Quadroped, backing away from the irritable woman.

"Don't speak until you are asked to do so," said the woman coldly. "Who are you anyway? *I* am Eunoe."

"I'm Quadroped," said the chastened pig. He stared doubtfully at Eunoe's severe face.

"So?" asked the lady indifferently. "Go away, pig. I'm busy." She bent to gather her fallen fruit.

Quadroped hesitated; Eunoe was unfriendly but she was the only creature around and Glasgerion was dying. "Please," he said, "you have to help me. My companion's been attacked by monsters. He's lying in the lake bleeding to death."

"There *are* no monsters in my lake," retorted Eunoe, turning to face the pig. "You are quite mad. I wish you would go away and leave me alone."

"You *have* to believe me!" cried Quadroped desperately. "I'm telling the truth. Oh, please come and see for yourself."

Eunoe looked closely at Quadroped; there was an almost hysterical gleam in his eyes. She noticed for the first time that it was not berry juice sprinkled all over his white skin. "You have blood on you," she said, surprised. "Perhaps I *had* better follow you. But I warn you, pig, this had better be serious. I am not a nice person when I am angered." Quadroped silently wondered whether she was *ever* a nice person. He snorted and ran back to Glasgerion. Eunoe picked up her basket and followed.

Eunoe gasped when she saw Glasgerion's body. The grass around his head was sticky with blood and his breath was faint and laboured. She knelt swiftly beside him, ignoring the blood that stained her dress, and began to inspect his wounds. Quadroped stood anxiously beside her. Eunoe pulled a small velvet bag out of her basket and took from it a roll of bandages, scissors and a pot of thick white lotion. Quadroped's spirits rose as he watched her begin to clean the wounds. Eunoe looked as though she knew what she was doing.

"He has been attacked by Death Wings," Eunoe exclaimed, pulling a tuft of fine grey fur out of a wound on Glasgerion's arm. She examined Glasgerion's shoulder. "And by a sword as well. You two have been down in the tunnel. I knew I should not have built my house here, but I thought it would be private." She fell silent and began to bandage the worst wounds. "There," she said at last, sitting back on her heels. "That should do for the moment."

"Is he going to be all right?" asked Quadroped.

"Yes," said Eunoe shortly. "Though why he had to pick *my* lake to bleed in . . ." She angrily tucked her tools into her basket.

"We couldn't help it," said Quadroped.

"That's what *you* say," retorted Eunoe. "What were you doing in the tunnel anyway?" Quadroped hesitated and looked at his feet. *"Don't* tell me then," said Eunoe nastily. "I'm sure *I* couldn't care less." She put her arms under Glasgerion's legs and shoulders and stood up, lifting his heavy body with no apparent effort. She began to walk into the woods. "Come on, pig," she said over her shoulder, "and bring my basket with you."

The basket was larger than Quadroped and he doubted that he could move it without spilling the berries. He grabbed the handle tentatively in his mouth and the basket suddenly shrank until he could carry it easily. *Oh dear,* thought Quadroped as he ran after Eunoe, *more magic*.

"Does this man have any relatives or friends who can come and nurse him?" asked Eunoe, when Quadroped had caught up to her.

"I don't know," said Quadroped. He suddenly realized how little he knew about Glasgerion. "I could . . ."

"You're too small," said Eunoe bitterly. "I shall have to waste *my* time looking after him. And you will need food and a bed until he's cured. Oh, how I hate visitors." Quadroped mumbled that he didn't wish to be any inconvenience. "You *are* an inconvenience," said Eunoe. Quadroped fell silent and began to wonder if there would be rats in Eunoe's dungeon.

"I know someone who *might* be willing to look after him," Quadroped said suddenly.

"Who?" asked Eunoe tersely.

"Morragwen—" began Quadroped.

"The witch?" demanded Eunoe.

"Yes," said Quadroped in surprise, "but I don't know how to reach her."

"I do," said Eunoe. "But I find it hard to believe that she'll come. She hates being bothered as much as I do." She looked at Glasgerion with new interest. "Is *this* Glasgerion?" she asked suddenly.

"Yes," said Quadroped.

"He certainly doesn't look like much," said Eunoe candidly. "I'll call Morragwen and see if she can't clean him up a bit." Quadroped wondered nervously what Morragwen would say when she heard that she was expected to wash blood and mud off Glasgerion. He wisely kept his fears to himself.

The woods suddenly parted to reveal a wide, shady lawn and a small white cottage. Eunoe's house was surprisingly cheerful. It was trimmed in blue, and red geraniums grew at all the windows. Bright flower beds framed the path to the door and there was a mat that said WELCOME in large friendly letters.

Eunoe left Glasgerion on a couch in her sunny parlor and conducted Quadroped to a small guest room on the second floor. "Get some rest," she told him. She closed the door and went away to summon Morragwen by some mysterious means.

The guest room, Quadroped noted with relief, was not covered with dripping moss or infested by rodents. It was clean, comfortable and the walls were decorated with blue forget-me-nots. The windows had cushioned window seats and blue check curtains. A large four-poster stood against the far wall. Quadroped lost no time clambering into the middle of the mattress and diving under the cool, clean sheets. *Eunoe has feather pillows,* he thought happily. In a few moments he was sound asleep.

It was late afternoon when Quadroped finally lifted his snout off his crumpled sheets. Sunlight poured through the curtains and danced across the polished wooden floor. Quadroped stretched, gave a great yawn and hopped onto the floor. He climbed awkwardly onto a window seat, pushed open the window and stuck his head out. In the shade of a large elm he saw Glasgerion. The bard was fiddling with a harp and looked unaccountably moody. "Glasgerion!" Quadroped called, waving a small hoof. "You're alive!"

Glasgerion looked up and smiled at the snout in the window. "Come on down, sleepy," he called, waving back.

Quadroped raced out of the room and down the stairs. He galloped across the lawn and hurled himself into Glasgerion's lap, only to belatedly recall that Glasgerion was wounded. With a grunt of dismay he started to climb down, but Glasgerion restrained him.

"I'm completely healed," he said. "There's not even a scar. Morragwen's magic works quickly."

Quadroped looked at Glasgerion. The bard's voice was decidedly chilly when he mentioned the witch.

"Is Morragwen still here?" asked Quadroped cautiously.

"I suppose so," said Glasgerion shortly. He began to tighten a string. The string snapped.

I wonder what's wrong, Quadroped thought. *I ought to tell Glasgerion about Toridon now, but he's so angry. What if he doesn't like me anymore when he learns what I've done?* He paused, wrestling with his conscience. "Glasgerion," he said, "I did something wrong."

Glasgerion glared at him. "You still have the Key, don't you?" he snapped.

"Oh yes," said Quadroped. He showed Glasgerion the Key.

"Then what is it?" asked Glasgerion impatiently.

Quadroped gulped; Glasgerion was very intimidating. "I released Toridon," he said quickly.

"What!"

Quadroped shrank. "I knew it was wrong," he said miserably, "but I couldn't let you *die*, Glasgerion. Toridon promised to help us. She carried us here. Do you hate me now?"

Glasgerion stared into Quadroped's unhappy purple eyes. He relaxed and smiled. "I don't hate you, Quadro," he promised. "I'm glad to be alive. You still have the Key and Toridon has carried us several miles ahead of schedule. It's bad, but not a disaster." Glasgerion hugged Quadroped to show he was forgiven. Then his face relaxed back into a frown.

"Did Eunoe give you that harp?" asked Quadroped.

"Yes," said Glasgerion, replacing the broken string. "She can be surprisingly generous. It's a lovely instrument."

"Where *is* Eunoe?" asked Quadroped. "I didn't see her when I came downstairs."

"Hiding from her guests," said Glasgerion. "She resents our company. I expect she'll return around dinner time." He looked up and his face grew dark. Morragwen was

walking towards them. Her face looked careworn and unhappy.

"Hello, piglet," she said and forced a cheerful smile.
"You've rescued Glasgerion twice now. You're becoming
quite a hero."

"I am? Goody," squeaked Quadroped, wiggling his ears
about in a ridiculous fashion and turning pink. Glasgerion
frowned at him.

"Quadroped released Toridon," he said grimly. "He
talks too freely and is too quick to trust strangers. He'll
make a mistake soon, and it will be fatal."

"Oh, I don't know," said Morragwen. "Quadro seems to
be an excellent judge of character."

"Is Morrag here?" Quadroped asked quickly. He sensed
that Morragwen and Glasgerion were about to fight again
and he wanted to escape.

"He is," said Morragwen. "He's somewhere inside the
house. Don't be alarmed by his appearance. He refused to
change his shape so I put a flying spell on him. He's floating through the air quite nicely now, but it can be a bit
startling when you first see him. Eunoe had a fit."

"Go along, Quadro," said Glasgerion. "Morrag has
been asking for you, and Morragwen and I have things to
discuss."

"There's nothing to discuss, Glasgerion," Morragwen
said sadly.

"There most certainly *is,*" said Glasgerion. "If you love
me, why won't you marry me? I'm tired of silly excuses. I
want to know the truth."

Quadroped did not wait to hear any more. He jumped
off Glasgerion's lap and ran towards the house shouting,
"Morrag!" From the equally powerful shout of "Quadro!"
that echoed out across the lawn, Glasgerion and Morragwen assumed that he had found his quarry.

"Good afternoon, Quadro," said Morrag cheerfully, as
Quadroped trotted into the front hall.

"Hullo, Morrag," said Quadroped. The eel twined
around his neck and gave him a friendly squeeze. "How
are you?"

"*I'm* fine," said Morrag complacently. They went into a small rose garden and sat down on a bench. "Tell me all about your adventures, Quadro," said Morrag. "Morragwen said there were Pitch Fiends . . ."

"Quadro," said Morrag when the tale was done, "I think you're foolish to try to reach the Gate. You've almost been killed three times and now there's another Warlord on the loose. The dangers will get worse as you approach the Gate. Goriel will use all his powers to get that Key and the easiest way is to kill you."

"But I *have* to lock the Gate," said Quadroped in surprise. "If the Black Unicorn escapes there'll be a terrible war."

"True," said Morrag, "but war is inevitable. They won't keep the Black Unicorn captive forever."

"I can keep him locked up for the next hundred years," said Quadroped, "and that's almost forever."

"No, it's not," said Morrag. "I've been alive five times that long and I don't even feel ancient yet. How do you know that the Black Unicorn deserves to be locked up?"

"He's evil," said Quadroped. "He started the Great War and he wants to start it again. He has to be kept in Chaos; Glasgerion says so."

"I know what Glasgerion says," Morrag replied, "but I've lived a lot longer than he has. It was a war between countries, Quadro, not between abstract forces of good and evil. There may be good people in Ravenor. There are certainly evil ones in the Kingdoms. Why did the war begin?"

"Glasgerion says that no one knows," said Quadroped.

"There must have been a reason," said Morrag. "You should find out why the war began before you condemn the Black Unicorn to another century in prison."

"But I can't find out," said Quadroped. "Everyone's forgotten. Glasgerion has spent his whole life studying the wars and he hasn't found a reason. Anyway, pigs aren't allowed in libraries and I don't have enough time. I have to lock the Gate, Morrag; it's the only safe thing to do. I can't let the war start again."

"Hmmm," said Morrag, "I suppose you're right. But you will be traveling near Ravenor, Quadro. Somewhere someone may tell you the reason why the war began; listen to them. But, Quadro, if you change your mind about locking the Gate, don't let Reander know. He will stop at nothing to lock the Gate and he is a dangerous enemy."

"Oh, I wouldn't," said Quadroped earnestly. "He might kill me. But I *am* going to lock the Gate, Morrag, if I reach it alive."

"All right, enough whispering, you two," said Morragwen, walking up to them. She looked as if she had just been crying. Morrag wrapped around her shoulders sympathetically. "He doesn't understand," she said. Quadroped was startled by the despair in her voice.

"How can he?" asked Morrag.

Quadroped snorted softly. Morrag and Morragwen seemed to have forgotten him and he did not want to overhear such a private conversation.

"Hello, Quadro," said Morragwen. "Eunoe's in the kitchen preparing dinner. She could use some help." Quadroped accepted this thinly veiled hint and retreated from the garden.

"What were you talking about for so long?" asked Morragwen of the eel.

"Nothing much," replied Morrag. "Just planting a few ideas."

"About the Black Unicorn?" asked Morragwen. "You shouldn't have, Morrag. If Quadro starts to doubt his mission he will be in danger. He is too young to act on his own."

"He won't have to," said Morrag. "Quadro will always have friends."

"I suppose so," said Morragwen. She pulled the eel into her arms. The two sat silently together on the bench until the sun went down.

The company reassembled at dinner. Glasgerion and Morragwen were both subdued and quiet. Eunoe, on the other hand, was in high spirits. "You seem to be fully recovered, Glasgerion," she remarked almost merrily during the fourth course. "Will you be ready to leave soon? I could help you pack in the morning."

"Thank you." Glasgerion summoned a polite smile. "We'll be off first thing in the morning."

"Leave as late as you like," said Eunoe graciously, "but I don't have enough food left to feed you lunch."

A genuine smile lit Glasgerion's face. "We'll leave as soon as it grows light," he reassured his hostess. "I'm grateful for your hospitality and only sorry that we had to disturb you."

"Well, you *are* a nuisance," said Eunoe, "and I don't really like guests, though you have not been as much trouble as I feared. If you need maps or anything, the library is across the hall. Feel free to—" She was rudely interrupted by a loud hammering on the front door.

"Go and see who that is," snapped Eunoe to a hovering servant. "If they want to come in tell them I'm dead. They can pay their respects at the funeral next week." She fixed Glasgerion with a chilly stare. "Do *you* know who that could be?" she asked. Glasgerion shook his head. "Well, I'm sure it's for you," said Eunoe, "for no one ever visits me."

The front door creaked open. "There's no one home," said the servant timorously. "Come back tomorrow."

"Stand aside," a deep voice said, "at once."

Glasgerion and Morragwen started up from their chairs. Glasgerion looked suddenly happier. Morragwen looked gloomier than ever. "Aha!" said Eunoe when she saw their faces. "I knew it was for you. Oh, let him in!" The front door slammed shut and heavy footsteps came down the hall.

"Who is it?" Quadroped whispered to Morrag, who was hovering beside him.

Morrag's reply was lost as the man strode into the room. He was tall, broad-shouldered and carried himself with an air of authority. Quadroped could make nothing else of the stranger for he was wrapped in a shapeless green cloak that hid his face from view. His clothing was freely spattered with thick globs of mud, as were his high leather boots.

"Oh for goodness' sake!" said Eunoe as mud fell on her clean rug. "Wipe your feet off before you come inside!"

The stranger ignored Eunoe and strode over to Glasgerion. "Greetings, Uncle," he said. "I'm surprised you're still alive. Have you managed to lose the Key yet?"

"That," said Morrag in dire accents, "is Reander." Quadroped shrank down in his chair until the tablecloth hid him from view. He was as reluctant as ever to meet Glasgerion's nephew.

Glasgerion hugged Reander, mud and all. "I *am* glad to see you," he said. "I'm weary of being hacked to pieces by assorted horrors."

"You are wounded?" Reander frowned. "We cannot afford any delay now. What happened?"

"Seven Pitch Fiends, the Manslayer and a pack of Death Wings," said Glasgerion.

"They wounded you?" Reander looked surprised.

"Yes," said Glasgerion defensively. "*I* am not a warrior, Reander. I'm supposed to sing about battles, not fight them. In any case, I am perfectly fit, thanks to Morragwen and Eunoe."

"Witches," said Reander darkly. His eyes fell upon Morragwen. "What are you doing here?" he demanded.

"Someone has to protect Glasgerion," said Morragwen sweetly. Reander's green eyes narrowed to angry slits.

"How did you reach us so soon?" asked Glasgerion quickly. "I thought you'd be in Essylt until the end of the week. Is the army all set then?"

"No," said Reander shortly, "it is not. Leave us, witch women. I must speak with Glasgerion and the Key Bearer in private. Where, by the way, is the Key Bearer?" Reander looked around, but Quadroped was invisible under the white tablecloth.

"Umm . . ." said Glasgerion. He was not eager to reveal the Key Bearer's true identity to his irascible nephew.

"I will *not* leave," said Morragwen, successfully diverting Reander's attention.

"Do not provoke my anger, witch," said Reander. "If you do not leave I shall throw you out."

"Why you . . ." Morragwen's skin and hair rapidly turned fiery red. Quadroped waited for Morragwen to turn Reander into a toad.

"Morragwen stays," said Glasgerion in a low, clear

voice. "The Key Bearer and I both owe her our lives." He met his nephew's stare steadily until, surprisingly, Reander's eyes fell.

"You are a fool to trust her, Glasgerion," Reander said. "She will betray us to Goriel."

"She has already had ample opportunity to do so," said Glasgerion persuasively.

"She may stay," said Reander. Morragwen's mouth curved into a smug smile and she resumed her previous shade of indigo blue.

"My," said Eunoe, "what a *pleasant* person your nephew is, Glasgerion." She rose from the table and flung her napkin down with unnecessary violence. "You may wish to talk to this person, Morragwen," she said, "but *I* certainly do not. I will bid you all good night and good-bye. Glasgerion, I trust you'll be gone by morning." She tossed her dark hair and left, slamming the door loudly behind her.

"I'm afraid you'll have to sleep on the sofa, Reander," Glasgerion said. "I don't think Eunoe will let you use a guest chamber."

"I shall conjure up a cot in your room," said Reander calmly. Quadroped silently thanked Eunoe for giving him his own room, a whole floor above Glasgerion's. "We have plans to make, Glasgerion, before the Gate opens. There are only eight days left."

"Eight days? Oh *no!*" squeaked Quadroped. He popped up in his seat and stared anxiously at Glasgerion.

"What is that?" demanded Reander sharply. Quadroped began to sink under the table again.

"That's Quadroped," said Glasgerion. "Now about the Gate—"

"First remove the animal," said Reander.

"How dare you speak to Quadro like that?!" said Morragwen. "He's the K—"

"Madam," said Reander with awful civility, "you may be fond of the creature—there is no accounting for taste— but this is no place for pets."

"Pet?" Morrag said wrathfully. He slid out from under

Quadroped's chair and glared balefully at Reander. "Quadro is the Key—"

"An *eel?*" said Reander angrily. "Remove these beasts
at once. This is a council of war, not a circus to entertain
the witch's ridiculous menagerie." Quadroped jumped
down and hid under Glasgerion's chair. Morragwen turned
dull orange and Morrag prepared to lunge for Reander's
throat.

"Stop this, all of you," said Glasgerion reprovingly.
"Quadroped will stay, Reander; he's the Key Bearer."

"The *pig* is the Key Bearer?" Reander sat back dumbfounded.

"He certainly *is*," hissed Morrag fiercely. "See? He
wears the Key around his neck. Quadro, come out here and
show this *human* your Key."

Quadroped reluctantly crawled out from behind Glasgerion's ankles and showed Reander the little Key. He was
careful to keep a safe distance from this violent man.

"Of all the *silly* looking creatures..." said Reander as
he examined the small pig before him. "He may stay then,
but this will make our task harder than I had supposed.
However did you manage to keep him alive this long,
Uncle? He looks extremely foolish to me."

"Quadro is not foolish," said Glasgerion, placing Quadroped safely on his lap. "He's a very useful companion.
He has saved my life three times already."

"Hah," retorted Reander uncompromisingly.

I knew he wouldn't like pigs, thought Quadroped miserably. He settled down in Glasgerion's lap and allowed his
ears to be scratched.

"If we have only eight days in which to reach the Gate,"
said Glasgerion, "we'll have to cross the Crystalline
Mountains."

"You'll have to cross Spiders Mere as well," said Morragwen.

"What *are* these places?" Quadroped asked Morrag.

Morrag slithered up the leg of Glasgerion's chair.
"Spiders Mere," he said, "is a big swamp populated by
spiders. The Crystalline Mountains form the border between Ravenor and the Kingdoms. They are the home of

Goriel, the Lord of the Snows, the most powerful of the Unicorn's Warlords."

"Oh no, more monsters," said Quadroped softly.

"Don't speak unless you are spoken to," said Reander. "The swamp and the mountains are the least of our worries." Reander paused, then continued. "Someone has set the Warlord Toridon free." There was a sudden, uncomfortable silence and everyone looked at their plates.

"Then all the warlords are free?" asked Morragwen.

"Perhaps," said Reander. "No one knows where the fourth Warlord is." He shrugged. "We will find out when we reach the Gate."

"Do you think you *will* reach the Gate?" asked Morragwen. "Goriel is a formidable enemy and now Toridon and the Manslayer assist him."

"I can handle the Warlords," said Reander coldly.

"That," said Morragwen, "sounds nice, but you've only got eight days."

"He can probably do it," said Glasgerion reluctantly.

"He *would!*" whispered Morrag to Quadroped. "He's exactly the type who can do anything *and* knows it."

"Yes, I am," said Reander; he had very sharp ears.

The discussion continued, maps were produced from Eunoe's library and complicated lists began to take shape. Quadroped and Morrag were sent to bed early. They had disgraced themselves by yawning loudly in the middle of a lecture on the dangers of Ravenor.

"I hope," said Quadroped as he crawled gratefully into bed, "that Reander will decide to like me."

Morrag, who had elected to share Quadroped's room, stared pityingly at the friendly, hopeful pig. "I'm sure he'll tolerate you," he said unhelpfully, "but I am not sure that even *you* can make friends with a man like Reander. Reander *has* no friends, except Glasgerion and one or two of the mightier heroes of the world. The trouble is that he has no equals. Everyone else is somehow inferior, and he doesn't waste his time getting to know anyone he can't respect."

"Oh," said Quadroped gloomily.

* * *

Glasgerion woke Quadroped up at dawn. Glasgerion, Quadroped noticed, looked tired. "How did Reander find us?" Quadroped asked. "We've been through so many tunnels that I don't even know where home is."

"Your home," said Glasgerion, sitting down on the edge of the bed, "is to the east; mine is to the north. Reander's a sorcerer, rather a good one in fact; he used a spell to find us." Glasgerion began absentmindedly to pull threads from his old brown cloak. "Quadro," he said slowly, "don't let Reander know that you freed Toridon; he wouldn't understand. He hates Morragwen . . ."

"Why?" asked Quadroped softly.

"She's a witch," said Glasgerion. "And she's lived for centuries without ageing. He believes that she is from Ravenor. Nothing I can say will convince him otherwise, not that it matters now. She still won't marry me."

Quadroped sat silently beside Glasgerion. There was nothing he could say. After a while Glasgerion pulled himself together and smiled. "I live in constant dread that he'll turn Morragwen into a frog," he said. "Don't say anything about Toridon. I couldn't cope with an amphibious Key Bearer; a baby pig is bad enough."

Quadroped looked hurt and Glasgerion ruffled his ears placatingly. "Don't worry too much about Reander, Quadro," he said, observing Quadroped's wrinkled nose and twitching tail. "He isn't all that bad. Everything will be easier now. Reander can zap a Death Wing out of existence with a wave of his hand, and he's a demon with a sword or a knife."

A knife, thought Quadroped, *is for use on smaller creatures like myself.* He looked gloomily at the checkered pattern of his quilt.

"Drat!" said Glasgerion, startling Quadroped from his reveries.

"What is it?" asked Quadroped nervously.

Glasgerion was staring angrily at a hole he had pulled in his cloak. He sighed and stood up. "Stop sitting in bed, you lazy slug," he admonished the comfortable pig.

"Glasgerion," called Eunoe from the garden, "haven't

you managed to wake that lazy pig *yet?* Your nephew is growing impatient."

"It won't hurt Reander to wait a while," called Glasgerion. "Tell him to meet me in the stables. We have to find a way to carry Quadroped." He stood up and walked to the door. "Come along, Quadro," he said. "If you dawdle, I'll ask Reander to come and fetch you."

Quadroped immediately forgot how nice and soft the mattress was and jumped out of bed. He paused only to wash his face and hooves before scrambling past Glasgerion and dashing down the stairs. He found Morrag in the kitchen, looking for breakfast.

"Good morning, Quadro," said Morrag cheerfully. "Have you come to your senses yet and decided to stay clear of the Gate? How can you bear to travel with Reander? I wouldn't stay in his company for five minutes, not even if I were offered two thousand crunchy minnows *and* a lifetime supply of toothpaste." The eel began to open the cupboards in search of food.

"Well, I don't want to travel with him," admitted Quadroped, "but I don't have much choice; I'm the Key Bearer."

"Mad, quite mad," muttered Morrag, scanning the shelves. "There appears to be no breakfast, Quadro," he said. "We'd better get to the stables or Glasgerion will start looking for you."

Quadroped and Morrag reached the stables and stopped. Morragwen and Glasgerion stood just within the doorway oblivious to all around them. They had apparently reconciled their differences.

"I wonder how she managed that," said Morrag, observing their ardent embrace. He coughed loudly and the couple moved apart. Glasgerion looked rapturous but Morragwen, Quadroped noticed, still looked sad and her eyes seemed haunted.

"There you are," said Glasgerion as Quadroped trotted into the stable. "Congratulations are in order. Morragwen has agreed to marry me after we lock the Gate."

"If you still wish it," said Morragwen softly, "and if Reander—"

"Don't be silly," said Glasgerion. "Of course I'll still wish to marry you. Reander has never been able to influence me, you know that. Why do you doubt me?" He began to look angry again.

"I don't doubt you, Glasgerion," said Morragwen, "but feelings can change." Glasgerion began to protest but she stopped him. "I should go now," she said. "I hear Reander coming. Do not tell him yet, Glasgerion."

"Why not?" demanded Glasgerion, exasperated.

Morragwen did not reply. She wrapped her arms around Morrag and faded from sight. This time no blinding flash of light marked her passage.

Glasgerion shook his head and turned his attention to the trip ahead. "Now, Quadro," he said, "I want you to look at your traveling arrangements. I considered putting you in my pack"—Quadroped looked faint—"but I've found a boxlike saddlebag instead. It may not be too comfortable but you'll be able to see out. It's cushioned so you should be protected from the worst of the jolts." Glasgerion walked back into the dark shadows of a stall. He emerged leading a huge roan mare who tossed her head and snorted with frightening energy.

Quadroped looked up at the small shallow box tied to the front edge of Glasgerion's saddle and gulped. "But it's so high up," he cried. "I'll fall out and be killed!"

"Nonsense. You'll get used to it," said Glasgerion.

Quadroped looked up at the horse, undoubtedly a vicious creature, and shuddered. "Hello," he said timidly. The horse did not respond.

"These horses can't talk, Quadro," said Glasgerion. He scooped Quadroped up, ignoring his desperate protests, and deposited him in the box. He led the horse out of the dark stable into the sun.

Reander rode into the yard on a huge dapple-grey stallion. He looked large and formidable. "Have you found the pig yet?" he asked.

"He's in his box, ready to go," said Glasgerion.

Reander looked at Quadroped and his expression was

stern. *He doesn't look much like Glasgerion,* thought Quadroped. Reander had the same high cheekbones and sharp aristocratic nose. But his face was free of laughter and his eyes were a cool watchful green. Reander carried himself with the assurance of a man used to command. His clothing was plain but neat and a golden circlet held his red-gold hair back from his broad strong face. *Reander looks like a* real *Prince,* Quadroped thought.

Quadroped's chain of thought was broken when Glasgerion swung into the saddle, causing the box to tilt sickeningly forwards. They rode towards the stable yard gate, and the box began to sway with a steady but disturbing motion. Quadroped curled into a tight, miserable ball and closed his eyes. They had not even left the yard and already he felt queasy.

The horse stopped with a jolt that almost spilled Quadroped onto the ground. He opened his eyes, eager to see what had caused the merciful stillness. Eunoe was walking towards them, a small bundle in her hands. "Well, you're finally going," said Eunoe, a smile wreathing her face. She came up to the horses and rubbed their noses gently.

"Stand away from the horses' heads," said Reander, "and we'll be off."

"I'm going," said Eunoe calmly. "I only came to give the piggy these blueberry muffins. There wasn't any breakfast and he shouldn't travel on an empty stomach, it will make him ill." Quadroped suddenly realized that Eunoe was a very perceptive woman. He thanked her politely for the muffins. "You've already eaten everything else in the larder," said Eunoe gruffly. "You might as well finish the job properly." She patted Quadroped gently and told Glasgerion to keep him safe.

"You've made another friend, Quadro," said Glasgerion as they rode away. He looked over his shoulder. "She's even waving good-bye."

Chapter Six

Quadroped and his companions rode through a beautiful countryside. Leafy groves, still lakes and meadows filled with wild flowers decorated the roadsides. The sky was a deep, unclouded blue, and the wind was filled with the sound of rustling leaves and the voices of birds.

Quadroped consumed the muffins Eunoe had given him and soon his stomach felt much better. He grew accustomed to the way his box swayed and bounced against the horse's flank. He found that he could curl up on the bottom of the box and still see over the side. For a long time he was content to look around and enjoy the warm sunshine on his skin. But eventually he became bored with the view, which did not change much despite its beauty, and began to stare at Reander instead.

Reander glared into the distance, his dark brows pulled down over his nose and his lips compressed into a thin, uncompromising, line. *I wonder what he's thinking about,* thought Quadroped. Then he decided that he didn't really wish to know. Thoughts that could disturb Reander so were probably extremely unpleasant.

"Must you scowl like that?" Glasgerion asked his nephew suddenly, as though he had followed Quadroped's chain of thought. "It makes me uneasy just to look at you. What are you thinking about anyway?"

"The Black Unicorn," said Reander.

"Oh? Well, stop thinking about him then," said Glasgerion. "From your expression, you'd think the world was about to end."

"It may," said Reander.

"Nonsense. It can't end for another week," said Glasgerion flippantly. Reander's eyes twinkled ever so slightly but he continued to frown. Reander, Quadroped realized, was determined to be gloomy. He tried to ignore Reander's depressing attitude and thought about acorns instead. He soon found it impossible to remain cheerful. Reander, for reasons known only to himself, suddenly decided to address Quadroped directly.

"Little do you dream, unhappy piglet," said Reander meaningfully, "what dark and gruesome perils await you at the journey's end. Think you to emerge unscathed from the dark shadows that shroud the ruined towers of haunted Illoreth?" Quadroped could think of no suitable reply.

Reander smiled and continued. "Nay, your very soul shall shiver before the terror that lurks in the empty silent halls. Think ye of the dread abomination that quivers and crawls through its noisome lair, batting feebly with its jellied appendages at the grisly bones that dangle, swaying gently in the icy air, from the root-infested roof stones. There is death and pain in the desolation of Illoreth the Accursed. Unmentionable are the—"

"If they're unmentionable then pray don't mention them," snapped Glasgerion. "Stop trying to scare Quadro, Reander; he'll be scared enough by the time we reach the Gate." Quadroped was grateful for Glasgerion's intervention but his words were not reassuring. "Don't shake so, Quadro," said Glasgerion with a smile. "Reander was only teasing you. Reander," he added disapprovingly, "has a morbid sense of humor." Quadroped noted that there was, indeed, a slight curve to Reander's lips.

"Ah, but *was* I teasing?" said Reander, giving Quadroped a long measuring look. He laughed darkly and sent his steed flying ahead down the road.

"Drat," said Glasgerion, watching as Reander disappeared over a hill. "I *wish* he wouldn't be so melodramatic. I had things to discuss with him."

"Oh," said Quadroped. He thought of the monster waiting to kill him at the Gate. The peace of the day had been shattered. Quadroped chewed absently on the Key and wished he had never found it.

Reander stayed far ahead for the remainder of the day, much to Quadroped's relief and Glasgerion's considerable annoyance. To pass the time, Glasgerion began to tell stories. Unfortunately, his thoughts kept drifting off towards Illoreth and the Gate.

"Once upon a time," Glasgerion would begin, "there lived a wise King. Now this King was a happy man, happy, that is, until his fair Queen drowned in the Black Bog. His children motherless and his heart weary with grief, he began to walk the parapets by night, gazing thoughtfully down at the waves which raged 'neath the battlements . . . I wonder what the Black Unicorn is doing now?" Glasgerion would fall silent, the story forgotten. After a long while he would shake himself and ask, "Where was I?"

"I don't remember," lied Quadroped upon this particular occasion, "but the story was getting sad."

"Yes, well maybe I should tell another one then," said Glasgerion. "I think the King gets eaten alive in that one."

"Yes, *do* tell something else then," said Quadroped, repressing a shudder.

"Once there was a lovely Princess who fell down a deep slimy well and was captured by a hideous troll . . ." began Glasgerion. So it went for the rest of the day, each story becoming gloomier and more disjointed than the last. At five o'clock Glasgerion stopped trying to cheer Quadroped up and fell silent. His expression made it clear that he was contemplating all sorts of horrible things which could do nought to cheer an already depressed pig. With a feeling bordering on relief, Quadroped saw Reander wheel his steed around and come thundering back down the road towards them.

"Hello, Reander," said Glasgerion in a melancholy tone. "What do *you* want?"

"It will be dark soon," said Reander. "We need a place to sleep, preferably on grass, for the horses need food."

"So does the pig," said Quadroped. He was firmly ignored.

"How about that hedgerow ahead of us?" said Glasgerion, pointing to a large privet hedge ten feet in front of them. A thin strip of grass separated it from the road. Reander nodded and the two men quickly dismounted and tethered the horses to the hedge.

"Let me down, let me down," squeaked Quadroped noisily as soon as the horse was still. He began to hop up and down, tipping the box to an alarming degree.

"Sit still a moment, Quadro," urged Glasgerion. "You'll spill out."

"Let me down," said Quadroped, hopping even harder.

"I'm coming, I'm coming," said Glasgerion. He quickly removed the troublesome pig from the saddle box.

"Ouch!" said Quadroped as Glasgerion picked him up. "Don't squeeze so hard. My sides are all sore from bumping around."

"They'll be even sorer tomorrow," said Reander with despicable cheerfulness. Glasgerion set Quadroped on the grass and the tired pig essayed a few steps. He fell flat on his nose, his legs too stiff to support him.

"Ouch," said Quadroped automatically. He was beyond caring what grievous injuries the callous world chose to inflict. "It's not funny," he said, staring reproachfully at Reander's rare smile.

Quadroped might have said more, but Reander forestalled him by conjuring up a dish of roasted acorns. The unexpected treat banished all of Quadroped's woes. There were, he decided as he munched contentedly on the nuts, some advantages to traveling with a sorcerer. Dinner finished, he curled comfortably up in Glasgerion's cloak and fell into a deep dreamless sleep.

* * *

Quadroped was awakened near midnight by a cold, tickling sensation in his left ear. All attempts to brush the perpetrator away proving futile, he reluctantly opened a single eye and glared up at the small, furry spheroid sitting beside his head.

"What are you?" asked Quadroped grumpily, wishing it would go away and let him sleep.

"My name is Fairfax," ruffled the strange creature. "I am a long-nosed hedgehog, of course." He poked at Quadroped with his long pale snout.

"What does a hedgehog do?" asked Quadroped, cautiously surveying the creature and hoping it was harmless.

"We hog hedges, silly," said Fairfax, clearly disgusted with such ignorance. He turned and began to poke at Glasgerion's knapsack.

"How does one hog a hedge?" persisted the sleepy piglet, vainly trying to distract the creature before it destroyed the contents of the bag with its rummagings.

"We push others out of our hedges," snuffled Fairfax from deep inside the knapsack. "We also," he added slyly, poking his nose out briefly, "bite people when we're hungry. *I* am hungry now."

"You are?" quavered Quadroped.

"*Very* hungry!" said Fairfax, eyeing Reander's sleeping form with a sinister smile. Quadroped hastily handed him a dried apple from one of Glasgerion's pockets. The thought of Reander's reaction to an attacking hedgehog was too horrible to contemplate. Fairfax eyed the battered fruit askance. "Not nice," he pronounced with awful finality.

"It's all there is," said Quadroped. "Reander made all the leftovers disappear."

"Ah," said Fairfax grimly. He nibbled halfheartedly at the old apple. "You're the Key Bearer," he remarked between bites.

"Yes," said Quadroped, beginning to feel nervous. Fairfax did not look particularly diabolical, but he supposed that agents of Ravenor were very clever with disguises.

"What are you doing in my hedge?" asked Fairfax.

"You're supposed to be locking the Gate." His tone was faintly accusing.

Quadroped briefly outlined his adventures to date. "I don't even know if I'll reach the Gate," he concluded. "There are all sorts of monsters and Warlords in the way."

"A pig is a silly sort of Key Bearer," Fairfax said thoughtfully, "but at least you're not a human. Now I am going to sleep." Fairfax carelessly tossed his apple core at Glasgerion's head.

"Oh, wait a bit!" cried Quadroped in alarm. "You can't stay here. Glasgerion made me promise not to talk to any more strangers. He'll be mad at me if he finds you here."

Fairfax ignored Quadroped's protest. He curled up into a tight ball and began to snore loudly. Quadroped gave him a feeble shove, but the hedgehog only snored louder and more convincingly than before. With a sad sigh, Quadroped gave up and lay back down to sleep. *I hope*, he thought, *that Fairfax is gone before Reander wakes up.*

"What is that!" a voice yelled into Quadroped's ear. He opened his eyes and stared into Glasgerion's angry face. Out of the corner of his eye he saw Reander prodding the hedgehog with the toe of his boot.

"That," said Quadroped gloomily, "is Fairfax."

"How many times must I tell you not to make friends with strangers?" asked Glasgerion.

"I didn't *invite* him to join us," said Quadroped. "He just wandered in around midnight. I don't think Reander should kick him like that."

"I'll do far worse than kick him if he refuses to unroll," said Reander.

"And a good morning to *you* too," growled a tiny voice. Fairfax slowly unrolled and sat glaring at his audience.

"What is your business in our camp, creature?" asked Reander, directing a brooding glance at Quadroped.

"I'm not a creature," said Fairfax. "I'm a hedgehog. I came because it's *my* hedge and I was curious. Now I'm going to leave."

"Stop!" said Reander in ringing tones, but Fairfax was already gone.

* * *

Breakfast was a silent affair. The food tasted like cardboard for, as Reander tersely informed them, it was a waste of energy to conjure up flavor as well as nutrition. Quadroped, acutely aware of Reander's disapproving stare, sat far apart in the shade of the hedge. This enabled Fairfax to sneak up behind him without being observed by the others.

"Help!" said Quadroped as the hedgehog nipped his ear. "Fairfax! What are you doing back here?"

"Shhh!" hissed the hedgehog angrily. "Do you want that red-haired monster to shake us again? I've brought you something." He showed Quadroped a glass jar full of golden liquid.

"What's that?" asked Quadroped.

"Honey," said Fairfax, thrusting the jar into Quadroped's hooves. "You'll need help, since you're only a pig. Now take it."

"Honey? Oh goody!" gurgled the famished pig. "Breakfast was simply *awful*." He began to pry the lid off with his teeth.

"Stop that!" ordered Fairfax impatiently, snatching the jar back and slapping Quadroped sharply on the nose. "You aren't supposed to *eat* that!"

"But what else *can* you do with honey?" asked Quadroped plaintively.

"You can save it for later," said Fairfax mysteriously. "Before tomorrow morning you'll be glad I gave you that."

"Yes but—"

"Shhh, the monster is coming," said Fairfax. He disappeared quietly under the hedge.

"Who were you talking to?" asked Reander, coming to stand over Quadroped.

"Myself," lied Quadroped gamely.

Reander looked sharply about, but Fairfax was well hidden. "Go stand by the horses," he said. "We'll be leaving soon." Quadroped looked at the horses and shuddered. They were stamping and pawing the grass in their eagerness to be off.

"Quadro, come over here!" called Glasgerion. Quadroped remained by the hedge. "Come here, at once," he said. "You've already caused enough trouble this morning."

Quadroped began to amble reluctantly towards Glasgerion. He had only gone a few feet when Reander, his patience at an end, wheeled his stallion about and charged down upon the disobedient pig. Quadroped's eyes opened wide as the monstrous war-horse galloped towards him. Reander looked furious. "He's going to trample me to death!" Quadroped gasped. "Glasgerion!" he wailed. "I don't want to be killed!"

"Stand still, you silly pig!" said Reander.

I'm not silly. I don't want to be dead! thought Quadroped reasonably. Still clutching the honey in his hooves, he ran as fast as he could, but the horse was faster. Without once breaking stride, Reander leaned down out of the saddle and scooped Quadroped up into the air. Riding back to Glasgerion he unceremoniously dropped the pig into his detested saddle box. "Ouch!" said Quadroped as he landed.

"It serves you right," said Reander. He rode up the road at a swift trot, Glasgerion close beside him.

"You shouldn't have scared Quadro like that," said Glasgerion.

"He needed a good scare," said Reander. "He won't disobey me again. We can't afford such delays if we are to reach Illoreth in time."

"But you could have hurt him," said Glasgerion.

"Hurt the Key Bearer?" said Reander. "Never! I need him until the Gate is locked."

What will happen to me after the Gate is locked? thought Quadroped. He sighed; the trip was not going to be an easy one.

Glasgerion and Reander began to discuss the journey ahead. Quadroped did not understand what they were saying but the Black Unicorn was frequently mentioned in a grave, hushed tone that frightened him. The jar of honey was lying beside him and he started to think about it instead. For a long while he puzzled over Fairfax's peculiar insistence that he save it until tomorrow. At length he concluded that there was only one possible explanation. Somewhere down the road something was lurking in wait for them and the honey was meant to protect them. How the honey could do this taxed Quadroped's imagination considerably. *Perhaps*, he thought ingeniously, *we are to meet a wild bear who can be placated with a gift of honey*. This explanation seemed plausible so Quadroped let the question rest and began to think of acorns instead.

Shortly after noon Quadroped realized that his theory about the bear was incorrect. The landscape had slowly changed from groves and meadows into boggy areas which grew larger and swampier. Lakes became a common feature of the landscape, and the road became soft and muddy. The tall trees which had grown beside the road became smaller and scarcer until all that remained were stunted, malformed trunks which bore few or no leaves on their sickly, twisting branches. He missed the trees for they had formed a cool canopy against the sun and without their shade the air became almost unbearably hot. Insects also became unpleasantly common, and in between mosquito chompings he decided that no wild bear would be caught dead in a damp, deforested steambath like this.

The colors soon faded away, leaving a dull unending vista of mud flats, stagnant ponds and dead trees. The whole was a symphony in beige, brown and olive grey. Even the sky ceased to be blue, becoming overcast with drab yellowish clouds. This sky was of so unpleasant an appearance that Reander was forced to remark that he hoped it would not rain, slime rather than water being the only possible product of such a sickly sky.

"Glasgerion, where are we now?" asked Quadroped.

"Spiders Mere," said Glasgerion.

"Is there a story about it?"

"The men who live on the edges of the swamp," said Reander in a low menacing voice, "tell terrible tales of the spiders that live here. At night, when travelers are asleep, the spiders crawl from their invisible webs. They swarm over their helpless victims and encase them in bonds of silk until they are ready to be eaten. It is not a pleasant way to die."

"Stop telling Quadro horror stories," said Glasgerion.

"He's only teasing you again, Quadro. The swamp got its name because the rivers and streams which flow through it form a pattern resembling a spider web."

The swamp stretched on, seemingly forever. When night fell they could only just see a dark line on the horizon, which Reander identified as the Crystalline Mountains. "The clouds will hide the moon tonight," said Reander. "We shall have to find a place to sleep, though I dislike this place."

"There's a patch of mud which looks a little drier than the rest just up ahead," said Glasgerion.

"It will do," said Reander. They dismounted and laid their cloaks down upon the damp ground. Reander quickly conjured three bowls of steaming food. Glasgerion took his and gazed at it distrustfully. "I hope," he said as he sat down, "that you have created taste as well as nutrition. I know you're tired, but I don't think I could stand another meal like breakfast."

"I have given it both taste and nutrition," said Reander.

The meal was not without its faults. Reander had ignored both color and texture. Quadroped, contemplating his bowl of nutritious acorn-flavored grey glue, felt rather nauseated but he tried it anyway. Reander, he decided, had certainly created an excellent flavor. But *nothing* could quite make up for the sensation of a wet jellyfish slipping down one's throat.

Reander and Glasgerion were asleep as soon as they were done eating, for they intended to rise before dawn. Quadroped curled up in his usual place next to Glasgerion, but try as he would he could not fall asleep. He was exhausted, but the irregular chirps of crickets and the loud bellows of distant bullfrogs woke him every time he began to drift off.

This is unfair, thought Quadroped, looking at the peaceful forms of Reander and Glasgerion. *If I stay awake any longer I'll feel horrible in the morning. I can't afford to waste any sleep.* "I *am* going to fall asleep," he told himself firmly. "I'm just going to lie down and relax and then drift gently off to sleep."

Quadroped lay down, closed his eyes and remained that way until his back began to ache. *There is a stone poking into my back,* he thought, *but I'm not going to move. I'm going to ignore it and stay still until I fall asleep.* He got up and moved to a more comfortable position and tried it again.

In the cold hours before dawn Quadroped remembered the jar of honey which Fairfax had provided. *I don't care what happens, I'm going to eat just a little honey to help me sleep,* he decided. He trotted over to the dark heap of the saddlebags and rummaged about for the jar.

Quadroped found the jar under the cushions of his box. He picked it up in his mouth and walked back to Glasgerion. He plopped down on the bard's cloak, the jar of honey in front of him, and peeled off the lid. He thoughtfully licked a sticky hoof and stared up at the paling sky. As he gazed at the stars he began to notice that the sky, rather than being any uniform color, was made up of light and dark splotches, with the dark splotches arranged in the general form of a spider.

How interesting, Quadroped thought, dipping his hoof back into the jar. *The clouds are shaped like an enormous spider.* He watched, fascinated, as the thin legs slowly moved around. It slowly dawned on Quadroped that he was not seeing a cloud. There really *was* a gigantic spider perched above his head.

I wonder how she floats there, Quadroped thought sleepily, too tired to be afraid. *She's so large; she must be very heavy.* As his eyes became accustomed to the early light he saw that the spider was not floating, she was crawling back and forth across a web which seemed to reach to the horizon.

The spider crawled directly over Glasgerion and began to drop a cloud of silken threads onto the sleeping bard. "Stop that!" said Quadroped, alarmed.

"Hello. What's this?" asked the spider, peering down at Quadroped with eight red eyes. "A little pig?"

"I'm Quadroped," said Quadroped bravely. "What are you?"

The monster clicked its mandibles together and replied in an unpleasantly soft voice, *"I* am a nasty spider."

"All spiders are nasty," said Quadroped disparagingly.

"A common belief which has no basis in fact," said the monster pedantically. "Most spiders are small inoffensive bugs who go about their daily drudgery without ever a malicious thought to occupy their tiny minds. Have you ever been pursued by a persistent fly and then, miraculously, found it gone? Undoubtedly it was devoured by a household spider trying hard, in her feebleminded way, to be helpful. Does this household spider ever hear a word of thanks? No! Let a human set eyes upon a spider and there is instant chaos. 'Yeek! A horrible hairy spider!' they cry as though the innocent bug were five feet rather than five centimeters tall. Then they commence crushing, stomping, mashing, grinding and pulverizing until the delicate spider is no more. I know: my mother fell victim to a velvet slipper."

"Oh," said Quadroped. He felt sorry for the dead mother spider.

"Now I," said the spider proudly, dropping a second cloud of silk onto Glasgerion, "am not to be compared with the common garden variety spider. No, I am an anarchistic arachnid, a sinister spider, a thoroughly disreputable and wicked individual. I am going to right the wrongs done my people once and for all!"

"How?" asked Quadroped with a sense of foreboding.

A sudden gleam of madness lit the spider's numerous red eyes. "I am undertaking a glorious crusade!" said the zealous spider. "I have sworn to eradicate every human I encounter."

"How?" asked Quadroped again. He felt a sort of morbid curiosity.

"Well," said the spider, sounding a trifle uncertain, "I had originally intended to jump on them until they were pulverized like Mother. But now that I see how large they are I think I shall have to eat them instead. The thought revolts me; I am generally used to a diet of insects. You don't suppose, do you," the spider asked, "that humans taste a bit like flies?"

"Oh no," said Quadroped hastily. "I'm sure they taste very different. You will probably find them horrible, indigestible."

"Alas! I had feared as much," lamented the spider. "The red-haired one looks bitter and they both look tough. But, sacrifices must be made." The spider stopped dropping silk on Glasgerion and gazed momentarily off into space brooding, no doubt, upon the nobility of her actions. Then she resumed weaving a cocoon around Glasgerion.

The silk began to cover Glasgerion's face. Quadroped began to feel frightened. He walked cautiously over to Reander and shook him. "Wake up," he whispered.

"They won't wake up until I'm done wrapping them," said the arachnid cheerfully, scrambling over the web until she reached the small pig. "I've put a spell on them."

"Oh dear," said Quadroped.

The spider finished packaging Glasgerion and began to work on Reander. Quadroped searched wildly for some topic of conversation which might distract her a little longer. "Why don't you stick to your web?" he ventured timidly, trying not to look at the spider clicking her hairy mandibles as she talked.

"My feet are especially designed to prevent such an occurrence," said the spider. "Do you see the way they taper into little hooks? Those are so small and delicate they can pick their way across the web without getting tangled. The strands aren't really sticky; it's just easy to get tangled in them."

"Could you get stuck in another spider's web?" asked Quadroped, an idea slowly beginning to form.

"Why yes, I suppose I could," said the monster pensively, "but spiders never trespass on one another's webs."

"Oh," said Quadroped. Suddenly he knew just what to do. He grabbed Fairfax's honey jar and threw the entire contents onto the web at the spider's feet.

"Yuk!" bellowed the spider as the sticky golden liquid adhered to her feet. "What *is* that?"

"Honey," said Quadroped. He scrambled away in case the spider came after him. The spider struggled and fought but her feet remained stuck to the honey-coated strands and her struggles only trapped her further. In her anger and alarm the spider neglected to maintain the spell which held her victims asleep.

The roars woke Reander. He struggled out of his cocoon and drew his sword. "What is going on here?" he asked. Quadroped told him what had happened. "That was well done," said Reander. "Now stand back while I finish this monster off. It has polluted the world too long with its noisome presence."

"Oh no!" cried Quadroped as Reander swung his gleaming blade high. The sword hissed through the air towards the now helpless spider. "Stop!" cried Quadroped and launched himself at Reander's sword arm. It was a truly magnificent leap that almost resulted in the loss of his right ear. Reander barely managed to swing the sword clear and his arm sent Quadroped crashing towards the ground.

"Are you all right?" asked Reander, lowering his sword. Quadroped nodded and Reander said in a voice more frightening than the spider's, "Don't you *ever* try anything like that again. Never put yourself in front of a sword; pigs aren't designed for warfare. Now go wake Glasgerion and let me finish this business."

"I'm sorry," gasped Quadroped, "but you *can't* kill the spider."

"And how do you think you'll stop me?" asked Reander angrily.

"I don't know, but I'll try," said Quadroped. "You can't kill the spider now while she's helpless!"

Reander smiled thinly. "You are being foolish," he said. "Five minutes ago this creature was trying to kill us. If I am merciful, if I let her go free, do you think she will reform her evil habits? That she will stop preying upon humans and eat vegetables instead?"

"But that's just it," said Quadroped stubbornly. "She doesn't eat humans! At least she *was* going to try and consume you, but that was due to noble motives. She really prefers insects."

"*What* could possibly be noble about murdering and devouring two travelers?" asked Reander. He wondered once more why Glasgerion was so fond of this deranged beast.

"Well, the spider is on a crusade to eradicate all humans," said Quadroped earnestly. Reander began to raise his sword once more. "People have done awful things to perfectly harmless spiders for ages," said Quadroped. "Her mother was crushed by a velvet shoe! You can't really blame her for wanting revenge. She hasn't killed anyone, at least not . . ."

"Yet," Reander finished with a frown.

"And I'm not going to kill any in the future either," said the spider. She had ceased struggling some time ago and was listening intently. "Humans," she continued, "are too violent. I'm sure you all taste revolting. I don't think I really *could* eat you, not even to avenge Mother. I shall eat nothing but flies from now on." Which statement left Quadroped wondering uncomfortably if there were gigantic flies in this region as well.

"Please don't kill her," said Quadroped again. "She isn't really evil. She can't hurt us now anyway."

"Very well," said Reander, "but I won't cut her free of that web. If she wants to live she can free herself. I don't want her following after us and frightening the horses." He walked away and began to cut the silk off Glasgerion.

"Can you get free by yourself?" asked Quadroped.

"Oh yes, I think so," said the spider, tentatively tasting a little of the honey. "This stuff tastes rather good," she said. "I should have myself cleaned off and out of this web in a few hours."

"Quadroped, get over here *now!*" said Reander.

"Why are you traveling with such a terrible person?" asked the spider.

"Well, I . . ."

"No, don't tell me," said the spider suddenly. "I see the Key around your neck. If you're the Key Bearer, that man must be Reander of Essylt and I have had a miraculous escape! If I'd known what kind of people you were, I would have stayed on the other side of the swamp."

"Quadroped! Come now!" said Reander.

Quadroped ran over to Reander and helped him clear the last silk threads off Glasgerion.

"What time is it?" asked Glasgerion, his mind still drugged with sleep and the spider's spell.

"Four in the morning," said Reander. "We have no time for explanations now. If we are not gone when that monster gets free I may be forced to kill her."

"What monster?" asked Glasgerion. He caught sight of the spider and gave a low whistle. "What's been going on here?" he asked. Quadroped explained what had happened while Reander saddled the horses. "But where," asked Glasgerion after the tale was done, "did you get the honey?"

"I was wondering about that also," said Reander, coming towards them.

"Fairfax gave it to me," said Quadroped. "He told me I'd need it before morning."

"I should have guessed," said Glasgerion. "You've just saved us again, Quadro." Quadroped blushed and Reander looked thoughtful. "Why didn't you kill it, Reander?" asked Glasgerion.

"Quadroped wouldn't let me," said Reander. He lifted Quadroped into the saddle box and swung into his saddle. "Let's go," he said. "Perhaps we can reach the foothills by nightfall."

"No breakfast?" asked Quadroped dolefully.

"No breakfast," said Reander. Quadroped grunted unhappily and curled up to sleep in his box.

Chapter Seven

They left the unending monotony of the swamp sometime after noon. Once again, tall trees arched over the road and cool shady glades lay beside it. The land was hilly; waterfalls and pools became increasingly frequent. Streams often ran across the road and down the gullies beside it.

"We are in the foothills of the Crystalline Mountains," said Reandor when they paused for lunch. "We should be in the mountains the day after tomorrow. That leaves us three days to reach Illoreth and lock the Gate."

"Where *are* the mountains?" asked Quadroped, looking around.

"We're in a valley now," said Glasgerion patiently, handing Quadroped another sandwich. "We'll see the mountains as soon as we start to climb these hills."

"Are we going to climb them?" asked Quadroped. He had never seen a mountain but he had heard they were all uphill.

"Yes, but we'll be on horseback, so it won't be too tiring," said Glasgerion. Reassured, Quadroped devoted his full attention to the sandwich, ignoring Glasgerion's sudden frown. "Reander," Glasgerion said, "we'll be in the mountains when the moon is full."

"What can we do?" asked Reander prosaically. "It's dangerous but we have no choice. There is no time to go around the mountains." Quadroped looked up from his sandwich with a puzzled frown and was ignored by the men.

"I wonder what the Lord of Snows is up to now?" said Glasgerion.

"We'll know soon enough," promised Reander darkly. Quadroped stopped eating and squeaked for an explanation.

"It's no use looking confused, Quadro," said Glasgerion. "I'm not going to tell you horror stories during lunch. You have enough to worry about. Finish that sandwich and let's be on our way."

"Just once," mumbled Quadroped to himself, "I would like to know what everybody is talking about."

"No, you wouldn't." Glasgerion laughed.

As the day wore on Reander began to revise his opinion of the small Key Bearer in his charge. Reander was not a patient man. He was a superb leader, brilliant strategist and a ruthless fighter but his very expertise isolated him from his fellows. He had few equals and this, combined with a naturally aloof nature, left him few friends. Quadroped's spirited defense of the spider had impressed him. Reander began to consider what it would be like to be a young pig, surrounded by danger, entrusted with the task of saving a world. Viewed in this light, Quadroped appeared as a singularly brave individual. Reander allowed himself to feel some affection for the pig and, in no time at all, he found himself worrying over the problem of Quadroped's abhorred saddle box.

Towards evening, Reander surprised everyone, including himself, by suggesting that Quadroped ride with him for a while. "Quadro can sit on the saddle in front of me and hold on to the pommel," he said. "I can easily hold him—it takes but one hand to hold the reins. We will be ascending a hill soon and the mountains should be visible from the summit. The view will be spectacular. It would be a shame if Quadro missed our first sight of the Crystallines, but his box is on the wrong side."

Glasgerion raised an eyebrow and contemplated his normally austere nephew. "Reander," he inquired gently, "do you feel all right?"

The proud glare that met this expression of tender concern assured Glasgerion that his nephew was himself. "As leader of this expedition I am responsible for the Key Bearer's comfort," said Reander. "Quadroped hates his saddle box. It is no inconvenience if he rides with me."

"You'll look very silly with a piglet on your saddle," said Glasgerion.

"Will I?" asked Reander indifferently. "How about it, Quadro? It will be far less bumpy than your saddle box."

"But it is so high!" wailed Quadroped. He was not happy with this turn of events. He was still afraid of Reander and horses. "There aren't any sides; what if I fall off?"

"You won't," said Reander. "I shall be holding you. Stop arguing and come along."

Quadroped eyed the huge grey horse with misgiving. He was about to refuse when Reander reached down and lifted him into the air. "Help. Put me down!" he cried. Reander placed him securely on the saddle and held him with one strong hand.

Reander urged his steed to a swift trot while Quadroped, eyes tightly shut, held on to the slippery leather saddle for dear life. They were climbing a steep hill and he slid backwards against Reander's stomach. His legs weren't long enough to reach the pommel so he clung on to Reander's hand instead. He was certain the horse would stumble on the loose, rocky slope and send him hurtling to the ground. "I don't *like* this," he said under his breath. "I don't like this at *all!*"

"Quadroped, stop being silly and open your eyes," said Reander imperiously. "This is supposed to be fun."

"Well, it isn't and I won't," mumbled Quadroped. He felt very sorry for himself.

"We're almost at the top of the hill and there is a marvelous view," said Reander. "Why," he added in tones of awe, "just ahead of us I can see a perfect example of a geosyncline and beyond that you can see the Crystalline Mountains. The mountains contain some very interesting examples of the ophiolite suite."

"Geowhats?" asked Quadroped, confused by the long words and intrigued in spite of himself.

"Geosynclines," said Reander in a low mysterious voice. "If you open your eyes, Quadro, you will see them."

"I won't," said Quadroped. "I'll fall off."

"As you wish," said Reander, "but you are missing a fine glacial erratic."

Quadroped slowly opened his eyes. "Where?" he asked.

"Just over there, beside the road," said Reander, grinning with triumph.

Quadroped eyed a large grey boulder with disfavor. "What's erratic about it?" he asked suspiciously. "It looks just like any other rock."

"Nonsense," said Reander. "It is pure granite, nothing at all like the rocks around us. It was carried here on an ice sheet thousands of years ago, before the Black Unicorn was even born."

"Ah." Quadroped nodded. He secretly felt cheated for it was, when all was said, a plain and ugly rock.

Quadroped's spirits rose as they breasted the top of the hill, for the view was truly marvelous. Gentle hills rolled beneath them, patches of blue, green and gold sewn together by the brown threads of roads. Far behind them he saw the blotchy shape of Spiders Mere and beyond that a glimmering of silver that Glasgerion said was Eunoe's lake. Ahead of them lay a long valley enclosed by steep grey cliffs. Towering over the valley, filling it with purple shadows, stood the Crystalline Mountains. Their peaks were white with snow that the summer sun could never melt. One mountain rose hundreds of feet above its brothers. Quadroped had to tip his head back to see its cloud-shrouded summit. "What mountain is that?" he asked.

"Heart of Ice," said Reander. "The snow up there never melts."

"Do you see the triangular notch just below the summit?" asked Glasgerion; Quadroped nodded. "That's the upper pass. It's the quickest way to get over the mountains."

"You mean, we're going to climb all the way up *there?*" asked Quadroped.

"Not if we can help it," said Reander. "We will use the lower pass, unless summer rains have made it impassable." Quadroped did not reply; he was staring with horrified fascination at the black notch in the mountain.

"Don't worry, Quadro," said Glasgerion, "it hasn't rained much this year. The lower pass should be free."

"Unless Goriel has closed it," said Reander softly. He spurred his horse on and Glasgerion followed close behind.

If possible, Quadroped decided, the journey downhill was worse than the journey up. Whereas before he had been tilted sharply backwards so he had been in no real danger of sliding out of the saddle, for Reander sat behind him and he was merely pressed tightly against the man's stomach. Now the danger of falling was real, for the horse's angle forced him to slide forwards and there was only the small, slippery hump of the pommel to prevent his tumbling over the horse's head.

Reander was aware of the danger and his grip on Quadroped's waist increased until Quadroped was sure his ribs were broken. The path was covered with loose stones and deeply rutted, and the great horse stumbled and lurched alarmingly. Were it not for Reander's expert horsemanship the horse would have fallen, crushing them both. When they reached level ground at last Quadroped could hardly stop shaking long enough to croak, "Box!" in strangled accents. Reander reluctantly complied with his request and Quadroped, safe once more in the bumpy saddle box, sighed with relief and began to calm down.

When day cooled into evening they rode into the long valley between the grey cliffs. A wide river, shaded by ancient willows and slender poplars, ran the length of the valley; its banks were covered with soft green grass. "We won't have to worry about lumps and stones tonight," said

Glasgerion cheerfully. They stopped for the night in a small clearing beside the river. They could see the water, but a sapling leaning far out over the stream hid their campsite from anyone walking on the other side.

It was summer; the days were long and they looked forward to an hour or two of pleasant twilight before building a fire. Glasgerion and Reander lost no time plunging into the river for a refreshing swim and Quadroped, realizing that dinner was not to be immediately forthcoming, seated himself on a stump at the shore and looked forlorn.

"Quadro, stop moping and come into the water," called Glasgerion when he finally noticed the lonely figure. "The water's just the right temperature."

Quadroped looked at the current swirling swiftly around the roots of his stump and shuddered. "I can't swim that well," he said. "I'll be swept downstream and drowned."

"You can't be drowned, Quadro," Glasgerion said. "You've just spent several weeks at the bottom of the ocean."

Quadroped recalled how he had been forcibly dragged under the surface of the duck pond and sighed. "What if fresh water's different?" he asked.

"It won't be," said Reander, swimming beside Glasgerion and staring accusingly at Quadroped. "Stop being silly."

"Well, even if I don't drown, I'll sink," said Quadroped. "I don't want to walk around on the bottom in all the nasty weeds. Swimming isn't fun unless you can stay afloat."

"Hmmm," said Glasgerion, "the current *is* a bit swift. But if you walk along the shore a bit, there's a log which has fallen into the water. The sand has piled up around it and the water's shallower there. The branches should keep you from being pulled into the middle. Anyway, if you do get into trouble, Reander or I can easily drag you out."

So Quadroped scrambled along the shore and soon he was playing happily in the water and building castles out of mud. He emerged at last looking very dirty and was carried out to midstream and washed before he was allowed to eat dinner. "I don't want to wake up covered with mud," said Glasgerion.

"You could always wash in the morning," said Qua-droped. He did not want to go out into the middle of the river.

"Ahh, but *you* could wash now," said Glasgerion firmly.

Reander felt unusually generous that night; the meal had color, flavor, texture and was piping hot. When dinner was done, he made a fire that looked cheerful but generated no uncomfortable warmth. Glasgerion brought out his new harp. Quadroped lay on his back and gazed up at the dark branches against the indigo blue of the night sky. All at once his attention was caught by a flashing green light dancing through the air above his head. He watched and soon another red light joined this one as it flickered through the trees.

"What are those?" asked Quadroped.

"Those are fireflies," said Glasgerion.

"Are they on fire?" asked Quadroped, wondering if the poor bugs were in much pain.

"No." Reander laughed. "They produce a cold fire in their tails; it is called phosphorescence."

"Like the sponges that Morragwen and the sea people use for lights?" asked Quadroped.

"Yes," said Reander. "Glasgerion, sing him that song about fireflies. You know, the one about how they were created."

"But that's gloomy," said Glasgerion.

"Play it anyway," said Reander.

"Why does everyone always want to hear gloomy songs?" complained Glasgerion. "The world's gloomy enough already." He tuned his harp and sang:

Islindril ran where the fountains played
When all but the moon was black
Though the trees stretched gnarled, protective hands
To snatch her shadow back;
The ground so dark, it fell away,
She trod a void of night,

Suspended o'er the cruel abyss
By slender shreds of light;
And Islindril shall not return,
Too soon the moon revolved,
Erased of color by the dark
She shivered and dissolved;
Then, when the fountains and the lawn
Lie dark beside the sea
A faint and fleeting star appears
Where shadows used to be.

Quadroped drifted to sleep with the melody in his ears. It had been a perfect evening that even the inevitable mosquitoes couldn't ruin.

When Quadroped awoke the campsite was shrouded by early morning mists rising from the river. It was chilly and his skin was damp, for the dew had settled on him. Silver beads of water coated the grass and sparkled like jewels in the light. The air was heavy with the scent of fresh water, earth and leaves. The birds had not achieved full volume but twittered softly in their green beds. The shade, which had been so welcome after the long ride, now seemed gloomy as though the glade clung tenaciously to night. Reander and Glasgerion both took quick swims after rising, but nothing would persuade Quadroped to dive into the cold water. They ate a quick breakfast and were soon mounted, eager to leave the shadows and ride out into the morning.

Beyond the glade it was quite warm, though the sun had not been up for two hours yet. It promised to be another fine day; already the morning clouds were fading from the sky. Looking towards the mountains, Quadroped noticed that they were almost invisible behind a curtain of pink haze. Glasgerion and Reander were both cheerful and there was no talk of the future that awaited them in Illoreth. Glasgerion told stories and Reander related the latest court gossip from High Essylt. Quadroped was so content that when Reander offered him another ride he agreed and discovered that, on a flat road, riding was fun.

They stopped for lunch in another woody clearing and during a quiet moment while everyone was relaxing and watching the river, Quadroped saw one of the most beautiful creatures he had ever seen standing quietly in the shadows watching them. "What is that?" Quadroped whispered, afraid his voice would scare the creature off yet anxious to know what it was.

"A unicorn," said Glasgerion and Reander looked up and nodded. Quadroped gazed at the lovely white horse with its silver horn.

"Is it evil? Will it come any closer?" asked Quadroped.

"No, it's a white unicorn," said Glasgerion. "I don't think it will come any closer."

"Is it scared of us?" asked Quadroped.

"Unicorns fear nothing," said Reander, "but they are solitary beings and rarely come near enough to be seen."

"If you are very quiet, Quadro, the unicorn might let you approach a little closer," said Glasgerion, "but don't try to talk to it. Unicorns are proud and it might be angered by your presumption."

Quadroped jumped off Glasgerion's lap and walked a few steps forwards. The unicorn did not move, but its eyes fixed on Quadroped and he stopped, feeling awkward and shy.

"Go on," whispered Glasgerion, "he doesn't seem to mind."

Quadroped walked slowly up to the unicorn. He was even more splendid up close, for his coat was not white but filled with the palest shades of the rainbow. It gleamed like a stained glass window, as though there was some great light within the beast. His horn was like ice and only looked silver in the reflections. The unicorn stared at the Key and then for a moment its dark eyes met Quadroped's. With a sudden motion it tossed its head and ran back into the trees. A warm hand fell on Quadroped's head and looking around he saw Glasgerion. The bard picked him up and carried him to the saddle box.

* * *

They left the valley in mid afternoon and started up into the mountains. The countryside was still grassy and wooded, but the road was steep and outcrops of grey granitic rock became increasingly common until the road began to cut through the stone. Dark pines dominated these forests. The air no longer smelled of grass and sun but of the winter scent of evergreens.

The pine woods were quiet; even the rare bird calls sounded foreign and unwelcome. Thin brown needles covered the forest floor instead of grass. A few wildflowers grew but only close to the roots of the trees, half hidden in the shadows. They were not the yellow and red colors of morning but deep purple violets and pale white blossoms. Mushrooms—beige, brown, red and blue—grew on the tree trunks and rotting logs; soft patches of emerald moss covered the bark and rocks. Lonely patches of ferns rustled quietly where the trees stood far enough apart to let the wayward sunbeams in.

Aedh would have liked this place, Quadroped thought. *It's like his study, all shadowy and filled with the smell of wood.* He felt suddenly sad as he recalled the exiled Prince.

They left the wildwood in late afternoon. The sudden warmth and brilliance of the sun hurt Quadroped's eyes and he had to stare down at the dark road until his eyes adjusted to the light. When he looked up, they were riding through a hilly daisy meadow. Below them, at the meadow's edge, lay a cluster of red tile and yellow straw roofs.

"What town is that?" asked Glasgerion.

"I don't know," said Reander. "This area is very close to Ravenor and has not been mapped well."

"It might be a good place to stop for the night," said Glasgerion. "The villagers can tell us if the lower pass is open."

"It is too late to climb the mountain today, in any case," agreed Reander.

They rode towards the town at a swift canter. As they passed the first building, they were hailed by a middle-aged man engaged in painting his front door.

"Welcome, strangers," said the man cheerfully, dropping his paint brush and wiping his hands on his pants. "What lands do you travel from? We don't often have visitors. Most people avoid the mountains, and the land beyond."

"We come from the south," lied Reander swiftly.

"Are you heading over the mountain?" asked the man. "Or are you lost?"

"We hope to cross Heart of Ice in the morning," said Reander.

The farmer frowned and stared hard at them. "Ravenor lies beyond Heart of Ice," he said. "Are you headed to that land?"

There was an uncomfortable silence, broken by the approach of a tall, white-haired man. "Gregor, to whom do you speak?" asked the newcomer.

"Greetings, Harmicah," said Gregor. "These are strangers."

"So I had observed," said Harmicah dryly.

"They head across the mountain, towards Ravenor, towards Goriel," said Gregor.

Harmicah smiled. His teeth were brilliant white and in amazingly good condition for a man his age. "Gregor," he said gently, "you must not question strangers so closely. These men do not look like creatures of Ravenor, do they?" Gregor fell silent and stepped back. "I apologize for my friend," said Harmicah. "We live too close to the borders of Ravenor to ignore the existence of Goriel and his servants. Do you seek a place to pass the night, or will you travel on this evening?"

"We were hoping to spend the night," said Glasgerion.

"You are wise to beware the mountains at night," said Harmicah. "Strange creatures prowl there, and tonight there is only the new moon. There is room for you in my barn."

Reander accepted the invitation and they followed Harmicah to a small white house with a large red barn on the side. "Stable your horses and come into the house," said Harmicah. "I'm sure you'll want some dinner after your journey."

The barn was warm and roomy; a ladder led up to a narrow, hay-filled loft which Reander decided was the best place to spend the night. They fed the horses and went into the house to look for Harmicah. They entered the kitchen, a large cluttered room decorated with spoons, pans, dried meats and a bewildering array of knives. A tall woman with black eyes was seated at the table peeling turnips. "Harmicah has gone to fetch the boys," she said to them. "Sit down, they won't be long."

"Can we help you?" asked Glasgerion.

"I can always use help." The woman laughed. She gave Reander and Glasgerion large white aprons and set them to slicing vegetables for the stew.

Harmicah and the "boys" returned half an hour later. Quadroped started involuntarily when he saw the sons of the house. They were large young men, larger than Reander, and their hair was dark and long, giving them a wild look. They had loud, rough voices and huge, calloused hands. Quadroped did not feel safe near them and took care to stay far away from them during dinner.

"I saw a harp on your saddle this afternoon," said Harmicah to Glasgerion when the meal was done. "Are you a bard?"

"I am," said Glasgerion.

"Play us something?" asked the farm wife. "That would be ample payment for the meal."

Glasgerion went quickly back to the barn and returned with hi harp. "What would you like to hear?" he asked.

"There's a song I haven't heard in years," said the farm wife, "but I don't know the name or words to it."

"Hum a little of the tune," said Glasgerion with a smile. The woman hummed a stanza of the eeriest tune Quadroped had ever heard; it made his skin prickle just to hear it. Glasgerion's smile faded. "I know the song," he said, "but it is not my favorite."

"Oh, please play it," said the woman.

Glasgerion could not well refuse his hostess and so he began to play. The farm wife's tune had been haunting, but when Glasgerion played it the tune was horrifying. Qua-

droped jumped onto Reander's lap for comfort. Glasgerion
sang:

> Goriel's Hounds are in the Hills,
> His chilling horn is sounding
> From the narrow mountain walls,
> Our destinies resounding;
> So fly together like the leaves,
> Until the forest gives you rest,
> As one upon another falls
> Into the graveyard of the blessed;
> Where footsteps never pass away,
> But stir the dry earth till it speaks,
> And once again through all the world,
> The deadly voice of winter creeps.

The farm folk thanked Glasgerion for the song and bid
their guests good night. Glasgerion carried Quadroped up
to the hayloft and together they piled the straw into two
comfortable beds. Quadroped liked the loft; it smelled
sweet and cozy. He could sit on the edge and look across
the floor, out the door to the back door of the house. He
peered down at the horses; Reander was saddling them.

"Glasgerion, why is he doing that?" Quadroped asked.
The bard was sitting beside him, swinging his legs over the
edge.

Glasgerion contemplated his nephew and shrugged. "We
have to start very early, Quadro," he said. "We're near
Ravenor," he added, "and Goriel may challenge us at any
moment. We will have no time to saddle the horses if Goriel attacks tonight. Now stop worrying and let's go to
sleep." He rolled onto his carefully prepared bed and Quadroped snuggled up next to him.

"Is Goriel *very* close?" asked Quadroped after a moment.

"Yes. He lives on the summit of Heart of Ice," said
Glasgerion.

"Where we're going tomorrow?" squeaked Quadroped
in alarm.

"Yes. Now go to sleep," said Glasgerion.

Quadroped rolled over and obediently closed his eyes.

Reander climbed up to the loft, pulling the ladder up behind him. Seating himself nearby, he began to polish his sword by an unearthly green light which seemed to emanate from a spot a few feet above his hands.

"Oh, for goodness' sake, Reander," complained Glasgerion after fifteen minutes, "can't you do that somewhere else? How can I sleep with that light in my eyes?" Reander moved to a shadowy corner of the loft and for a moment all was quiet and peacefully dark. Then the peace was broken by a harsh, metallic grating; Reander was sharpening his sword. "Stop that!" said Glasgerion. After another fifteen minutes the noise stopped. Reander came over and lay down to sleep, extinguishing the strange light.

"It's best to be prepared, Glasgerion," said Reander.

"Yes. We need all the sleep we can get," said Glasgerion crossly. "A sword won't help against snowstorms or Goriel."

"I did not like our hostess's choice of music," said Reander. "There may be trouble before dawn."

Quadroped whimpered softly and huddled closer to Glasgerion. "Stop scaring Quadro," said Glasgerion automatically, his voice slurred with weariness. "He's only teasing, Quadro."

Quadroped awoke suddenly; he was being smothered. A large strong hand was clamped tightly over his mouth. "Lie still," Reander hissed. He removed his hand and let Quadroped sit up.

It was still dark. Quadroped could only see a dark patch where Reander crouched. He looked around and saw Glasgerion's shape lying low in the straw, looking over the edge of the loft. "What—" he began.

Reander put his hand against Quadroped's mouth again. He was listening to something. Quadroped stretched out his ears and soon heard soft voices outside the door of the barn. The voices were deep, sinister and bestial. The sound sent shivers running up and down his back. He burrowed down into the straw and wished he could snuggle up to Reander for reassurance. But Reander was very tense and clearly he would not be very patient now with a frightened pig. Glasgerion came silently back to them and sat down.

"Well?" whispered Reander, so softly that Quadroped could hardly hear him.

"I don't know," said Glasgerion. "Whatever they are, they're hostile. I couldn't identify them; they're new horrors to me. I think the attack will be claw and knife stuff though; they were talking about blood and tearing. No mention of magic."

"How many are there?" asked Reander.

"Four that I could hear," said Glasgerion. "There could be more but they were keeping quiet."

Reander nodded and drew his sword; his long dagger he gave to Glasgerion. "Quadroped," he said, "we'll be fighting in the dark and I want you well out of the way. Go to the far wall and stay there. When I call you, go to the ladder and wait for us to join you. We travel tonight." Quadroped did as he was told, crouching down with his back pressed against the damp, splintery boards.

Glasgerion and Reander piled the straw into the shape of two sleeping figures and covered them with blankets. Then they retreated to the walls to await the attack. The creatures were entering the barn; Quadroped could hear their padding footsteps and the slow heavy breathing. They walked silently under the loft until they were diretly below the entrance.

"Where is the ladder?" growled one. Quadroped looked at the ladder leaning against the wall beside him and silently thanked Reander's foresight.

"They must have pulled it up," said another. "We will climb."

The hay rustled as the monsters slunk to the walls and then Quadroped heard the terrible sound of long nails digging deeply into the wood. He wanted to scream but there was a wall deep in his throat, crushing his lungs and keeping him quiet. The monsters climbed stealthily up the walls. When the first head appeared over the edge of the loft, Quadroped closed his eyes. The monsters did not crawl onto the loft; they continued to climb towards the ceiling. Then they crawled along the huge rafters that stretched over the loft until they crouched directly over the spot where Glasgerion and Reander had slept.

For an awful moment nothing moved; then, with ferocious howls, the monsters leapt. Their sinister shapes fell unnaturally slowly and made no sound when they landed. Before the monsters could recognize the trick, Reander and Glasgerion were upon them. Quadroped could not see the battle; the tangled shapes were all the same size and the voices seemed to come out of the air with no relation to figures. In an agony of apprehension he listened to Reander's curses and heard an occasional cry of pain from Glasgerion.

The fight lasted only a few minutes. The monsters were strong, but Glasgerion had spoken truthfully when he had praised Reander's fighting skills. Virtually single-handedly, for Glasgerion was not much help, Reander over-powered and slew three of the monsters.

The fourth monster was the strongest and engaged Reander in a lethal wrestling match. Glasgerion hurried to help him, but the two were locked too tightly together and moving too fast. He could not strike for fear of killing his nephew. The interlocked figures fell to the floor and the boards shook with the impact. At last, with a horrible gurgle, the monster lay still in Reander's hands. It was not dead. Its eyes gleamed wickedly, but Reander held it helpless, one powerful arm wrapped around its throat.

"It looks like a wolf," said Glasgerion.

"A bit," agreed Reander. "Did Goriel send you, beast?"

"Of course," snarled the monster. "You were so easy to identify with your northern speech and your pig. Poor Gregor, he thought you were Warlords traveling to Illoreth. He was disappointed when I told him the truth. It would be a great honor to host Lords of Ravenor." The monster laughed cruelly then gasped as Reander's arm tightened about its throat.

"Does Goriel know we are here, or did you act on your own?" asked Reander.

"The Lord of Snows knows all," said the creature devoutly.

"Why did he send you to attack us?" asked Glasgerion.

"He must know that creatures like yourself are no match for my nephew. He could not hope to kill us."

"Goriel does not underestimate the Princes of Essylt," sneered the monster. "There are many, many more of us. Enough to delay your arrival in Illoreth until the Gate opens. Listen, I hear them coming now. Run away, humans; my brothers will slay you."

"They can try," said Reander. His arm tightened again. There was a *crack* as the beast's neck snapped in two and with a soft gurgle the monster died. A mournful, ululating, cry rose into the night from somewhere in the hills. "They wait for us on the road," said Reander. "We must take the upper pass across the mountain."

"Is that wise?" asked Glasgerion.

"No, it is not wise," snapped Reander. "It brings us too close to Goriel's palace but we have no choice. These monsters are easy to kill, but they could delay us as planned. They don't expect us to brave the upper pass. By the time they realize where we've gone we'll be far ahead. Quadro, come here." Quadroped rose on shaky legs and half stumbled to the ladder.

Glasgerion drew a sharp breath and Quadroped stopped. "What is it?" he said. Glasgerion was staring at the monster, and his face looked pale in the darkness.

"The monsters," said Glasgerion softly, "they were werewolves."

Quadroped gazed slowly at the fallen bodies. On the bloodstained straw lay Harmicah, his wife, and their two boys.

"We must go," said Reander sharply. "There are more of them outside."

"I'll go down first, Reander," said Glasgerion. "When I'm down, hand Quadro to me. He can't climb the ladder in the dark." He descended with surprising speed. Reander almost threw Quadroped to him and jumped down, ignoring the ladder completely.

Glasgerion tossed Quadroped into the saddle box, and flung himself into the saddle. The two men galloped from the stalls and crashed through the half open door of the barn into the cold night air. Wordlessly they raced down the dark streets of the town. A wailing cry floated on the wind behind them as the werewolves gave chase. But Reander had chosen their path wisely and the wolves were far behind.

The cold, thin air lay clear between the earth and stars; the hills glowed dim and blue in the hostile light of space. A bitter wind blew off the frozen slopes, stirring the unpacked snow in swirling ashy shapes that glided ghostlike upon the pearly hillsides. It was a night when the earth went on forever. The mountain reached down into the distant valley still untouched by summer ice. There, only a few dim shapes could be resolved: two men on horseback and the metallic flash of water as the rivers, which had carved the land, twisted under the glare of the sky. Farther up, the open whiteness faded in a maze of thick trunks. The pine trees stood impassively upon the hilltops and marched like dark trolls in long uneven lines towards the high mountain. The forest loomed above the land, an impregnable jagged fortress darker than the sky. The pines enclosed the pure, crystalline slopes and preserved their mysteries. Through the ragged tips the deep blue night crept in and gazed, dispassionately, at the glistening world.

The wolves ran noiselessly through the dark, their open mouths red and steaming. Smiling beneath the knife-thin edge of the setting moon they ranged across the countryside, hunting the men who had slain their comrades. In a moment of impossible stillness the cold voice of death echoed out across the sky, and the leader paused. His fur shimmered silver where the snow light touched it and his tongue hung from his mouth. Yellow eyes, pale and baleful, roamed the landscape, searching one last time for the prey that eluded him. Clean water smells of snow and pine, untainted by any fleshly perfume, drifted past. He growled softly, softer than the constant hushed conversations of the woods. He could find them, but he would need time. The deadly notes of the horn echoed out once more; there would be no more time. With a throbbing snarl he turned and faded back into the woods, the pack following close behind. Lord Goriel of the Snows stretched his swan pinions and smiled benevolently down upon the earth. His hounds had done their work well.

Chapter Eight

The long night paled to sulky grey dawn and Reander drew to a halt. "The werewolves are far behind," he said. "Now that the sun has risen they will be in human form again."

"Let's rest then," said Glasgerion. "You'll need all your strength in the upper pass, Reander. I have the strangest feeling that Goriel is waiting for us."

"We can rest until noon, but no later," said Reander. "We must cross the pass before nightfall. That clump of pines over there should shelter us from the wind and from our enemies' gaze." He led them to a shadow-filled grove.

Glasgerion scooped Quadroped out of his box and they lay down on his cape. Reander made a strange fire that warmed without emitting light or smoke that might betray their presence to their enemies. While Glasgerion and Quadroped slept, Reander kept watch over the empty snowfields.

* * *

Reander woke Glasgerion and Quadroped at noon and gave them cups of a hot bitter liquid which, he claimed, would give them enough energy to get through the rest of the day. Quadroped tried a little sip of his, but it burned his nose and the taste was terrible. He set the cup down behind a large stone and wandered a few feet away to play.

Quadroped had never seen snow before and was fascinated at the way it could be packed into castles and snowballs. It tasted better than the stuff Reander had provided and he discovered he was very thirsty. He began to eat snow until his teeth ached and chattered from the cold.

"Quadroped, come back here," Reander called. He had been watching the pig's antics for several moments and was frowning. Quadroped hastened to comply, recalling the last time he had dawdled. Reander seemed much friendlier now, but he was still a little frightening.

Reander did not scold Quadroped. "Drink your breakfast, Quadro," he said mildly.

"But it tastes horrible," said Quadroped, "and it burned my nose."

"Well, it won't burn you now," said Reander. "It has probably frozen solid."

Quadroped retrieved his cup and found that there was indeed a thin, slushy coating of ice forming over the liquid. He took a tentative sip and nearly choked. Reander chuckled at his expression. "Here, give me that," he said, taking the cup from Quadroped's hoof. Quadroped watched closely to see what Reander would do to the drink, but he just held it in his hand without doing or saying anything. "Now try it," said Reander.

Quadroped was positive that it would taste the same, for Reander hadn't done anything. "It's warm!" he gasped as he touched the cup. He lapped a little up and found that the stuff was now sweet, a little like apple juice only not as good. Still, it was drinkable and he drained his cup quickly. When it was all gone he looked down into the empty depths of his cup a little wistfully. He was about to ask for more when the cup suddenly vanished. "How do you do that?" he asked Reander curiously.

"Practice," said Reander. He went to resaddle the horses.

Quadroped started back to play in the snow but Glasgerion told him to stay put. "You're the same color as the snow, Quadro," he explained. "If you fall into a drift, we'll lose you and you'll freeze to death." Quadroped went and played with the fallen pinecones instead.

They rode higher and higher until they left the trees below and entered a world of grey lichens and black stones. The only living things they saw were white rabbits that flickered across the snow and the tawny eagles which shrieked overhead, hunting the fleeing rabbits. The path continued to climb until even the eagles were left far below with the clouds. The air was thin and so cold that knives of clear ice seemed to stab into Quadroped's lungs every time he took a breath.

Reander noticed Quadroped shivering and took off his own cloak, wrapping it tightly around the pig. Quadroped could not move his legs, but he was too cold and tired to protest and the woolen cloth helped keep out the wind. Glasgerion was also shivering and with much difficulty managed to extract a blue, fur-lined cloak from the saddlebag behind him without falling off his horse. He pulled the hood so far down that only his nose protruded beyond the shadowy depths. The clouds of steam which emerged when he breathed made him look like a lumpy blue dragon. Reander, now cloakless and wearing only a cotton shirt and pants, should have been dying of hypothermia but he seemed unaffected by the temperature. *Perhaps*, thought Quadroped, *he has a magic spell to keep him warm. I wish he'd share it with the rest of us*.

"I'm sorry, Quadro," said Reander, correctly interpreting Quadroped's expression, "but it takes much more energy to warm up a pig than to heat a cup of juice. I can't afford to use so much power right now. My cloak will have to do."

They reached the upper pass by four. At least, Reander claimed it was only four; Quadroped was sure that it must be later. The sky was dark grey and it was hard to see the

path in the dim light. He looked up and realized that while
the sky was overcast, the clouds were not thick enough to
cause the twilight.

"This will be Goriel's doing," said Glasgerion. "Should
we wait? The pass will be very dangerous in this light and
if it gets much darker it may be impossible to travel without falling off the cliffs."

"We can't wait," said Reander. "Goriel is aptly named
the Lord of Snows. We are lucky the weather isn't worse.
We'll go as far as we can until Goriel makes it impossible
to travel."

Glasgerion sighed. "Hold on to the box tightly, Quadro," he said as the horses started into the pass. "This will
be a difficult journey; the horse may stumble a bit." Quadroped freed his front legs from Reander's cloak and held
on to the side of his box as hard as he could.

The walls of the pass were sheer, black cliffs which
clawed up into the air like fingers. This part of the pass,
Glasgerion explained, was the safest. With walls on either
side there was no way to be seriously hurt. The black,
gigantic rocks loomed overhead like menacing giants.
Quadroped did not feel safe at all.

When they reached the middle pass, Quadroped understood why Glasgerion had called the first part safe. The
outer cliff dropped away and they rode a threadlike path
along the right cliff face. A strong wind blew up from the
world below and pressed them hard against the rocks. "The
wind," Quadroped assured himself, "is holding us to the
cliff." But the sensation of being pushed in such a dangerous place, even if it was in the direction of safety, made
him feel dizzy.

"Close your eyes, Quadro," Glasgerion said. "You'll
feel better."

It grew darker, and the men were forced to dismount
and lead the horses along the treacherous path. When they
could no longer see the path, Reander created a ball of
green fire, like the one he had used in the barn. He handed
a piece to Glasgerion and in the hellish green glow the two
men walked on. Glasgerion was invisible in the darkness;
Quadroped felt very vulnerable. He chewed the Key ner-

vously. Neither man spoke and the sound of their footsteps was drowned by the rushing of the wind. Quadroped began to believe that he was all alone with the horses.

The wind rose steadily, and it brought the snow. A few large wet flakes first; then more until the travelers found themselves battling against a blizzard which threatened to tear them off the cliff. Quadroped began to panic. He wanted to scream for help but he knew that he would not be heard over the storm. Even if he could attract Glasgerion's attention, his voice might startle the bard into a fatal misstep.

"Reander!" Quadroped heard Glasgerion say in the distance, "I felt something large brush past me. It wasn't the wind." Quadroped never heard Reander's reply for the thing that had touched Glasgerion was standing beside his box. It froze his screams deep inside his chest.

A gaunt spectre towered high above Quadroped's head. It was almost invisible against the dark air and seemed to be made of grey ice. The phantasm had no features, only a great black opening for a mouth that opened to the night at the creature's back. It was as thin as the pale, slender birch trees that grew in the valley. It had four long arms; its hands were large and white.

Quadroped cowered in the corner of his box, trying to get far away from the phantasm. He was on the cliffless side of the path and if he jumped he would fall off the mountain. "Glasgerion!" he cried. His voice came out as a tiny whimper, and Glasgerion never heard.

The phantasm reached down and the ghostly fingers sank deeply through Quadroped's skin and into his side. There was no blood and the pain was not that of a wound, just a mind-absorbing ache where the fingers were embedded. Quadroped remembered that Toridon had also been partially intangible. *This must be Goriel,* he thought.

The phantasm lifted Quadroped from his box and Quadroped tensed, waiting for the monster to toss him into the howling storm. The phantasm did not release him. It turned and carried him up the treacherous path. They passed Glasgerion and Reander. Quadroped struggled and cried, but neither man looked up. "Reander," he heard Glasgerion say, "I felt that thing pass me again." Reander did not reply, and Quadroped was carried off into the storm.

It was a terrible journey. Occasionally the phantasm set Quadroped down and changed hands. At first Quadroped tried to run away when the fingers were pulled out of his side, but he never got far. Eventually he was too tired and miserable to try anymore. The phantasm carried him like a bowling ball, usually with an arm on the drop-off side. Once the phantasm switched him to a cliffside hand and he was battered against the sharp rocks of the wall.

I will never be rescued, Quadroped thought. *I've always had a friend to help me, but there isn't anything friendly living in these mountains. Goriel is even worse than the Manslayer. He was horrible, but at least he* looked *human. Goriel will kill me and take the Key. The Black Unicorn will be freed.*

Quadroped knew that even if he tried to fight he had no chance of surviving for long. *Goriel* mustn't *get the Key,* he thought. *There must be something I can do.* He was on the cliffside; if he slipped the Key off his neck it would land on the path. Glasgerion and Reander might find it. Even if they never did, it would not belong to Ravenor. Some future hero could use it to recapture the Black Unicorn.

Quadroped breathed a little faster; his hoofs were free and the phantasm had no eyes to see what he was doing. With trembling hooves he reached up and began to slide the Key's chain over his ears. He gasped as the phantasm gripped him tightly. The pain in his chest increased until he was forced to drop his hooves away from the Key. The agony intensified until he lost consciousness.

Quadroped awoke to clear, blinding daylight which made his eyes tighten into narrow slits. He was still being carried but ahead of him he could see the summit of the mountain, and on the highest point stood a fantastic palace of spun glass. It was a fairy-tale castle of tall towers and minarets, thin graceful arches and bridges, tall imposing ramparts. It caught the sun; like a prism it turned the light into brilliant rainbows, colors so pure they made Quadroped's heart ache with the desire to hold them.

The phantasm carried Quadroped to a black iron door set in the rocks below the palace, which opened with a loud pain-wracked groan. The sudden transition from daylight to the dimness of the passage was too fast for Quadroped's eyes to adjust to, and he could not see where they were going. All he knew was that it was not far, for before his eyes were accustomed to the reduced light, the phantasm opened another unoiled door, flung him ungently onto an icy floor and locked him in.

The room looked like the prison cell in Seamourn. Quadroped decided that he was in Goriel's dungeons below the ice palace. There was a partially disintegrated wooden cot against the wall opposite the door. It looked like a good place for bedbugs and other vermin, but he decided it was much too cold for bugs; icicles were growing on the windowsill and ceiling. He crept onto the bed and curled into a very tight ball. Goriel did not seem in a hurry to kill or torture him and it was too cold and frightening to stay awake and worry. He tucked the Key safely into his mouth, silently prayed for rescue and fell into an exhausting, nightmare-filled sleep.

Quadroped was awakened by a very human hand. *I wish Reander wouldn't always wake us up so early,* he thought. He tried to snuggle closer to Glasgerion's warm side but instead of Glasgerion he felt freezing stone. With a gasp, he opened his eyes and stared into the icy, dark blue eyes of a strange man. The man was pale as snow and dressed in black. He picked Quadroped up without a word and carried him out of the cell, up a long, sloping tunnel.

The tunnel emerged, as Quadroped had suspected it might, inside the palace in a large circular room with transparent walls through which the sky and mountains could be seen. This room had doors set every few feet around its walls; pairs of men and women all dressed in black and of the same fair complexion as his captor stood before each door. They held long, many-pronged spears and collections of swords and daggers at their sides. *They must be the palace guards*, thought Quadroped. He wondered uneasily what lived behind the doors that needed such constant guarding.

Quadroped's captor took him to an ornately carved wooden door a little larger than the rest, and after a hushed conversation the guards stepped aside and opened the door. The room they entered took Quadroped completely by surprise, for it was the last thing he expected to find at the heart of this crystal palace. It was made of obsidian, a glassy black stone that reflected the light of the red torches set in iron brackets in the walls. Tall, twisted pillars of obsidian supported the vaulted roof and the floor was of bloodstone, black with thin veins of red running through it. There was only one piece of furniture in the room, a vast throne set against the far wall. The throne was made of obsidian as well, and as Quadroped approached he could see that it was decorated with black opals which sparkled with the red, blue and green lights of a stained glass window.

The throne was empty and so, it appeared was the room. *Maybe Goriel doesn't want to see me today,* thought Quadroped; his spirits rose slightly at this unexpected respite. A dark figure emerged from the shadows behind the throne and approached the guard. It was an old man, dressed in black like the guard.

"*He* wishes to see the pig in the council chamber," said the old man. It was the first voice Quadroped had heard since his capture and it startled him with its normalcy. He had unconsciously assumed his captors were mute.

The guard looked ill at ease and Quadroped began to tremble. Anything that could unnerve these people was probably terrible. The Key was still in his mouth. He clamped it hard between his teeth and resolved not to give it up, no matter what was waiting for him in the inner chamber.

With slow, reluctant steps the guard followed the older man to a small door hidden behind the great throne and walked through it. The council chamber was a smaller version of the room they had just left. The guard set Quadroped down on the freezing floor and left, glancing neither left nor right. Quadroped looked around in confusion; the room seemed to be empty. He took a few cautious steps backwards towards the door, when a sound behind him made him stop and turn.

A voice from the corner, a whisper of implacable ice, drew Quadroped inexorably into the far shadows. The shade seemed to melt away from a vast presence seated there. A hand, white as silver, reached down to him, rested gently with the pressure of a falling world on Quadroped's upturned head. Feathers of wind brushed across Quadroped's ears, hardly touching yet exerting a terrible, relentless strength. Goriel, Lord of the Snows, the January Angel with night in his eyes, looked quietly down at the small pig and his great wings of mists and silver ice fluttered softly. Quadroped looked up into the alien infinity of Goriel's eyes and felt himself falling forwards like a leaf. The Key fell from his open mouth.

Goriel smiled his sleepy, serpentine smile and spoke in his deep compassionate voice. "So, little Key Bearer," he said, "you have come into my mountains on your way to Illoreth; on your way to rechain the Black Unicorn to Chaos." Quadroped nodded, still staring with fascination into Goriel's brilliant eyes. "You must realize, little one," said Goriel, "that I can't let you do that."

Quadroped shook himself free of Goriel's mesmerizing gaze. "I won't give you the Key," he said.

Goriel smiled dispassionately. A note of infinite sorrow entered his lovely voice. "You are foolish, little one," he said, "for I offer you your life. You are young, you have many years to live. I have no desire to kill you." Quadroped looked into Goriel's colorless face and shivered. "Trust me," said Goriel. "Give me the Key. You have helped a Warlord before. Toridon has told me of her escape."

"I had to free her," said Quadroped. "Glasgerion was dying. She promised to help us."

"Had you truly cared about the war," said Goriel, "you would have left Glasgerion to die. Give me the Key willingly and I shall spare Glasgerion again."

"I *do* care about the war," said Quadroped. "I won't give you the Key."

"You have no choice," said Goriel dispassionately. "If you do not give me the Key I shall take it from you. Your only choice, piglet, is to live or die."

Quadroped tried to say, "Then I'll die!" in a brave, strong voice like Reander would, but he could only whisper. He waited for Goriel's terrible hands to reach down and break his neck.

Goriel sighed and stood. "I should eliminate you now," he said, "and take the Key, but Toridon has asked me to be lenient. She is reluctant to slay one so young and misguided. Come, I will show you my gardens." Quadroped was dumbfounded; it was the last thing he had expected Goriel to say. But gardens did not sound dangerous. As he was not eager to be executed, he followed along quietly at Goriel's heels.

Goriel led Quadroped through the glassy halls of his palace. "We are now in Ravenor," said Goriel at one point. Quadroped looked around but everything seemed just the same as in the Kingdoms. They walked out of the palace; behind them the towers rose like huge icicles shining out against the deep blue of the sky. They passed over a slender bridge and came to a high glass door in which was set a small gate. Beyond the gate lay the strangest garden Quadroped had ever seen.

It was desolate: filled with dead trees, stagnant pools and rocks encrusted with malignant lichens and mosses. Neat paths bordered with precious stones ran through the wilderness, pale marble statues and dry, silent fountains stood in small enclosures surrounded by the spectral trees. As they passed through it an occasional deer, half starved and gaunt, would come out to stare at them before returning to nibble desperately at the dry plants. Once they stopped by a pond which was nearly empty and Quadroped saw two goldfish flapping helplessly as they suffocated. Before he could stop himself Quadroped asked, "Why didn't you give them some water?"

Goriel's face darkened and Quadroped instinctively cringed backwards, afraid that Goriel would strike him.

But Goriel only said, "Because there is no water," and his face became impassive once more. "Come," said Goriel, "I will show you the other side." Quadroped did not want to see any more of the garden, but he didn't want to die right away either.

Goriel unlocked another gate and Quadroped gasped. The garden beyond was breathtakingly lovely. The trees were ancient and green; flowers bloomed everywhere; the fountains and pools were full of sweet water, and their unscummed surfaces reflected the clouds and sky.

"You are in the Kingdoms once more," said Goriel. "Can you explain what you see?"

"Well," said Quadroped hesitantly, "Glasgerion told me that Ravenor was a wasteland where nothing could grow. He believes that the Black Unicorn started the war because he wanted to rule our lands, which are green and pleasant to live in."

Goriel looked silently down at Quadroped. "That is what your comrades truly believe?" he asked.

"Yes," said Quadroped.

"Let me tell you another story, piglet," said Goriel. "I am the eldest of the four Warlords of Ravenor. I alone was alive before the Great War began. The world which bore me was like this garden: beautiful, green and ancient. When first I built my gardens here it was impossible to tell Ravenor from the Kingdoms and so I built that gate to mark the border. All lands were alike in those days, save for one major difference. Ravenor is a world permeated by magic; all its folk are magical. This is why many of our people still live who remember the Black Unicorn, while your kings have passed away and left their wars to distant descendants.

"Glasgerion was correct when he told you that Ravenor was first a desert. Before the Black Unicorn arrived nothing lived in Ravenor; it was a barren world. Then the Black Unicorn came. He made Ravenor a magical land. He made the valleys and the mountains green and caused the springs to flow. He was our life force. While the Black Unicorn dwelt among us, Ravenor was the fairest land in the world. When he left us, driven into Chaos by ignorant men from the Kingdoms, Ravenor withered and dried. No longer are we immortal, though our lives are aeons long. While the Black Unicorn lives some life will remain in Ravenor. But Ravenor will remain a wasteland until the Black Unicorn walks his land once more."

"But," said Quadroped, "if Ravenor was a nice place to live, why *did* the war start? And why doesn't anyone else know what Ravenor used to be like?"

Goriel shrugged. "The reasons are complex. Ravenor was not the guilty party, and that is all that matters. When the wars ended the Kings saw only the blasted fields of Ravenor. They assumed that it had always looked so. They could not remember how it had looked a thousand years before their birth, when the war began. No one beyond the borders of Ravenor has ever known the true nature of the Black Unicorn. The wasteland theory was plausible when the true reasons for the war had been forgotten."

Is it true? Quadroped wondered. *Maybe Glasgerion believes a story made up by his ancestors and not the true history at all. Reander would tell me not to trust a Warlord, but the story makes sense.*

"Give me the Key, piglet, and you shall be spared from the Black Unicorn's vengeance," said Goriel.

"No," said Quadroped, the reminder of the Black Unicorn's vengeance shattering his thoughts.

"You puzzle me, piglet," said Goriel. "I sense that you half believe what I have told you. If you are willing to accept the truth you must see that the gate must be allowed to open. Are you cruel enough to condemn a world to this unending death?"

"I don't wish Ravenor to die," said Quadroped, "but if I give you the Key it won't really make anything better. The Black Unicorn will be free and maybe Ravenor will be alive, but then you'll try to destroy the rest of the world. I won't let you make the Kingdoms look like the other side of your garden."

"And should the Kingdoms not be punished for our suffering?" asked Goriel. His eyes grew dark as storm clouds and his voice was cold. "Are we not entitled to our vengeance? For hundreds of years we have lived in *hell*. Those goldfish, did you think they just started suffocating? Oh, they will die—someday. But they have gasped there in agony for over five hundred *years!*" Quadroped gasped in revulsion and Goriel smiled soulessly. "That, Key Bearer, is the fate of the lucky ones, the strong ones who survived. Some were more delicate, could not live in the devastated world. I had a wife and twin daughters once; they died in the first year."

Quadroped did not know what he could say. If Goriel had really lost his whole family then he had good reason to want revenge. *The whole palace,* Quadroped realized, *is in mourning, has been in mourning for hundreds of years. Why else would he build such a light, lovely place and then have everyone dress in black?*

"I'm sorry," said Quadroped, feeling it was a very inappropriate remark under the circumstances. "But I won't let you have the Key. It isn't right to destroy a whole world in revenge. Besides, nobody in my world was responsible for the war; they weren't alive then. It's wrong to destroy people just because their ancestors harmed you."

"Each time the Gate is locked the crime is committed," said Goriel inflexibly. "If you lock the Gate, you and your generation will be as guilty as your forefathers were."

"I won't give you the Key," said Quadroped.

"So be it," said Goriel. "We will take it from you then. Come." He returned to the palace and Quadroped followed in a cloud of misery. He could not help the Warlords destroy his world. But the choice was made at the expense of another world which was, perhaps, more deserving of life. It had been dying while his world thrived. "How can *I* judge which world is best?" cried Quadroped silently. *Perhaps,* he thought, *it is best that I should die. That way I won't betray my world and Ravenor won't suffer for my decision because they'll get the Key anyway.*

It's so silly, thought Quadroped. *If they didn't want vengeance I could free the Black Unicorn. Then everything would be all right for both worlds, just like it was before the war.* He was wise enough to realize that the people of Ravenor had lost too much to ever forget the past. *It must be awfully hard to forgive,* he thought, *if your family has been killed*. He knew he would hate anyone who killed his parents or brothers.

Goriel led Quadroped back into the council chamber, and after the daylight and beauty of the garden it was like entering a tomb. *Which,* Quadroped reflected gloomily, *is what I'll be entering soon anyway.* The room was not empty; someone was seated in the shadows and with a start of fear Quadroped recognized the ferocious form of the Manslayer, perched incongruously on a plain wooden chair that was much too small for him. Goriel acknowledged his colleague's presence with a silent nod.

"Well, will he join us?" a woman's light voice asked. The room was lit by a reddish glow as Toridon entered the room and stood beside the Manslayer. Apparently she could alter her gigantic stature at will, for now she was no larger than the other Warlords.

"He has refused," said Goriel, "and so he shall be killed." The three Warlords glared down at the small pig. Quadroped wanted to curl into a small ball and scream out his terror and helplessness.

"But did you not show him the gardens?" asked Toridon. She looked more puzzled than angry.

"I showed him," said Goriel.

"Piglet, if you have seen Goriel's gardens, how can you refuse?" asked Toridon. "Don't you understand what you would be doing if you locked the Black Unicorn into Chaos for another hundred years? How can you be so indifferent to the fate of our whole world?"

"I'm sorry," said Quadroped, wishing there was some phrase more appropriate to discussions of this sort. "I don't *want* your world to die. I don't want *my* world to die either. I wish you would all forget about the war. Then I could let the Black Unicorn go free and both worlds could live like before."

"*Nothing* can be the same as before!" The Manslayer rose, the muscles of his neck tensing with rage. "Your world must pay for its crimes in full. We shall never be satisfied until your world suffers as we have suffered!"

"The people of my world aren't responsible anymore," Quadroped said. "It was our ancestors, hundreds of years ago, not *us!* What they did was awful but even Goriel admitted that they didn't know about the Black Unicorn. The people you hate aren't alive now. The men who hurt you died hundreds of years ago! You don't have to forgive them, just us. We haven't hurt you."

"You *are* them," said the Manslayer. "Do you think it matters that generations have passed? Your world is the same; its people are the same. Do you believe that people can change? Do you think Reander is any different from his ancestor Rhiogan? They even look alike! Given the same situations, Reander would do the same things."

"Glasgerion would not allow you to tell Reander who freed Toridon, would he?" asked Goriel.

How does he know that? thought Quadroped.

"Quadroped," said Toridon, "if Reander knew about that, do you think he would ever forgive you? He is your friend now, but he would kill you if he thought you would unlock the Gate. He is no more merciful than his ancestors were." Quadroped considered Reander's opinion of the Black Unicorn and silently admitted that there might be some truth to this. After all, Reander even hated Morragwen. Yet Reander was not an evil man. He could be very kind to a frightened pig. He was a good ruler and he was passionately devoted to saving the lives of his people from the Black Unicorn's vengeance.

"This is pointless," said the Manslayer. "The piglet is of no consequence. Let us kill him and take the Key at once. We could have the Black Unicorn free again by morning, long before those fools, Reander and Glasgerion, can reach Illoreth to stop us."

"No, wait," cried Toridon.

"The Manslayer is right, Toridon," said Goriel. "We can do no more; the pig has chosen."

"But there *is* a way to change his mind," said Toridon. "*She* is a friend of his, but he doesn't know what she is yet."

"Then tell him," said Goriel.

"Quadroped," said Toridon, "my sister is the fourth Warlord and her name is known to you. She is called Morragwen."

Quadroped stared at Toridon in shock. "No!" he shouted. "It's not true! It can't be true! Morragwen is our friend. She told Glasgerion how to find out where the Gate was. She saved us from the Pitch Fiends and she cured Glasgerion after his battles with Manslayer and the Death Wings."

"As an ally she does leave something to be desired," said Goriel dryly, "but I suppose we can all be grateful that she didn't tell Glasgerion where the Gate was herself. Morragwen has much to answer for, but she is the fourth Warlord. She will be waiting in Illoreth when the time comes."

"No!" said Quadroped again. But it all made horrible sense to him. This was why Morragwen had refused to marry Glasgerion. She knew that she could not marry him once he learned her true identity. Reander had been right all along. Quadroped's legs suddenly came to life and before he realized what he was doing, he began to run.

"Stop him!" cried the Manslayer.

Six hands reached towards the fleeing pig but in his grief, he managed to elude them all. Quadroped ran out the door and through the palace before the Warlords or the palace guards could collect their scattered wits.

Quadroped ran out of the palace and into the gardens without thinking; but when he felt the icy mountain air on his face, he took note of his surroundings. *I'm escaping*, he thought and his grief was replaced with the fear of being captured. Black garbed guards poured out of the archways behind him. *I have to hide. I can't outrun them. They'll have horses; Goriel has wings and Toridon can grow so large*. He started towards the green side then stopped; they would search hardest for him in his own country. *They'll think I'll try to run straight towards Reander and Glasgerion*, he decided, *so I'd better find a hole to crawl into on this side*. He searched about frantically and at last he found a hole in the ground at the base of a crumbling fountain, which was just large enough for him to squeeze into.

It was wet and muddy in the hole, for the spring which fed the fountain still contained a little water. But Quadroped thought it was the nicest, most comfortable hole he had ever crawled in. He could see the black boots of the guards as they raced by, but nobody found his hiding place. A huge shadow fell over the ground and with dismay he watched as Goriel alighted directly in front of the entrance, to be joined by the flaming feet of Toridon and the voice of the Manslayer who was standing out of sight off to the left.

"We must *find* him!" cried the Manslayer. "Goriel, you have magic spells—use them!"

"I have no spells which can find the Key or its bearer," said Goriel. "I have tried for centuries to develop them but the Key is invisible to magic and makes its bearer so."

"This is all your fault, Toridon," said the Manslayer. "You should have guessed he would try something foolish when he heard the truth. If I had killed him we should not be in this mess. Oh, I know he's just a little, silly pig, a baby at that; I wouldn't have enjoyed the execution, but he is the Key Bearer and must die. You are as bad as Morragwen, a softhearted fool!"

"How dare you?" cried Toridon. "You, who let him escape your minions *three* times?! I suppose you think I agree with Morragwen that the pig should be allowed to reach the Gate and make his own decisions. Or do you think that my loyalties, like those of the witch, are torn? Perhaps you think I too yearn for the grey-eyed bard, or perhaps you think Reander holds my affections. Idiot! Don't dare accuse *me!*"

"Enough, both of you," said Goriel. "We have no time to lose. The pig must be found."

"Hah," said Manslayer. "Toridon will find him and carry him to Illoreth so he won't tire his poor little hooves. Or Morragwen will pop in with that eel of hers to take him to her miserable bard."

"I said enough." Goriel began to sound angry. "Morragwen will answer to the Black Unicorn for her crimes. She is not responsible to us. It is enough that she will stand by us at the Gate. Start looking again. He can't have gone far. He's hiding somewhere in the garden." The three Warlords moved off, Manslayer cursing softly under his breath.

If I'm found, Quadroped thought, *I hope it's by Toridon*

*or Goriel. Manslayer would probably kill me very slowly
for causing him such inconvenience.*

The Warlords did not find Quadroped. He lay, shivering
and cold, in his hole all through the day while searchers
raced back and forth around him. The search ended in the
dark, depressing hours of twilight.

"We can waste no more time," said Goriel, standing
once again in front of Quadroped's hole.

"But the pig still has the Key!" protested the Manslayer.

"What does it matter?" asked Goriel coldly. "He is
trapped in the gardens; the guards will catch him if he tries
to leave. Even if he escaped, the Gate opens the day after
tomorrow; he can never reach Illoreth in time. We must go
to the Gate; Reander and his meddlesome uncle will be
there soon." There was a blinding flash of light, similar to
the ones Morragwen was so fond of, and the Warlords were
gone.

I have to get out of here, Quadroped thought. There
were lots of guards in the green garden but very few in this
desolate section. Quadroped watched the nearest gate and
in an hour one of the guards fell asleep. Moving as softly
as he could, Quadroped crept past the guard and ran down
the mountainside, into the bleak land of Ravenor.

Quadroped scrambled down the steep mountainside all
night. The way was slippery with melting snow and loose
gravel, and several times he lost his footing and slid several heart-stopping feet before he could grab on to a
boulder and break his headlong descent. The night was
cool and dark; the moon had set earlier in the evening, and
now only the proudly distant stars lit his path with their
cruel light. Around him, huge boulders rose as jagged
black outlines against the dark, inky blue of the midnight
skies.

"Ouch," Quadroped cried as he stubbed his hoof against
a sharp stone. The stone came loose and he tumbled down
a steep slope. Around him rocks rolled noisily away; listening to them Quadroped froze, for far below him he
heard a series of gentle thuds. The rocks sounded as though
they had fallen over some sort of precipice. Tentatively he

kicked another small stone and listened carefully as it rolled, quieted and then clanged sharply somewhere far below his hooves. Nervously, Quadroped started to push small stones in every direction, becoming more and more frantic as he slowly realized that the only safe place was the slope behind him. He was standing at the edge of a long, narrow projection over a drop of unknown height. Quadroped suspected that the drop was fairly far, the air was clear and the night so silent that the sounds could be deceiving. With a sigh, Quadroped turned around and retraced his steps up the steep, skree slope he had just slid down.

The journey back was exceedingly difficult. The material was loose and for every few feet Quadroped managed to climb he slid swiftly backwards towards the drop behind him. Worse still, he had begun to tremble violently, both from exhaustion and fear. It was horrible, sliding and rolling backwards, wondering if this time the momentum of the fall would be enough to pitch him over the edge into the darkness below. He was making a terrible amount of noise in his frantic efforts to climb off the ledge. Loose stones were rolling and clattering all around and three or four large boulders had come bouncing and roaring over his head, crashing into the ledge with tremendous force.

At last Quadroped felt the slope level slightly and knew he must be getting near the top. With a gasp of relief he relaxed slightly and allowed his tired muscles to rest. But his noisy climb alerted the creatures that lived among the mountain ledges.

With the speed of the wind, two huge white owls swooped over Quadroped's head, their talons just grazing his back in a sinister caress, their butter-yellow eyes gleaming down upon him. Terrified, Quadroped huddled close to the slope and lay as still as he could, but a white pig against a dark slope was an easy target for the great owls. With a haunting wail, the larger of the two dived down and fastened his talons into Quadroped's tender back. With a scream of fright and pain Quadroped began to struggle, but his hooves could not hold on to the slope and he was raised inexorably into the chilly air.

"Quiet," said the owl in a voice which reminded Quadroped of Goriel.

"Help," whispered Quadroped to the pitiless stars. "What are you going to do with me?" he asked, dreading the answer but hoping desperately that the birds were friends.

"Shhh," soothed the bird. "Quiet, soon it will be over."

"What will?" asked Quadroped, twisting helplessly. The pain where the talons were embedded in his skin was almost unendurable, and he could feel his blood starting to dribble in thin, ticklish threads down his side.

"Now," said the second owl calmly and with a shriek, Quadroped felt the talons opening and himself falling swiftly through the air.

Chapter Nine

Quadroped rolled and tumbled quietly through the air; he had fainted as soon as he realized his awful fate. With a dull thud he landed on a narrow ledge, several hundred feet above his intended destination, on a pile of soft grass and twigs.

"Ow! Oh! Help!" cried several clear, flutelike voices. "Mommy!" wailed the highest voice repeatedly.

"Stop that," said a deeper voice. "They won't be back. They're hunting."

"I want Mommy," wailed the voice on a rising note.

"Oh hush," said another voice. "Look, it isn't moving. I think it's safe." Tentatively the ledge's occupants edged closer to the limp body of the unconscious pig.

"It's quite soft," whispered the one with the deep voice.

"Mommy," wailed the other.

"Be quiet, do!" said the third. "They won't be back for hours yet. Let's try and push it off the ledge." Three soft bodies pushed valiantly against Quadroped's flank, but no amount of pushing could move his inert form.

"Now what do we do?" asked the deep voice crossly. "I'm not going to sleep with that thing on our ledge."

"We'll have to sit and wait then," said the other.

"Mommy!" wailed the third.

"HUSH!"

The pale light of dawn flickered across Quadroped's face and with a groan he began to slowly wake up. With effort he opened his eyes and stared around him, then quickly shut them again and tried to pretend he was still asleep.

"Good morning," said a deep voice in dry tones. Quadroped sighed and opened his eyes. Seated on a rock beside his head was a gigantic eagle with brilliant yellow eyes and a long, curved beak which could kill a piglet with very little effort.

"You are, I think, a pig," said the eagle. "It is not often that we have a pig for breakfast."

"Oh," said Quadroped, "but I don't want to be breakfast. Are you going to eat me?"

"I shouldn't think so," said the bird. "Should you like to eat it, kiddies?"

"Ugh."

"Mommy!"

"Daddy, no!" Three small voices chorused; and rolling his eyes sideways, Quadroped saw three balls of fluffy down, all equipped with small sharp beaks, staring at him with undisguised horror.

"Hello," said Quadroped in a whisper.

"Say hello," commanded another voice sternly and a second eagle, a little smaller than the first, walked daintily out of the shadows.

"Hello," said the chicks dutifully. "Can we get rid of it now, please?"

"That depends on who it is," said their father calmly, "and why it was dropped on our ledge. Although somehow I doubt it was intended for us; I think it was supposed to land at the bottom." The eagle stared piercingly at Quadroped who nodded faintly.

"I'm Quadroped," he said, "and two white owls tried to kill me."

"White owls?" repeated the eagle so sharply that Quadroped wished he had kept quiet. "Speak," commanded the eagle, "or I will drop you over the edge right now. What business does a pig have with Goriel's white owls?"

"None. I . . ." Quadroped gulped nervously and stared at the eagle who was glaring down at him and ruffling up the bronze feathers around his neck. With a small gurgle, Quadroped decided to risk all and quickly told the eagles how the ice phantom had snatched him away from Glasgerion and how he had escaped from Goriel down the mountain. He omitted all mention of the Key.

"Those awful owls," said the mother, soothing her three young who had sidled up to her during Quadroped's tale and were now pressed close against her warm feathers.

"Hmmm," said the father, considering Quadroped carefully. "You are not telling us all the tale, piglet," he said. "Goriel does not kidnap pigs on a mere whim, nor does he send his servants to hunt them down and slay them unless he considers it important. But why he should find a piglet of interest is beyond my powers of imagination. We will not dwell longer upon the subject as you are obviously reluctant to tell me why Goriel wants you dead."

"You said you were traveling with a man called Glasgerion?" asked the mother. "We knew a man named Glasgerion once, didn't we?"

"We did," said her mate. "He was, I think, a bard . . . that was some years ago. Tell me, piglet, is your Glasgerion a bard? And what does he look like?"

"Well, he's very tall with white hair and grey eyes," said Quadroped thoughtfully, "and he used to have a harp all carved with serpents and flowers and birds, only the Manslayer broke it."

"The Manslayer!" The mother eagle looked alarmed.

"So, it is not just Goriel who wants you dead, piglet," said the father eagle menacingly. "What are you then, that you have become prey for the Warlords of Ravenor?"

"Don't ask him that," cried the mother. "It is better if we don't know; it will only bring us trouble. The man he described is certainly the one who rescued you so long ago. Let us leave him safely at the base of the cliffs and he can find his own way home."

"You are right," said the eagle, "for I think this pig is headed for Illoreth."

"Take him away quickly then," said the mother, a sharp note of fear in her voice. "It is unsafe to shelter him this long. If Goriel finds out—"

"Climb onto my back, pig," said the eagle hastily, "and grab hold of my feathers in your teeth." Quadroped stood and winced at the sudden pain in his back where the owls had wounded him. With great effort he climbed onto the great bird's back and grabbed on to the long bronze features on the bird's neck.

With a hop the eagle dived off the ledge and fell swiftly downwards for many feet until, just as Quadroped closed his eyes for the crash, the eagle opened his magnificent wings out wide and wheeled upwards to glide in circles over the land below. They flew under the shadow of a towering cliff that rose from the red sand floor of a flat, unending desert.

The morning was clear and far below Quadroped could see the thin gnarled branches of thorn trees and the deep green of cactus and sagebrush. The ground was rocky, and there was no water or shade anywhere in sight. As Quadroped looked he was overwhelmed with despair. *I'll never be able to walk out of this place and find Glasgerion*, he thought. *The Black Unicorn returns tomorrow.*

The eagle landed gently beside a large boulder and Quadroped climbed off. "Good-bye," said the eagle, "and good luck,"

"Which way *is* Illoreth?" asked Quadroped, staring helplessly around at the inhospitable environment. But the eagle was already gone, a thin gold line high above his head. Quadroped looked around him very carefully, but there was no clue to the direction of Illoreth. *I wish there was somebody to ask,* he thought. Then he remembered that even if he met anyone he could not ask because they would be suspicious and would, in all likelihood, just hand him over to the nearest Warlord. *I'm in Ravenor,* he realized. *I can't expect people to help me anymore, especially not if Goriel told me the truth. The eagle only helped because he owed Glasgerion a favor, and he didn't help very much.*

Quadroped was about to pick any direction at random when he heard a scrambling behind him. Turning around he beheld a strange man peering at him from behind a large boulder. The man had a powerful build and a rather savage expression. A necklace of teeth gleamed around his neck and he looked very hostile. Turning to flee, Quadroped stopped dead, for another man was crouched in front of him. Quadroped heard a low chuckle and saw that a woman stood to his side. *They've surrounded me!* he realized. *Help!*

The people remained motionless, staring at Quadroped intently from luminous brown eyes, as though they had never seen a pig before. Quadroped thought this was all too likely—pigs and deserts were not often found together. Quadroped stared hard at his captors. They were short but exceedingly muscular, though their appearance was not as stocky as that of dwarfs. They looked, he thought, a bit like Reander, only on a smaller scale. They were all clothed in animal skins and wore a great deal of jewelry, mostly made up of bones, teeth and clay beads; although the woman wore gold earrings and the man in front of him wore a silver buckle on his belt. They were also heavily armed with long daggers which hung at their waists. Their skin was greyish and their hair the deep red of the desert soil. From their thin eyebrows and long ears, Quadroped deduced that they were not humans but some kind of desert spirits, a thought which did little to comfort him.

"Hello," Quadroped said at last, deciding that he had very little to lose by speaking. "I'm Quadroped."

"It talks!" gasped the woman, drawing closer. "What is it?"

"I'm a pig," said Quadroped, "and I'm not dangerous," he added helpfully.

At this, the man before him chuckled and grinned, exposing a row of neatly pointed teeth. "We had not supposed that you were," he said in a deep voice, "but we are relieved to have our guess confirmed. Tell me, pig, why are you wandering in our desert and riding about on the back of an eagle? Surely this is not normal behavior for your kind? I had thought pigs were rather lazy creatures, dwelling far to the east in the acorn woods."

"They are," said Quadroped, "only I'm different."

"So I see," murmured the man. "Tell me, pig, where were you going a moment ago? What business have you here in our desert?"

"None," said Quadroped vehemently. "I just want to get out of it." Then he blushed; it was a rude thing to say to people who lived in the desert and no doubt considered it a nice place to be. The man was not offended; he smiled again and asked where Quadroped was headed. This question put Quadroped in a quandary: he was afraid to tell the truth, but he had no other choice. If he lied they would surely discover it and he would be in more danger than before.

"I'm trying to get to Illoreth," he said nervously. "It's very important."

An appalled silence greeted his words and Quadroped, staring around at the shocked faces, felt that he had, perhaps, made the wrong decision. Still, he could do nothing about that now. "Could you tell me which way to go?" Quadroped asked hopefully. "I'm lost."

"Why do you desire to reach Illoreth?" asked the man suddenly. "If you are an idle sight-seeker I warn you that Illoreth is a dangerous place to seek in these days."

"I need to get there," said Quadroped in a very small voice.

"Oh, let's help him," said the woman impulsively, coming forward to the man. "Look how small and frightened he is; he can't do us any harm."

"But he heads to Illoreth," the man reminded her harshly. "The situation there is dangerous. I do not know what is going on but the Warlords are gathering there. If the pig is harmless he has no business in Illoreth, and if he is not . . . well, then we may bring the wrath of the warlords upon our people. No, I think we should keep him with us until we can hand him over to someone who knows more of this business than we do."

"Oh no!" squeaked Quadroped in terror. Surely he had not come so far to be stopped by people who did not even know about the Black Unicorn's imminent arrival?

"Look how scared he is," said the woman. "You know how cruel the Warlords are; they would kill him. He can't be dangerous; just look at him."

The man looked and reluctantly agreed that Quadroped did not look villainous. He felt a little ridiculous arresting a piglet on the grounds that he might have some nefarious purpose at Illoreth. "Why do you need to get to Illoreth so badly?" he asked, his resolve weakening as he gazed into Quadroped's unhappy purple eyes.

"My companions are there," said Quadroped, daring to say no more. The Princes of Essylt were too well hated in Ravenor to risk mentioning his companion's names.

"What are *they* doing there?" asked the second man suspiciously.

"I don't know," said Quadroped. He felt terrible about lying but what could he do?

"What does it matter?" asked the woman. "He is just their pig and he has gotten lost. What harm can it do to return him? Even if his owners are up to no good, the return of their pig can hardly signify. It's not as if the pig were anything important."

Only I am, thought Quadroped miserably, but he kept silent.

"Very well, Andvari," said the man suddenly, "if you wish to, return him. You may take him as far as the walls and from there he must find his masters on his own. I will not risk the lives of any of my people inside that accursed place. Go, and be quick." With a swiftness which left Quadroped blinking, the two men vanished, leaving the woman staring down at him with a kindly smile.

"Well then," said Andvari. "Come along, little pig. We have a bit of a walk ahead of us, I'm afraid. Now, what did you say your name was?"

"Quadroped," said Quadroped obediently, trotting at the

woman's heels as she walked quickly onwards. "People usually just call me Quadro," he volunteered.

"Very well, Quadro. I am called Andvari."

"How far *is* Illoreth?" asked Quadroped anxiously; there was not very much time left.

"Oh, ten miles or so," said Andvari. "We should be there by nightfall."

Quadroped gasped; he had not realized he was so close, nor that Illoreth would be in the middle of the desert. *I must have run down the opposite side of the mountain,* he thought. *I wonder if Glasgerion and Reander have even arrived yet. I suppose I shall have to tell Glasgerion about Morragwen.* Quadroped wished suddenly that Illoreth were thousands of miles away.

"Was Illoreth always in the middle of the desert?" asked Quadroped after a while. "It seems such a strange place to build a city."

"Yes," said Andvari, "and the builders had good reason to build it here. You see, in the old days before people became unfriendly, Illoreth was the great trading city between this land and the lands across the border."

"But what did they trade for?" asked Quadroped, looking around the wasteland for anything of value.

"Minerals," said Andvari. "Gold, silver, copper, telurium, lead, zinc—all of the precious metals. There was also sulphur, cassiterite, zircon, salt and so many other valuable things I can't list them."

"But where?" asked Quadroped.

"All around us," said Andvari. "The earth below us is rich in all of these things, and in the old days we mined them and took them to the city where they were traded for cloth, wine, wooden tools and furniture, spices, fish and all the other things which the desert could not provide and which were too costly to ship from the other side of Ravenor. Of course now," she added bitterly, "we can't get them from the far lands of Ravenor, for all has been laid waste."

"But there are still all of those things across the border," said Quadroped. "Why can't you trade for them?"

"Because they would kill us first and then steal our minerals," said Andvari. "That is, after all, how it began."

"What?" asked Quadroped.

"Why, the Great War," said Andvari. "The people of the other place were greedy and stole our minerals, rather than paying for them honestly. So we were forced to steal in turn from them those things which we needed."

"Oh," said Quadroped nervously.

"Didn't you know that?" asked Andvari. "You haven't been very well educated. It is all about to be changed now though."

"It is?"

"Yes," said Andvari. "The King is to be returned to us. Surely you must know that even now our greatest heroes have gathered at Illoreth to welcome him home?"

"No," said Quadroped, amazed to hear the Warlords referred to as heroes.

"Yes," said Andvari, looking happy, "our King is coming home and all shall be as it once was. The far lands will be fertile once again and the mines here shall be opened and we shall be able to have wood and fish and cloth and all sorts of marvelous things. I have always wanted to taste the things called fruits; soon I will be able to. It will be wonderful!"

No, thought Quadroped unhappily, *it won't. When the Unicorn gets free there is going to be another war and people will fight each other for hundreds of years and all the fields and orchards will be ruined. I have to stop the Black Unicorn*, he thought firmly. *Another war would be terrible for everyone, even the people of this land.*

Quadroped's guide chattered happily on about the wonderful time before the Great War, oblivious to his distress. *Oh I wish it could be like that again*, he thought miserably. *Goriel was right: the Black Unicorn really was the life of Ravenor.* Andvari's descriptions of the far lands were horrific; people there lived lives of misery and starvation and many had resorted to savagery and violence. It was terrible to keep their Black Unicorn in Chaos, but he remembered Goriel's garden and knew with certainty that the "heroes" would never renounce their vengeance.

*Even if I could persuade the Black Unicorn to make
peace,* Quadroped brooded, *Reander would probably
refuse. He hates the Warlords as much as they hate him.
He hates Ravenor and everything in it, and he hasn't even
been imprisoned for thousands of years.*

It was growing darker now; the dome of the sky had
darkened to black and above the pale orange of the horizon
the new moon arose, huge and horned. Andvari quickened
her pace, uneasy now that Illoreth was so close. She
claimed that the city was haunted by vengeful ghosts and
that monsters lurked around its walls. She had picked
Quadroped up earlier in the day, for he was too tired after
his flight from Goriel to walk for long. From her arms he
gazed out at the darkening desert and shivered slightly as
the air cooled with night.

"Look," said Andvari, "you can see the city now."

Quadroped looked and saw the dark outline of a city
ahead of them. Illoreth was huge and walled; rampart upon
rampart it rose upwards to tower over the desert, a mighty
fortress dark and forbidding. Where the moonlight struck
its stones it glowed palely as though embued with its own
ghastly luminescence. Before them, two massive doors
made of wood and iron carved in the shapes of men and
monsters were set in the stone. *It's bigger than the cliffs,*
he thought frantically. Somewhere in its shadowy heart lay
the Gateway into Chaos.

"I have to leave you here, Quadro," said Andvari when
they stood below the walls. "There's a small door in the
side of the gate which is partly open; you can enter there.
Be quick; it is not safe to linger outside at night. It is not
safe inside either," she added, "but with luck you will find
your masters. Besides," she added cheerfully, "with so
many great heroes inside you can't come to harm."

Quadroped shuddered at the thought of what would
happen to him if her "heroes" caught him but said nothing.
"Thank you, Andvari," he said and watched as she slipped
silently away into the shadows. Looking up at the walls
above him, Quadroped had the uneasy feeling that they
were leaning menacingly towards him, falling. Dizzy, he

looked down again and walked carefully through the small door into the dead city of Illoreth.

Before him lay long lines of ruined, roofless houses, each almost thirty stories high. Their masonry lay in ragged piles along the silent grey streets. The air was deathly still; the black, empty holes of shattered doors and windows stared back at him malevolently, silently blaming him for their condition. "I don't like Illoreth," he said aloud and his voice sounded flat in the hideous silence.

The city was darker than the desert; its walls shut out the sinking moon and the buildings cast sinister shadows in the queer light the merciless stars provided. Quadroped walked a few steps down the street in front of him and bumped into an invisible heap of bricks. *I'll have to look for Glasgerion and Reander in the morning,* he decided. Normally he would have been too scared to stop searching, but he was afraid of telling Glasgerion about Morragwen and any respite was welcome. Curling up beside a large stone Quadroped began to wash his ears, an occupation so normal that he began to feel less frightened and even managed to think wistfully about acorns and hot soup, for he had not eaten in a long, long time.

Quadroped's comfortable thoughts were abruptly shattered by a freezing draft of dank air upon his head. Looking up, he was horrified to see a ghastly apparition hovering some five feet away and some three feet above the ground. With a scream Quadroped jumped frantically backwards, only to collide painfully with the sharp bricks behind him. Rubbing his rump, Quadroped froze and looked carefully at the thing in front of him.

The creature was composed of a vaporish, glowing mist which formed the hazy outline of a human figure. The details were hard to see, for it was nearly transparent and the buildings behind it obscured the lines of the figure. Its head seemed to be a little more solid, having a milky appearance, and by staring very hard Quadroped could just discern its features. The apparition was of a young man, eighteen or so, with long disheveled hair. Its eyes looked very sad and there was a despondent droop to its mouth.

Quadroped was afraid to move, lest the spirit attack

him; so he remained where he was, staring up at the creature with large, frightened eyes. *It must be a ghost,* he decided, remembering Andvari's warnings. *I wish Glasgerion or Reander was here.* But as neither of his companions was likely to appear, he gathered up what was left of his courage and whispered, "Hello."

The result was startling; with a sudden jerk, the spirit rose into the air and began to retreat hastily down a street, bathing the buildings in a pale blue glow. "Why, it's scared too," said Quadroped. "Come back. I won't hurt you," he called after the fleeing spectre. In a moment the ghost had disappeared and began to timidly rematerialize in front of Quadroped, staring sadly at him from its transparent eyes. "My name is Quadroped," offered the pig, "but most people just call me Quadro. Who are you?"

The ghost did not reply but floated a little closer, causing Quadroped to shrink back in alarm. But the spirit did not harm him, only hovered and stared fixedly at him for a long time. After several attempts to speak to it, Quadroped gave up. "I shall call you Ghost," he declared. He felt curiously disappointed in the spirit, for he had never met an otherworldly being and would have liked to talk to it. Sensing the pig's disappointment, the ghost looked, if possible, more woebegone than ever and began to hesitantly fade away.

"Oh stop," begged Quadroped, aware that he had somehow injured the ghost's feelings. "You don't have to go away. You can hover there as long as you like. It's rather comforting to have someone else around; this city frightens me." The ghost sighed and quickly solidified again, looking a bit happier. Uttering a sigh of contentment in a voice that sounded like dead leaves in empty corridors, it hovered closer to the ground and began to hum softly to itself in an off-key monotone. "So you *can* speak," said Quadroped with some satisfaction; but the ghost said nothing, only hummed a bit louder. Quadroped gave up and curled up for sleep. *Ghosts,* he thought, *are certainly peculiar, but it's nice not to be alone anymore and the hum is sort of soothing.*

* * *

"Well, well, well," a familiar voice said, somewhere above Quadroped's head. It was morning and Glasgerion was standing over him with a broad smile on his face.

"Glasgerion!" Quadroped cried. He scrambled to his feet and was scooped up and hugged firmly. To his dismay, he found himself sobbing hysterically into the bard's shoulder as all the horrors of the past two days finally overwhelmed him.

"It was so horrible," said Quadroped. "A phantasm grabbed me and they tried to kill me and the owls—"

"Shhh, it's all right, Quadro, you're safe now," said Glasgerion. He seated himself on a fallen pillar and rocked Quadroped gently in his arms. After a time, Quadroped's tears stopped and he began to breathe more normally. "Are you all right now?" asked Glasgerion.

"Yes." Quadroped nodded, smiling shakily at the bard. "It's just that I'm so glad to see you."

"We thought we'd lost you," said Glasgerion; a look of pain crossed his face for a moment and then was gone. "You have been injured." He was looking at the talon marks on Quadroped's back. "Tell me what happened to you. How did you manage to find Illoreth? We thought you'd fallen off the cliff."

I should tell him about Morragwen right now, Quadroped thought, but Glasgerion looked so happy that he couldn't find the courage. Instead he climbed into Glasgerion's lap and allowed Glasgerion to put some salve on his cuts while he told him all about Goriel, the eagles and the desert spirits.

"How do you like Illoreth?" Glasgerion asked when Quadroped's tale was done.

"I don't like it at all," said Quadroped with a shudder. "It's too gloomy. I thought it would be all covered with vines and be full of birds and animals."

"Ah," said Glasgerion, "but it's much safer this way. Nothing lives here at all. We are better off having only a hostile atmosphere to combat, rather than hordes of wild animals. And traveling through a jungle of thick vines would be impossible; we should never find the Gate."

"Where *is* the Gate?" asked Quadroped.

"I don't know yet," said Glasgerion. "Reander is off searching for it now. So was I, but I found you instead, which was nicer."

"How much time do we have left?" asked Quadroped anxiously.

"None at all." Glasgerion frowned. "The Black Unicorn arrives at midnight tonight." He might have said more, but at the mention of the Black Unicorn the ghost, which was still hovering around, gave a horrible scream and began to wave its misty arms.

"What was that?!" demanded Glasgerion, springing to his feet and spinning around to face the ghost.

"That," said Quadroped, "is Ghost. He is rather nice really. Oh, Ghost, do stop that. Glasgerion didn't mean to upset you." The ghost looked infinitely sad and stared suspiciously at Glasgerion who frowned back. Uttering a heartrending sigh, the ghost drifted off and resettled itself on a wall above their heads and began to hum again.

"It seems harmless enough," said Glasgerion, sitting down again.

"Who do you think he is?" asked Quadroped, "or was?" He was unsure what tense to use when discussing a ghost.

"Who knows?" said Glasgerion solemnly. "Probably just another victim of the Great War against the Black Unicorn. Sorry," he added as the ghost began to wail again.

"Do you think there are lots of ghosts?" asked Quadroped.

"Undoubtedly," said Glasgerion. "This city was once the largest in the world. More people lived here than in any other city, even Essylt."

"What happened to them all?" asked Quadroped.

"Some left when the war began; others were killed in the fighting and still haunt the streets like this ghost," said Glasgerion.

Quadroped looked around at the empty, blackened buildings. They no longer seemed menacing, only terribly, awfully lonely. Glasgerion placed a hand on his head, comforting because it was warm and alive. "What is the tune Ghost keeps humming?" asked Quadroped curiously. It was a nice tune.

Glasgerion listened to the monotonal humming for a minute and then he sang:

The morning sun sings a forgotten song
As it dances on unseen sands,
Aloud cried the wind when the last wave broke
And wept in its cold crystal hands;
Tears for the towers that never shall rise
Are few as the tears for the sky,
None weep for the ruins that never saw stone
But died in the architect's eye;
Who marks the passage of works of the hand
When those who first dreamed them are gone,
When the wind fills the windows with curtains of
  sand
While the builders are sucked into dawn?

"How depressing," said Quadroped. "Do you have anything to eat? I am terribly hungry."

"Reander can fix you up something when we find him. In the meantime, I still have a nutritious protein tablet left," said Glasgerion unpromisingly. "I had a dried apple somewhere but it seems to have vanished."

"Fairfax ate it," said Quadroped over a mouthful of capsulized yeast extract. "When I get home I'm going to *stuff* myself with acorns."

"Hmmm," said Glasgerion absently, staring off into the distance with a brooding expression. "Let's go find Reander." He rose and placed Quadroped on his shoulder. Then he started off down a narrow street to the left. Behind them the Ghost stopped humming and looked anxious. Then it floated off the wall and hurried after them.

I have to tell Glasgerion about Morragwen right now, Quadroped decided firmly. *It's better to tell him before we find Reander. He's going to be heartbroken and if Reander knows, it will make things worse.* "Glasgerion?"

"What is it, Quadro?" Glasgerion paused and looked enquiringly into Quadroped's miserable face, "What's wrong?"

"Well . . ." Quadroped stopped in confusion. He did not know how he could tell Glasgerion the truth. Then he closed his eyes and said as fast as he could, "Morragwen-is-the-fourth-Warlord."

"What!"

"Or at least," Quadroped amended, "that's what Goriel and Toridon said. Only, Glasgerion? I think it's true."

"Quadro! Do you know what you're saying?" Glasgerion demanded, raising a hand as though to strike the piglet. He looked so angry that Quadroped squealed and grabbed at the nearest ear, certain he was about to be dropped on the hard cobblestones. But the hoof on his ear brought Glasgerion back to his senses. "Sorry, Quadro," he said, lowering his hand once more. "I cannot believe that Morragwen is a Warlord. But if you think it is true then I will listen. Tell me everything Goriel told you on the mountain." Glasgerion sat down on a pile of stones and drew Quadroped onto his lap for the second time that morning. He was pale and Quadroped could feel his body shaking.

"First," Quadroped began, "they wanted me to give up the Key and so they started trying to convince me that locking the Gate was wrong."

"Why didn't they just kill you and have done with it?" asked Glasgerion.

"I think Toridon had something to do with that," said Quadroped. He told Glasgerion all about Goriel's garden and the Black Unicorn and all his doubts about locking the Gate. When he was done, he gave a great sigh of relief, for it felt good to have someone to discuss it with at last. "*Is* Morragwen the fourth Warlord, Glasgerion?" he asked timidly, when Glasgerion made no reply.

Glasgerion buried his face in his hands and his voice was low and muffled. "I don't know but . . . yes, I think she may be," said Glasgerion. "But *why?* She could have sabotaged our mission a hundred times! She's helped us all along. How can she be a Warlord?"

Quadroped knew that Glasgerion didn't really expect an answer, but he told Glasgerion what Goriel had said to the Warlords about Morragwen's dilemma. "She does love you," he said.

"That makes no difference," said Glasgerion heavily. "If it's true, we must oppose each other. She will stand by the Black Unicorn when the Gate opens; he is her King. I would think less of her if she betrayed him. But I am a Prince of Essylt; I am not free to choose. I must stand by Essylt and by Reander, who is my ruler as well as my nephew. This is why she refused to talk of marriage. But she was wrong, Quadro; I still want to marry her. I love her." His shoulders shook and Quadroped thought he was crying.

"Glasgerion, is it right to lock the Gate?" Quadroped asked after a long while.

"I don't know anymore," said Glasgerion bleakly. "Once, only an hour ago, I was certain. Now neither choice seems right. I can't tell you that one country deserves death more than another. Reander, the Warlords, Morragwen and I all had our sides chosen at birth. You, Quadro, have no such ties of loyalty to make your decision easier. But you must make a choice, and soon."

Quadroped looked helplessly up at Glasgerion. He had been so sure that Glasgerion, who was so wise and knew so much, would have an answer for him. "How *can* I make a choice like that?" he wailed desperately. "No matter what I do my decision will be wrong!"

"I know." Glasgerion sighed. "Quadro, we must end this talk. If I'm gone too long Reander will look for me. If he knew you had doubts he would leave you no choice. Reander has come to like you, but he will not let you free the Black Unicorn. So let us keep this secret."

"I don't think Reander will like our ghost, do you?" asked Quadroped, obligingly changing the subject. He looked over Glasgerion's shoulder at the spirit who was still doggedly following them.

"Reander is most certainly *not* going to like your ghost, Quadro," said a deep voice and Reander stepped towards them out of a doorway, the smile on his face softening his words. "Quadro," he said joyfully, taking the pig from Glasgerion and hugging him briefly. "He is all right?" he asked Glasgerion, searching Quadroped carefully for any serious injury.

"His back is cut up a little and he has a few bruises," said Glasgerion, "but they'll heal quickly enough. I have put an antiseptic on them already."

Reander nodded and turned his attention to the ghost which was hovering behind Glasgerion's left shoulder and had paled into almost total invisibility. Quadroped sympathized with the creature; he had often wished to be invisible when Reander scowled at him.

"It's not dangerous, Reander," said Glasgerion placidly. "And it watched over Quadro last night."

Reander shrugged and turned back to Quadroped. "Have you eaten?" he asked.

I hope Reander didn't hear us talking, Quadroped worried. *I'm sure he didn't; he doesn't look upset.* He shook his head and looked hopeful. "Acorns?" he asked. Reander smiled and produced a bowl of hot acorn mash which he presented to the hungry pig.

"Have you had any luck?" asked Glasgerion as they waited for Quadroped to finish his meal.

"Not yet," said Reander shortly. "The city is huge."

"What do we look for?" asked Quadroped, licking the last remnants of his meal out of the bowl.

"A stairway running down into the caverns beneath the city," said Reander.

"Caverns?" gulped Quadroped, remembering the caves at the bottom of the sea with alarm. "I thought the Gate was in Illoreth."

"No," said Glasgerion.

"You don't think, surely," said Reander caustically, "that the magician would have opened the Gate up in the middle of a public street?"

Quadroped blushed and mumbled that that would be inconvenient. "Will there be trolls?" he asked nervously.

"No, these caves are uninhabited," said Glasgerion.

"They *were* uninhabited," Reander corrected him grimly. "By now I expect the Warlords are there." Reander got up and began to peer methodically into ruined doorways, and after a moment Glasgerion and Quadroped followed him.

* * *

By midday, Quadroped was sure that the city contained several million houses each larger than the last. He had peered into so many windows and been pushed into so many small crevices that his head was spinning. *And we haven't even searched a tenth of the city,* Quadroped thought in despair. *By the time we find the passage the Black Unicorn will be free. It's hopeless!* After another hour of fruitless effort both Glasgerion and Reander were ready to agree with him.

"The passage is well concealed." Reander sighed, resting upon a ragged wall. "We must think of another way to search; this will take too long."

"Can't you use magic?" asked Quadroped, who had been wondering about that all morning.

"The Warlords have put a spell on the passage," said Glasgerion. "Reander could break it, but he says it will take too much of his strength. If we have to we can use magic, but it is better if Reander saves his strength for tonight."

Quadroped nodded; he certainly didn't want Reander to be in a weakened condition when he had to face the Warlords. Quadroped rubbed his aching hooves and talked quietly to Ghost, who had followed him all morning, an expression of curiosity replacing his habitual air of melancholy. Quadroped had learned that it was best to talk and complain to Ghost, who always looked properly miserable, than to Reander or Glasgerion, who either ignored him or told him to keep quiet.

Reander watched Quadroped with a scowl of annoyance that suddenly vanished to be replaced by a look of discovery. "Ghost!" he exclaimed in a voice which made Quadroped jump and Ghost temporarily vanish. "Ghost, come here," said Reander. "I would talk to you."

The spirit reluctantly condensed before him. "You have dwelled here for some time, have you not?" asked Reander.

The spectre looked very gloomy which Reander interpreted to be an affirmative.

"You have, perhaps, been here since the Great War?"

The spirit howled and groaned and wrung its vapor hands.

"Enough," said Reander sternly, ignoring the ghost's pathetic sighs. "You must know where the passage that leads to the Gate into Chaos lies. Therefore, I charge you to tell us where lies the passage!" At these words the ghost began to shake and howl so terribly that Quadroped felt shivers run up and down his spine.

"Please help us, Ghost," said Quadroped. "It's very important. We have to find that passage soon or it will be too late. The Black Unicorn will escape and the Great War will begin all over again. People will die! You don't want that to happen, do you?" The ghost ceased its cries and looked thoughtful.

"Please?" asked Quadroped simply. With a sob, the ghost rose into the air and glided slowly away.

"So much for that idea," said Reander.

"No, look," said Glasgerion, "it's beckoning us to follow."

Quadroped looked and saw that the ghost had halted a few yards ahead of them and was waving its arms impatiently. "Hurrah!" cried Quadroped, doing a little skipping hop and running towards the ghost. "He's going to help us." Reander and Glasgerion, both fully aware of the dangers ahead, had little trouble containing their own joy and followed him at a more sedate pace.

The ghost led them quickly through a complex maze of twisting alleyways and halted before a small building whose doorway was almost completely obscured behind a pile of debris. Working quickly, Reander and Glasgerion soon cleared a space large enough for them to fit through. Inside it was dark, but the faint light which crept in was sufficient to show them an empty chamber without any doors or other means of egress.

"There isn't anything *in* here, Ghost," said Quadroped in disappointment.

The spectre looked grieved at this lack of faith and gestured towards the blank wall at the far end of the room.

"We can't *go* through walls," said Quadroped sadly.

"I don't think he wants us to," said Glasgerion suddenly, crossing to the wall and examining it carefully. "I think . . . ah, yes, this is it." He pressed against a portion of the wall and to Quadroped's amazement his hand passed right through the stone and disappeared. "Don't look so shocked, Quadro." Glasgerion laughed, withdrawing his hand. "The Warlords have just disguised the passage to look like a wall; there is actually an opening here."

"Ah," said Quadroped wisely, but he thought that the wall certainly looked solid enough.

"Thank you," said Reander to the ghost, who was so pleased with this praise that it began to hum once again.

The ghost stopped humming abruptly when it saw Reander begin to conjure up a light. As the glowing sphere of light began to form above Reander's hand the ghost began to look worried and drifted about in nervous circles. Reander stepped forwards, the light floating just in front of him, and was just about to pass into the passage when the ghost floated in front of him, barring his passage.

"Out of my way," said Reander but the ghost shook its head and pointed at Quadroped, indicating that they should leave the pig behind. "Quadro comes with us," said Reander shortly. "Stand aside."

The ghost remained obstinately still and gave a heart-rending shriek.

"Don't be melodramatic," said Reander coldly. "The pig is the Key Bearer and will come with us. Now move or we shall walk *through* you!"

The ghost shrieked and moved aside.

"It will be all right, Ghost," said Quadroped bravely as he followed Reander into the wall. "I'll come back, you'll see." With a wave he trotted into the wall and passed through into the darkness, Glasgerion following directly behind him. In the small empty room the ghost began to sob softly to itself.

Behind the wall lay a narrow passage, its stone walls glistening wetly in the macabre green light. At the end of the hall a long flight of stairs wound down into the blackness below. "These stairs may be slippery, Quadro," Glasgerion warned, "so step carefully. I don't know how far the bottom is and if you fall you could be seriously hurt."

"I'll be careful," said Quadroped. He soon found that although Reander's light illuminated the stairs several feet below them, it was unwise to look down unless one wished to become dizzy. He gazed at the walls instead.

The stairwell was carved into the solid rock; and as it sliced through the earth, veins of gold, silver, copper and other precious metals were revealed. Looking at their swirling outlines, Quadroped wondered if the rock had not been liquid at one time, for the patterns on the walls and steps looked like the rainbow designs created by oil upon water. When Quadroped asked Glasgerion about this he only chuckled and said that the rocks had been deformed by internal pressures. Quadroped did not understand what that meant so he gave up trying to analyze the structures and simply observed them instead.

Occasionally they passed huge beds of crystals, growing outwards from the walls. These came in an astounding variety of shapes and colors, and Quadroped wished that he might take one with him to show his family if he ever got home again. But when he asked Glasgerion if he would snap off a lovely white one, the bard broke out laughing.

"It would take more strength than I possess." He chuckled. "Those are diamonds, Quadro."

"Oh," said Quadroped, disappointed. He supposed that all the others were gemstones as well, and while the idea of so much treasure was staggering, Quadroped wished they had just been ordinary crystals so that he could pick one.

Although the geology of the staircase was interesting, Quadroped soon began to wish fervently for the end. It seemed that they had been climbing down forever, yet the bottom was nowhere in sight. Once Reander stopped and threw a rock down ahead of them. Quadroped could hear it rolling down until the noise was too faint to hear.

"We have a long way to go," remarked Reander. With a sigh Quadroped began to climb downwards again. The stairs had been constructed for tall men with long legs, and this presented quite a problem for the small Quadroped. Where Glasgerion and Reander found them the perfect height, for Quadroped they were far from satisfactory. He had to walk carefully to the edge of each step and then dive head-first onto the next, bumping his nose repeatedly in the process.

Quadroped began to reflect bitterly upon the difficulties of climbing stairs if one was a small pig. Reaching up a sore hoof to rub his even sorer snout, he failed to look where he was going and stepped blithely off the edge of a step and began to somersault down the stairs, squeaking, "Ouch!" each time he bounced off a step.

"Quadroped, stop!" cried Glasgerion, as the pig hurtled past him.

"I can't," wailed Quadroped miserably.

"You must—you'll be killed!" Glasgerion called after him.

But reassuring as that thought was, Quadroped continued to pick up momentum and had soon rolled out of sight, his cries becoming muffled and faint in the distance. With exclamations of alarm, Glasgerion and Reander raced down the stairs after the disappearing pig.

I should have carried him, Glasgerion thought sadly. He was certain that he would find Quadroped dead and broken at the bottom, not a cheering prospect. "I'm coming, Quadro!" he cried, but no reply came back. He began to take the steps three or four at a time.

When they reached the bottom Glasgerion and Reander paused to catch their breath before raising the light higher and gingerly viewing the grisly remains. The grisly remnant was sitting somewhat dazedly in the middle of the floor, sucking its hoof and looking *very* unhappy about life. "Quadroped, you're alive!" said Glasgerion delightedly.

"I am?" asked Quadroped dubiously. It was a hard fate that had provided only a stone floor, rather than a heavenly cloud, upon which to rest his aching limbs.

Glasgerion quickly got down on his knees and, drawing the small pig onto his lap, hastened to assure himself that no bones were broken. Quadroped was all in one piece, and with a sigh of relief Glasgerion set him down again and rose to his feet. "You seem to be fine," he said. "Although you may be sore for quite a while. You should be thankful."

Quadroped reflected that Glasgerion's mind was deteriorating if he considered a whole body full of aching muscles being fine. As for being thankful . . . "Do we have to climb back up again?" he asked gloomily.

"I'm afraid so," said Glasgerion.

Noticing Quadroped's unhappy expression, Reander said, "Cheer up, Quadro! After all, we may never return."

Quadroped looked at Reander in silent amazement. *Reander,* he thought, *may find the prospect of death cheering but I, for one, wish he would keep his morbid thoughts to himself. Still, when compared to that staircase . . ."* Quadroped left the thought unfinished.

The staircase had ended in a vast cavern. In the eerie green glow the cave was an awesome sight, an intricate cathedral of glistening limestone. Stalactites grew from the ceiling like melted candles colored white, pink and pale green or brown. Formations which looked like waterfalls flowed turbulently down the walls, frozen in motion by rock. Glasgerion called these "flow stones" and said they had formed over thousands of years, not through the instantaneous transformation of a waterfall. Delicate crystal flowers of sugary white dolomite grew upon the walls. Calcite cave coral covered the limestone pillars and was impossible to tell from the real corals Quadroped had seen on the sea floor.

The floor was covered with shining calcareous gravel that had the lustre of pearls and lumpy round balls that looked like popcorn. Huge stalagmites grew up off the floor, twisting like snakes and covered by frozen waves of flow stone. The glowing red eyes of large cave spiders gleamed evilly off the walls and white, troglodytic cave crickets scurried across the floor at their feet. Far overhead, Quadroped saw the twisting, quivering brown bodies of bats, disturbed by Reander's light.

As they walked through the cavern, the still air began to blow until there was a raging tempest blowing against them. Quadroped was not strong enough to fight the wind and found himself pushed roughly backwards into a patch of cave coral.

"Ouch!" squealed Quadroped upon impact; the cave coral was as sharp as real coral.

"Be careful, Quadro," said Glasgerion.

"And stop squeaking," added Reander.

"I don't squeak," said Quadroped, "and I didn't do it on purpose."

"It *is* a little windy," said Glasgerion, tucking Quadroped under an arm. "Now, I wonder where the Gate is. I can't see a thing."

Quadroped grunted. The storm was flinging huge clouds of grey dust into the air, reducing the visibility to zero. After a moment's hesitation, Reander faced directly into the wind and, shielding his eyes with one arm, began to walk slowly fowards, Glasgerion struggling along in his wake.

"I think I can see the Gate ahead," called Reander encouragingly, but Quadroped only whimpered. The winds frightened him with their incessant howling and sinister strength. More than ever, Quadroped did not want to be anywhere near the Gate or the Black Unicorn or the four powerful Warlords who would surely try and kill them very soon.

"There it is, Quadro. We've made it!" said Glasgerion joyfully.

"Don't celebrate too quickly," said Reander dauntingly.

Peeking out from under Glasgerion's arm, his eyes watering from the wind and dust, Quadroped caught his first sight of the incredible Gate. It was a work of art, forged of black iron twisted into vines and strange symbols backed by dark wood . . . and it was only four feet high! Worse, it was set in the middle of a neat little white picket fence.

Chapter Ten

"Glasgerion," said Quadroped, "that *can't* be the Gate. It looks like the fence around the vegetable patch at home. How can it stop the Black Unicorn? The one at home can't even stop *turtles!*"

"Its form is deceptive," said Glasgerion. "The magician who made it had a strange sense of humor. That Gate has held the Black Unicorn in Chaos for hundreds of years, with luck it will hold him for hundreds more. It will start to open in an hour and then you can lock it."

"What if the Black Unicorn pushes?" asked Quadroped.

"We'll help you," said Glasgerion. "Don't worry."

"I can't help worrying," said Quadroped. "I . . . help!" The wind had died without warning. A cloud of viscous black smoke coalesced before the Gate and advanced towards them, spreading like oil upon the dusty air. "This is how the Water Demon appeared," cried Quadroped.

The cloud parted, revealing the sinister form of the Manslayer. "Welcome to Illoreth, Quadro," he said. "We've been waiting for you."

I wish he wouldn't use my nickname, thought Quadroped.

A hot orange glow lit the cavern as Toridon slowly materialized beside the Manslayer. "Hello, Quadro," she said. "Have you reconsidered yet? We don't really *wish* to kill you. Give us the Key and you and your companions may return to the surface unharmed."

"You shall never have the Key, Warlord," said Reander. "You underestimate my power. Quadroped will lock the Gate and live to reach the surface."

"That's ridiculous," said Toridon. "No single *human* can defeat all four of us. Or have I miscalculated the odds? Does Glasgerion have some secret power we've not heard of? Or do you look to Quadroped to help you?"

"Quadro has escaped your combined might once already," said Reander. "I wouldn't be surprised if he outwitted you again; but he won't have to. I will slay you long before the Gate opens. But there are two Warlords still missing. Are they afraid to fight me?"

"They'll be here soon enough," said the Manslayer. "But let's fight a little now; your confidence intrigues me."

"I'm agreeable," said Reander. "It won't take long to kill you." The Manslayer smiled and drew his sword.

"Wait," said Toridon; she grabbed the Manslayer's arm. "Don't be so hasty; let's wait for Goriel."

"Since the lady is nervous," said Reander, "let us wait. Perhaps I could arrange a light picnic? You'll both feel easier when Goriel arrives and the odds are more even."

The Manslayer shook free of Toridon's grasp and stepped towards Reander. "Don't let him provoke you, Manslayer," said Toridon. "The Gate opens in an hour and the Key Bearer is at hand. Together, we can defeat him, but he may be powerful enough to best us in single combat. Goriel warned us that this might happen."

"Goriel is a cowardly fool," said the Manslayer. "Why should I wait when I can solve the problem now? The glory of slaying the Prince of Essylt and the Key Bearer shall be mine alone!"

"If you're determined to fight, then I'll join you," said Toridon.

"I don't want your help," said the Manslayer. "The Prince is mine."

"Your thirst for glory blinds you, Manslayer," said Toridon. "The Prince can defeat you easily."

"If you're done quarreling," said Reander, "I'd like to get started. There's a Gate to be locked."

"Very well, woman," said the Manslayer. "We'll kill the man together."

"The fight will be between the three of us alone," said Reander. "Glasgerion and Quadro must not be harmed."

"There'll be time enough to harm them afterwards," agreed the Manslayer.

Reander quickly took off his cloak and shirt and gave them to Glasgerion. "Get as close to the Gate as you can," he said. "I don't expect to lose, but the chance is always there."

"Are you going to kill Toridon?" asked Quadroped anxiously.

"I can't afford to spare her, Quadro," said Reander. "All the Warlords must be destroyed if we're to lock the Gate."

But I'm not sure we are *going to lock the Gate*, thought Quadroped, but he remained silent.

The cavern was deathly quiet as the fight began. Reander and the Warlords stood in a triangle, motionless as stone. The Manslayer moved first; his sword slashed at Reander's stomach, and the silence was shattered by a red flash and a thunderous explosion. Reander's sword was heavier than the robber chief's sword had been, yet in his hands it seemed to have no weight at all. He parried the Manslayer's thrust with ease, twisting as if he performed some graceful dance rather than a battle to the death. The great broadswords met and slithered past each other. Fiery explosions filled the air. The noise was so great that Quadroped had to cover his ears.

"I thought the Manslayer wasn't a very powerful magician," Quadroped yelled.

"He's not," shouted Glasgerion. "These fireworks are nothing. The most deadly magic is Old Magic. It needs no words or gestures and makes no sound or light."

Toridon suddenly engulfed Reander in a sheet of flame

that sprang from her hands. Her fires were cold; the temperature dropped and their breath misted in the air. "Toridon's hands were cold when she carried me out of the tunnel," Quadroped remembered. "Maybe it's another kind of phosphor-whatcha-macallit, like the sponges and the fireflies."

"It's not," said Glasgerion. "It's magical."

"Is it Old Magic?" asked Quadroped. "It doesn't make any noise and she isn't moving."

"No, but it's higher magic than the Manslayer uses," Glasgerion replied. "You'll see Old Magic at work when Goriel arrives."

"I wonder where he is," said Quadroped.

"Looking for Morragwen," said Glasgerion. "I hope he never finds her."

Quadroped avoided that topic. "Toridon's magic doesn't look any better than the Manslayer's," he said. "Reander's paying no attention to her at all."

"Yes, he is," said Glasgerion. "Her fires are weakening Reander's magical powers, but you can't see it happen. See, he's fighting her now."

An aura of blue fire flickered to life around Reander's body. The envelope of light expanded, forcing Toridon's flames back. The blue light ran and danced across Reander's chest, over his outstretched arms and wreathed through the air towards Toridon. As the strange fire approached her, she retreated and made a series of intricate gestures with her hands. "She's in trouble now," said Glasgerion. "Magicians never use hand gestures unless they're very weak."

Toridon's wall of fire turned slowly blue, the color starting at the top and dripping down like water. The color advanced until it reached her burning fingertips and began to creep up her arms like a serpent. Toridon shook, as if in pain, and the cave grew hot. The rocks at her feet melted like tar. Huge jagged cracks appeared in the floor and boiling lava poured forth.

The lava lapped at Reander's ankles but could not burn him. The Manslayer turned and scaled a tall stalagmite. He perched there like a vulture, watching the battle in impotent range. The waves of lava rolled towards the Gate. Glasgerion tucked Quadroped under his arm and jumped to his feet. "Hold on, Quadro," he cried and jumped onto the slippery-smooth side of the nearest stalagmite. He climbed swiftly to safety, but just as he reached the top, his foot slipped. Quadroped fell out of his arms towards the boiling bubbling floor.

"Quadro!" cried Glasgerion.

Reander never heard Glasgerion's desperate shout but Toridon heard. With a frantic gesture, she cooled the rocks below the plummeting pig. Quadroped crashed onto the hard stone and lay there, stunned. When he opened his eyes the blue fire was gone, and Toridon lay silently on the floor. With her death, the floor had become cold and hard.

The Manslayer leapt at Reander, and once more fireworks exploded through the air. Glasgerion grabbed Quadroped and sat down by the Gate. "Are you all right, Quadro?" he said. "You're crying."

"She saved me," said Quadroped, wiping the tears off his nose. "Maybe if she hadn't done it she'd still be alive."

"Stop that right now," said Glasgerion. "Her fate was sealed when she decided to fight; she was never a match for Reander. You can mourn her later, when the Gate's locked. Look, the Manslayer's beginning to falter."

The Manslayer's movements became slower and clumsier. He was gasping for breath and it seemed unlikely that he could stand much longer. But just as Reander moved in for the mortal blow, a pressure wave swept through the air, forcing the combatants apart.

"Enough," cried a voice. Goriel appeared and looked silently around the cavern. Then his eyes fastened on the Manslayer. "You *fool!*" he said. "I warned you to wait for me. Now you are too weak to fight, and Toridon is dead."

"If Toridon hadn't saved the pig creature, she'd still be alive," said the Manslayer.

"What does that matter?" asked Goriel. "She is dead and now Reander rests and regains his strength. You are useless to me!" The Manslayer began to argue and Reander slipped away unnoticed and rejoined Glasgerion.

"Are you all right?" asked Glasgerion.

"I'm fine," said Reander, "and the longer they argue the better I'll be; but I could use a drink of water." As Glasgerion bent towards the knapsack, Reander stepped swiftly up behind him and hit him sharply across the back of the neck. With a soft groan, Glasgerion collapsed on the cavern floor.

"Glasgerion!" cried Quadroped. Instinctively he raced to Glasgerion's face and began to lick it.

"Quadro, leave him be," said Reander. "Morragwen will soon be here. I cannot spare her, but Glasgerion need not see her die."

"How did you know?" gasped Quadroped, backing away from the Prince.

"I have always known Morragwen was from Ravenor," said Reander. "I wondered if she was the mysterious fourth Warlord. You confirmed my suspicions this morning. You *will* lock the Gate, Quadro." Quadro stared into Reander's green eyes and suddenly he was moving towards the Gate, unable to turn away or stop. Reander released Quadroped abruptly and he stumbled. "You see, Quadro," said Reander sadly, "you have no choice at all."

Quadroped felt obscurely relieved. One world was going to suffer no matter what happened, but now he didn't have to choose which. *Maybe the next Key Bearer will find a solution*, he thought.

Reander approached the arguing Warlords. "Gentlemen," he said, "cease your quarrel and tell me how much longer we must wait for Morragwen. Or has she had a change of heart?"

"She *was* somewhat reluctant to join us," said Goriel coldly, "but I managed to . . . persuade her." He raised his arm and a white flash suddenly illuminated even the farthest reaches of the cave. Quadroped blinked and looked up. Morragwen stood beside Goriel, her eel wrapped tightly around her waist.

"Morrag!" cried Quadroped. He was glad to see the eel again, despite everything.

"Hullo, Quadro," said Morrag. "So you've gotten to the Gate after all."

"Yes, and—"

"Quadroped! Be silent," said Reander.

"Hello, Reander..." Morragwen's greeting trailed off into silence as she took note of Glasgerion's limp form. "What have you done? You—"

"Monster?" supplied Reander. "Glasgerion is fine; he's only resting. He will wake up in an hour with a stiff neck. Join me and I shall let you revive him right now. I do not relish being your executioner, Morragwen; you have saved his life too many times."

"Don't fret, Morragwen," said Goriel, "since your lover's asleep, we have no cause to harm him. You may have him when the battle's done. Come stand beside me; let us kill the Prince."

"I..." Morragwen said in confusion.

"Reluctant?" asked Goriel. "I thought you loathed the omnipotent Reander. Who will avenge your sister, Toridon, if you do not? *I* fight only for Ravenor."

Morragwen gazed at Toridon's still form, lying crumpled near her feet. Her eyes filled briefly with tears. "I'll fight with Goriel," she said.

"Then let us begin," said Reander, "unless you think the odds too great?"

"Do not mock us, Prince," said Goriel gravely. "The odds are not fair. We do not fight for honor and glory, but for our King's freedom and life for Ravenor."

Reander went to face the Warlords in the center of the cave. Another strange battle of flashing lights began. This time the Manslayer did not use his broadsword lest it distract Goriel and Morragwen. Though the Manslayer's spells still exploded with terrifying noise and violent sparks, no light, sound or motion came from Goriel, Reander or Morragwen. Quadroped was mesmerized by the battle until his attention was distracted by a slippery body curling up beside him, "Hullo, Morrag," he said nervously. He wondered if Morrag would try to prevent his locking the Gate.

"Hullo, Quadro," said Morrag. "You looked worried. Have you grown to like that monster?"

"Yes," said Quadroped, "very much. Reander's not bad

when you get to know him. He even lets me ride on his saddle sometimes."

Morrag curled comfortably next to Quadroped. "I wish I could sympathize, Quadro," he said, "but Reander's trying to kill Morragwen."

"She's trying to kill him too," said Quadroped, "but I understand. Everyone except me knows what side he's on."

"Have you decided what you're going to do yet?" asked Morrag.

"No," said Quadroped. "But I'm not going to have a choice anyway. If Reander wins he'll force me to lock the Gate; if he loses, Goriel will kill me and let the Black Unicorn out."

"What if they're still fighting when the Gate opens?" asked Morrag. "You'll have a choice then."

"Will I?" asked Quadroped. "Won't you try and stop me from locking the Gate?"

Morrag fell silent and looked guilty. "Quadro," he said at last, "if you want to lock the Gate, I won't stop you. It's your choice; you're the Key Bearer."

"Promise?" asked Quadroped.

"Promise," said Morrag. He stiffened and Quadroped glanced quickly upwards. Morragwen and the Manslayer were staggering under Reander's assault. A fountain of blue-green sparks was playing around Morragwen and her face was tight with pain. The Manslayer was similarly besieged by a shower of exploding fires. Quadroped doubted he could last much longer.

"Why doesn't Goriel help them?" Morrag hissed anxiously. He curled his body nervously around Quadroped and began to contract.

"Maybe he can't," said Quadroped. "Maybe he's fighting for his own life. Morrag, don't squeeze so hard."

"Not him," said Morrag, relaxing slightly, "he's just watching. You'll feel it when Goriel starts to fight; he uses Old Magic."

Quadroped patted Morrag helplessly. Morragwen began to shiver uncontrollably; the aquamarine fires turned blood red around her feet. Morrag suddenly tightened again, knocking all the wind out of Quadroped's lungs and causing his eyes to tear in pain. Morragwen and the Manslayer were engulfed by a wave of golden fire. When the fire died, they lay in a heap on the floor.

"How melodramatic," said Goriel. He strode forward and prodded the bodies with his toe. "But I shall not repine. The Manslayer was useless to me, and Morragwen was a traitor." Morrag cried out and sprang at Goriel.

"Morrag, don't," cried Quadroped. He grabbed Morrag halfway down his body and tugged him backwards.

"Hold on tightly, Key Bearer, if you wish your friend to live," said Goriel.

Morrag half dragged Quadroped across the floor, but he hung on valiantly. After a few minutes, Morrag's wild rage died into sullen resentment. He curled up in a tight coil and fell silent. Quadroped released him and sat down beside Glasgerion again. It would be best, he decided, to let Morrag alone for a little while.

"I'll have to speak to the Black Unicorn about that eel," said Goriel. "It is a sullen creature."

"Leave Morrag alone," said Reander. "He served Morragwen faithfully."

"As you wish," said Goriel. "When you're dead the eel and the pig will pose no threat. I'll be generous and let them live."

Quadroped noticed that Goriel and Reander were both smiling. They seemed to find some grim satisfaction in this confrontation. The eel was peeking out from beneath his tail and Quadroped was somewhat comforted to see that Morrag looked just as unhappy and nervous as he did.

Reander and Goriel faced each other in silence, their bodies slightly relaxed. The air around them flickered like a heat wave. Neither man spoke or moved, but Quadroped could feel their magic at work. The air felt alive; it made his skin feel tight and crawly. A note too deep to hear shook the floor and echoed through his chest and stomach.

Then the air became heavy and pressed upon him from all sides. His mouth suddenly tasted of metal and his eyes began to water and blur. The walls were creeping towards him; their colors too bright to look at. He cried out in terror and moved back, hurtling towards the terrible walls at fantastic speeds. Then he was stuck, as if in glue, and the walls grew towards him like carnivorous plants eager for a meal.

Quadroped shut his eyes and he was caught in a dark whirlpool, spinning around and around. He could not breathe; the water covered his mouth like a tentacle. *The Water Demon*, he thought and cried out, "Glasgerion!"

"Shhh, I'm here," said Morrag.

Suddenly the world stopped spinning; Quadroped found himself held tightly in Morrag's coils, his snout pressed against the cool scales of the eel's stomach. "What happened?" he asked.

"You're feeling the Old Magic," said Morrag. "It draws on forces which are not of this world. The brain tries to interpret them in terms of the five senses, with frightening results. It will be easier now; it just takes a little getting used to."

Quadroped looked at the battle again. Reander and Goriel seemed to be miles away, though he could see them with unusual clarity. "They're waving around like snakes," he said.

"No, they're standing still," said Morrag. "Relax, don't let the magic disturb you."

Quadroped relaxed and found that it did help. Everything seemed normal again, although Reander had inexplicably turned orange and Goriel had leaves growing on his arms. Reander reeled as though he had been struck a heavy blow and staggered backwards. The cave became both freezing cold and burning hot. Goriel smiled and Reander fell to one knee, an arm flung out before him, as if to ward off a blow.

Reander shuddered, and his head dropped to his chest. Goriel towered over him. Rainbows shone on his feathers and formed a halo of light about his head. It was a splendid sight, but the feathers were wriggling with a life of their own, which was incredibly ghastly. An expression of triumph shone upon Goriel's lordly face. He stretched to his full height and his wings spread to form a brilliant cape cascading from his shoulders.

"Reander," cried Quadroped, "get up."

"He can't hear you," said Morrag. "He's too deep in the Old Magic. But I think I know something that will help."

"What?" asked Quadroped suspiciously. Reander had, after all, killed Morragwen. "I thought you wanted Goriel to win."

"I hate to admit this, but I'd rather have Reander around than Goriel," said Morrag. "Besides, he'll be too weak to use any spells on you if you decide to open the Gate."

"What can you do?" asked Quadroped.

"Sometimes pain can reach people, even through the Old Magic," said Morrag. "I'll bite Reander on the heel. With luck that will bring him to his senses."

"But won't Goriel blast you?" asked Quadroped.

"No, he's too wrapped up in Old Magic to see me," said Morrag.

Quadroped held his breath as Morrag slithered silently over the cavern floor to Reander's foot. He struck with blinding speed and Quadroped could see blood seeping through the leather of Reander's boot. Reander did not react; he knelt before Goriel as his life visibly drained away. Morrag drew back his head and struck again.

Reander shuddered; then his chin lifted imperceptibly. Goriel staggered backwards, his expression incredulous. Reander got to his feet. Goriel's back arched and broke with a horrible crack. His body fell limply to the floor. Reander also collapsed, but his eyes were still open. Quadroped ran to him.

"I'm all right," said Reander. "There's five minutes left, Quadro, just enough time." He struggled to his feet, swaying slightly.

"That's one thing I like about Old Magic," said Morrag. "It kills you or it fades away quickly."

"Not quick enough," said Reander, paling and starting to shiver. "Let's get that Gate locked. Goriel almost killed me, and his powers are supposed to be weaker these days. The Black Unicorn is even stronger. If he escapes today, I won't be able to fight him." He sounded tired and somehow defeated.

"Four minutes left," said Morrag. "Have you decided what to do yet, Quadro?"

"He has no decision to make," said Reander, taking a deep breath. Quadroped heard the familiar note of icy command with mixed feelings. "He will lock the Gate. I owe you my life, Morrag, but if you oppose me in this I will kill you."

"Quadro should be free to make his own choice," said Morrag. He raised himself up on his tail, until his glowering red eyes were level with Reander's, and hissed.

"Stop it!" said Quadroped. He tugged at Reander's boot, but Reander refused to look down. "Morrag, you'll be killed!" he pleaded, pushing hard against the eel's smooth body with his snout. Morrag hissed again.

Then, everything stopped. Reander and Morrag were frozen, their gazes locked, their breaths and heartbeats stilled. Silence filled the cavern until Quadroped could hear his blood pulsing behind his ears.

A sound whispered through the cavern; so soft that Quadroped only gradually became aware of it. *The Gate,* he thought. *It's starting to open!* The black iron groaned and creaked as the bolt, worked by invisible forces, turned and began to slip free. Light began to flow through the iron, casting weird, twisted shadows on the walls. Reander and Morrag remained motionless as the light swirled around them. *They must be under a spell,* thought Quadroped, *but why doesn't it affect me?* The answer came to him suddenly. *The Key must be protecting me,* he thought. *I do have a choice. Help! I have to lock the Gate!*

Quadroped ran to the Gate. The keyhole was far above his head. Even when he stood on his hind legs, bracing his front hooves against the iron, his nose only barely reached the bottom of the keyhole. But the intricate designs in the iron made excellent hoofholds and he quickly climbed to the lock. He tucked his hooves around the twisting iron, grabbed the Key in his mouth, and slipped it slowly into the lock. Then he stopped.

"Well?" A deep voice echoed through the air.

Quadroped peered over the Gate as a shadowy form moved towards him through the curtain of light. The Unicorn was night black; his horn was crystal clear and sparkled in the shadows. Quadroped began to turn the key.

"Free me," said the Black Unicorn. "Let Ravenor live again." His huge neck arched high above Quadroped's head and his red eyes gleamed down at the frightened pig.

Quadroped almost dropped the Key and caught it just in time. *I'll never get it locked in time*, he thought. He braced himself for the crash when the Black Unicorn broke free.

The great beast waited until Quadroped stopped trying to get the Key into the lock and looked up. "I have suffered for thousands of years," he said. "Am I evil to seek revenge?"

Quadroped felt a pressure in his mind. He saw shapes and scenes too horrible and lovely to comprehend. Strong winds hit him until his body ached and he could not tell up from down. He felt pain and heat and bitter cold. Loud noises shook him and hurt his ears. It was many times worse than the Old Magic; his identity was slipping away into madness.

"Stop!" cried Quadroped; and he was back in the cavern, staring into the red eyes of the Black Unicorn. "Was that Chaos?" he asked.

"Yes," said the Black Unicorn. "Set me free from this prison."

"But if I free you, you'll attack the Kingdoms," said Quadroped.

"If you free me, Ravenor will be green again," said the Black Unicorn. "It is time to avenge a world."

"No," said Quadroped holding the Key a little tighter, "there must never be another Great War. The Kingdoms didn't know that Ravenor needed you. Reander knows about Ravenor now; he'll find a way to help your people."

"Only I can do that," said the Black Unicorn. "There must be justice. Too long has your world thrived at the expense of my own."

"No, I won't free you," said Quadroped. "Your revenge isn't just! It's wicked, and . . . selfish."

"Selfish?" said the Black Unicorn with a snort. "I have suffered in Chaos for thousands of years while my Kingdom withered and died."

"You're selfish," said Quadroped firmly. "I don't know how the war started—maybe the Kingdoms *did* steal your minerals—but instead of trying to solve the problem peacefully you decided to kill everyone in the Kingdoms. That was *evil*, and now you want to start all over again! If you want Ravenor to live, stay in Chaos and let Reander feed your people. They won't have time to farm once you're free; they'll all be off fighting. You can bring life to *two* lands, if you'll stop trying to get revenge. What good are green plants and water if everyone's at war?"

Quadroped gazed morbidly at the Black Unicorn's strong white teeth. The teeth gnashed together, sparks flew, and he cringed. "Perhaps," said the Black Unicorn, "I should reconsider."

"What?" said Quadroped faintly.

"Once, long ago, I was a creator not a destroyer," said the Black Unicorn. "I am the Life of Ravenor; perhaps I should be less willing to shed its blood. You say my captors did not know how they wounded my land; I will believe you."

Quadroped stared at the Black Unicorn in confusion; his arguments had never swayed the Warlords. The Black Unicorn gave a strangely pleasant laugh. "I lived before the Kingdoms held life," he said. "I knew the price of war, and I forgot it. Free me quickly or lock the Gate; the worlds begin to part. In a hundred years I shall have forgotten your words. Chaos is a place of anger; it has no room for hope."

"Will you make peace with the Kingdoms?" asked Quadroped.

"Yes," said the Black Unicorn.

It might be a trick, Quadroped thought anxiously. *He changed his mind so suddenly. But maybe he always does? How can I judge a creature who has been alive since the world began, who created Ravenor? But Morragwen and Morrag love him, and Ravenor needs him.*

"I'll let you go," said Quadroped. With a shaking hoof he pulled the Key from the lock.

The Black Unicorn sprang forwards. The Gate rang like a bell as his powerful body crashed against it. The rusty hinges screamed aloud and the Gate flew violently open. Quadroped was thrown high into the air and landed painfully on the stone floor, his teeth aching from the vibrations of the iron. The Black Unicorn's sharp hooves passed over his head.

"I am free!" said the Black Unicorn. His voice whispered through the cavern like wind.

"What have I done!" wailed Quadroped. The Black Unicorn reared and pawed the air with cloven hooves. Quadroped tried to think of a way to trick the Black Unicorn back into Chaos before it was too late. But the lock was broken and the Gate smashed.

The light died; Reander and Morrag blinked and moved apart. Reander's eyes fell first upon the broken Gate. "Quadroped! What have you done?" he cried and raced forwards, sword drawn. Morrag raced after him and Quadroped wondered dimly if Morrag would be able to grab the sword before Reander executed him.

"Oh dear," said Quadroped weakly. He curled into a tight white ball and covered his eyes with his hooves. Reander grabbed him and began to shake him roughly. Then the painful grip suddenly relaxed and he landed on the floor. He opened his eyes and found the Black Unicorn standing over him. Morrag retreated, unnoticed, to Morragwen's body.

"Who dares shake the Key Bearer?" asked the Black Unicorn. "He should not be tossed about in that manner."

Quadroped decided that he did not like to hear Reander scolded. He deduced from Reander's thunderous expression that the Prince did not like it either. "Oh, but I'm just a pig," he told the Black Unicorn, "and Reander's a Prince. He told me to lock the Gate and I didn't." Reander glared at the Black Unicorn.

"Do not frown at me, mortal," said the Black Unicorn. "It could be dangerous." Reander's eyes narrowed and his sword arm tensed. The Black Unicorn placed the sharp tip of his horn against Reander's breast. "Who are you?" he asked. "You look familiar, but we could not have met."

"I am Reander of Essylt," said Reander coldly. "It is

said I resemble my forefather Rhiogan." Quadroped recalled that Rhiogan was the Prince who had trapped the Black Unicorn in Chaos. He wished Reander had not mentioned his relation.

"Yes, you *are* much like Rhiogan," said the Black Unicorn calmly, "proud, noble and suicidal. Put away your sword; I will not spill your blood."

"What?" Reander lowered his sword and looked utterly confounded. "Is there to be no war between us? Or has Quadro made some foolish bargain for the life of his friends? If you seek to destroy the Kingdoms, you will have to slay me."

"Ravenor shall not go to war," said the Black Unicorn. "The Key Bearer made no mention of you or his other friends, though I surmised that one so young did not make the journey to Illoreth alone. Is this another of your friends, Key Bearer?"

Quadroped peered between Reander's legs and saw Glasgerion's blue boots approaching. "That's Glasgerion," he said. "He's Reander's uncle and a Prince but he doesn't act like one. He's a very good bard."

"A bit muddled, but essentially correct," said Glasgerion. He calmly reached between the Black Unicorn's forelegs and picked up Quadroped.

"The Black Unicorn will make peace with the Kingdoms," said Reander. "Quadro arranged it." If he hoped to surprise his uncle he was disappointed.

"Good work, Quadro," said Glasgerion.

"I am in no ways displeased to meet the Princes of Essylt," said the Black Unicorn, "but I am somewhat at a loss to explain your presence here. I had thought my Warlords sufficient to prevent such an occurrence." There was a long uncomfortable pause as all eyes turned towards the bodies lying scattered and silent upon the floor.

Glasgerion was the first to speak. "Morragwen!" he cried. Quadroped fell forgotten to the floor as Glasgerion ran to the witch's side. He knelt beside the witch and drew her head onto his lap. "She's dead," he said dully. "Reander, did you . . . ?"

Reander spread his hands. "I had no choice; neither did she. Toridon was her sister."

"Morragwen, Toridon, Manslayer, even my Goriel, all dead," said the Black Unicorn sorrowfully. He bent over the bodies, touching them gently with his glittering horn. "I did not think a mortal could slay them." He bowed his head briefly to Reander. "You served me well, children," he continued, "but there will be no more battles for you now; there is too much work to be done. Get up."

"They can't get up," said Quadroped reasonably, "they're dead."

The Black Unicorn stared at Quadroped for a moment and laughed. "Key Bearer, if you believe that I can bring a land to life why should you doubt my power to restore my children? They will wake now; quickly if they know what's good for them. Prince Glasgerion, Morragwen will feel better if you stop shaking her."

Morragwen's eyes began to open. Quadroped looked around and saw Toridon's ribs begin to rise and fall with her renewed breaths. "Are they *all* alive now?" he asked nervously, staring at Goriel.

"You looked worried, Key Bearer," said the Black Unicorn. "There is no need. They are your allies now." Quadroped remembered Goriel's dead family and his hatred of everything in the Kingdoms and wondered. His fears grew as Goriel slowly rose to his feet and approached the Black Unicorn. The Warlord knelt briefly before his King. Then he stood and looked at Reander.

"My liege, why have you not slain this man?" he asked bitterly, turning to the Black Unicorn. "Have you so easily forgotten the wounds inflicted by his kind? What of revenge?"

"My Goriel," said the Black Unicorn, resting his horn upon the Warlord's shoulder, "there will be no revenge, only peace and life."

"My family is dead," said Goriel harshly. "That is a pain peace cannot heal." Goriel pushed the horn away and it returned to press against his throat.

"Resign yourself to this, my child," said the Black Unicorn, "or return to earth. I do not ask you to forget the

THE PIG, THE PRINCE & THE UNICORN 213

pain. I ask you to endure it, without the solace of revenge, for the sake of the people of Ravenor. You are a Prince. This is the price a leader pays for the welfare of his subjects. The past is immutable; do not let the present be its mirror."

Goriel turned away and they watched in silence as the muscles of his back rippled and tensed, reflecting his conflicting emotions. When he turned again his eyes held no love for Reander, but the hatred was gone. "I doubt that I shall ever call a creature of the Kingdoms friend," he said, "but I will accept the peace."

"Perhaps they'll break treaty with us," suggested the Manslayer hopefully. He had risen and was helping Toridon to her feet. "I'd like a chance to kill Reander."

"As if you could," scoffed Toridon loudly.

"Essylt has never broken a treaty," said Reander proudly, "and while I live the other Kingdoms shall follow her example."

"I am reminded," said the Black Unicorn suddenly, "that not one of my Warlords managed to prevent two mortals and a piglet from reaching Illoreth. That is a dismal failure indeed."

"Morragwen helped them," said the Manslayer vindictively. "She told Glasgerion the way to Illoreth, she killed my Pitch Fiends and she cured Glasgerion of the wounds I had inflicted upon him in battle."

"That is most disturbing," said the Black Unicorn. His burning eyes fell upon Morragwen where she lay in Glasgerion's arms.

"Please don't hurt Morragwen," said Quadroped anxiously.

"Let her be," said Goriel unexpectedly. "She stood by us at the end. She will not return to Ravenor with us in any case."

"You do not wish to return, Morragwen?" asked the Black Unicorn in surprise.

"Not really," said Morragwen, raising her head from Glasgerion's shoulder. "Glasgerion has asked me to marry him, even though I *am* a Warlord. I'd like to stay with him." Glasgerion hugged her and whispered something in

her ear that made her blush. Reander and Goriel both
looked faintly disgusted with the cooing couple.

"So be it," said the Black Unicorn. "I will pardon you,
Morragwen, on the condition that you remain in the Kingdoms as my ambassador." He tossed his head and the three
remaining Warlords quickly gathered around him. "It is
time to go home," he said and there was a wealth of long-
ing in that last word.

"Wait," said Quadroped suddenly, "you've forgotten
something. I mean," he added shyly, "I think you'd better
take this; I don't want it anymore." He slowly removed the
small Key from his neck and held it out to the Black Unicorn.

The Black Unicorn lowered his head and Quadroped
slipped the Key's chain around his horn. "What shall I call
you, piglet, now that you are no longer the Key Bearer?"
he asked.

"Call me Quadro," said Quadroped.

"Thank you, Quadro," said the Black Unicorn, "and
good-bye." With a great cry the Black Unicorn reared, his
hooves slashing the air. His mighty form grew misty and
he and his three Warlords faded slowly from sight.

Epilogue

The sun would soon rise. Quadroped sat on the front steps of the palace and watched the sky. The northern lights danced like rainbows on the night, leaving a dripping fringe behind. Above him the bells rang out, a solemn, joyous sound. Glasgerion and Morragwen were wed and all Essylt rejoiced. He had left the celebrations early; he felt lonely and unhappy. In the month he had spent at court he had made many friends but now he wanted to go home. He rarely saw Glasgerion without Morragwen and when they were together he felt like an intruder. Reander was always busy making his kingdom's treaties with Ravenor. Reander had sent a message to his parents, telling them that their son was safe, but Quadroped missed them. He wanted to see them and tell them about his adventures. He thought of acorn trees and duck ponds, and sighed.

"Hullo, Quadro," said Morrag, gliding down the steps. "What's wrong? You've been moping for days."

"I want to go home," said Quadroped.

"Ah," said Morrag wisely. He curled beside Quadroped

215

in companionable silence and together they watched the sun rise. When the sky was pink, Morrag turned to Quadroped and said, "Let's go."

"Where to?" asked Quadroped doubtfully.

"Home."

"But I can't just leave," said Quadroped, "Glasgerion . . ."

"I left a note," said Morrag.

"But how do we get there?"

"I have a map," said Morrag.

"But you don't even know where I live," said Quadroped.

"Whistlewood Forest," said Morrag promptly. "I made enquiries. I thought you'd get homesick soon. We'll follow the same route you took here. I'm sure Fairfax and Pseudo-Polyp are eager to hear about the Black Unicorn. There's Eunoe, Murg, the eagles, Andvari, the spider and Ghost. You owe them all a visit and I want to meet them. Then we'll go home, and after that? Well . . . There's a whole world to see." He glided away down the stairs. "Aren't you coming?"

"Oh *yes!*" said Quadroped. His ears began to wag and his purple eyes shone. "More adventures!" The two set off in the early morning, the golden towers of High Essylt in the northern ice gleaming fondly behind them.